SECRETS

SECRETS

SECRETS

FERN MICHAELS

WHEELER PUBLISHING
A part of Gale, a Cengage Company

Copyright © 2022 by Fern Michaels.
Fern Michaels is a registered trademark of KAP 5, Inc.
A Lost and Found Novel #2.
Wheeler Publishing, a part of Gale, a Cengage Company.

ALL RIGHTS RESERVED
This book is a work of fiction. Names, characters, businesses, organizations, places, events, and incidents either are the product of the author's imagination or are used fictitiously. Any resemblance to actual persons, living or dead, events, or locales is entirely coincidental.
Wheeler Publishing Large Print Hardcover.
The text of this Large Print edition is unabridged.
Other aspects of the book may vary from the original edition.
Set in 16 pt. Plantin.

**LIBRARY OF CONGRESS CIP DATA ON FILE.
CATALOGUING IN PUBLICATION FOR THIS BOOK
IS AVAILABLE FROM THE LIBRARY OF CONGRESS.**

ISBN-13: 978-1-4328-9719-2 (hardcover alk. paper)

Published in 2022 by arrangement with Zebra Books, an imprint of Kensington Publishing Corp.

Printed in Mexico
Print Number : 1   Print Year : 2023

SECRETS

SECRETS

Dear Diary,

When I started this six months ago, I promised I would write something every day. So much for that idea. It's been four months since the last entry. I guess I've been distracted, looking forward to graduation. Tomorrow is the big day. Can't wait to get out of here. Don't know what I am going to be doing, and I got a prob. K. and I have been getting very serious. He's been hinting about us blowing "Casa Aluminum." That's what he calls it. It's considered a mobile home, but we aren't going anywhere. Not in this thing. He keeps reminding me. He says he has big ideas. A future with us. Wants to make money but doesn't have a plan. He tells me to trust him. Do I have a choice? Truth is, I don't know what I want. That's a problem. I don't even know what I like. I suppose I should have put more thought into it, but now here I am, done with high school, and I have no clue what to do next. My head hurts from thinking about it. I sure can't ask Mom for advice. She's rarely sober enough to string a sentence together. Forget Dad. He's out driving his truck somewhere. Yep. Can't wait to get out of Casa Aluminum. What to do . . . what to do . . .

But there is good news! We'll have this double-wide to ourselves Saturday. I'm going to have my own graduation party for me and some friends. Mom is going to visit her sister, and Dad isn't around. But then there's my brother. With any luck, he'll take his pizza to his room, pull on his headphones, and zone out. What else does a twelve-year-old do anyway? I'll give him $20 to stay put and keep his mouth shut.

Bought some aromatherapy candles to set the mood. Wow. This is the most I've written all year. Just in case I don't get back to these pages, here's to a super weekend, and congratulations to me!

V.C.

CHAPTER ONE

The B.A.R.R.N.
Bodman-Antiques-Retro-Restoration &
  Namaste Café
Buncombe County, North Carolina
Present day

A delivery truck pulled up to the rear entrance of Cullen Bodman's restoration workshop. He wasn't expecting anything, but the driver handed him a printed version of the bill of lading and began to haul a crate with a dilapidated steamer trunk off the back of the van's motorized lift. Cullen eyed the document. It was addressed to him, but there was no return label. He looked up at the deliveryman. "Do you know where this came from? There's no return address."

The guy shrugged. "I picked it up at the hub. It was on my route ticket." He stopped at the door. "Where do you want it?" Cullen looked around the workshop, pointed to a space against the far wall, and moved out of the way.

"Is there some way I can find out where this came from?"

"Beats me." The guy wiped his forehead with his sleeve. "Please sign this." He handed Cullen an electronic clipboard and a stylus. Cullen scribbled his name and repeated the question. He didn't get any further.

"You can call the dispatcher if you want." The driver turned, hopped into his vehicle, and drove off, leaving a very perplexed Cullen standing in the doorway.

Like clockwork, Luna Bodhi Bodman arrived at the café at her typical time, nine A.M. On her way, she stopped at the Flakey Tart and picked up her usual basket of scones and muffins. Even though the Tart had its own kiosk at the art center, Luna served their delicious delights with coffee and tea during the day.

At the age of thirty-three, she was a dabbler in paranormal psychology and an amateur medium. Dabbled is probably an understatement. She didn't want her unconventional way of thinking and feeling to be a detriment to her brother's restoration business. But she certainly looked the part

10

of a New Age psychic if there was such a thing. Her hippie wardrobe, waist-length hair, and granny glasses were a huge clue that she was not your run-of-the-mill barista. The café had been her brother's idea. She had agreed to run it because doing so gave her the opportunity to do her readings as well as be of assistance to him. Plus, with the café being right next door to his shop, he could keep an eye on her. Not that she couldn't take care of herself. But Luna had a way of generating more excitement than was either necessary or expected. But that, too, was part of her charm.

In addition to the readings her unconventional talent allowed her to engage in, she was an artist and design consultant. When called upon, she worked with her brother Cullen, assisting customers engaged in redecorating or refurbishing parts or all of their homes.

Cullen heard the bell that signaled that someone had walked into the showroom. He checked his watch — 9:15 A.M. He was looking forward to one of the Flakey Tart's blueberry scones. He knew it was a bad habit, but they were too delicious to pass up. The days the center was open, Luna would bring Cullen his morning coffee and his favorite breakfast pastry.

11

Luna was a bundle of energy, spinning her light into the room. Cullen, who was not and never had been a morning person, marveled at how bright and effervescent she could be so early in the day.

"Namaste, brother." She gave a little bow as she handed him a tray holding a cappuccino with an extra shot of espresso and that blueberry piece of heaven.

"Good morning, sunshine." Cullen gave her a slight bow in return.

"Something smells a little smoky." She sniffed the air and turned to her dog, Wiley, a border collie. "What do you think, fella? Something smells different."

Cullen cocked his head in the direction of the far wall. "Somebody had an old trunk delivered. It's still in a crate."

"Smells like someone had a fire sale." Luna would never let her curiosity go unsatisfied. She inched her way toward the mysterious parcel. She kept inhaling and turned to Cullen. "Well, what are you waiting for?" Her eyes grew wide in an accusatory fashion.

"Jeez. Can I please have a sip of my coffee first?" Cullen gave her a playful sneer.

"Considering I made it special for you, yes, please do." Luna crouched to get a better look at the crate. The crate was open-sided, so part of the trunk could be seen. "Hmmmm . . ." she murmured quizzically. "Where did it come from?"

"I have no idea. Neither did the delivery-man." Cullen took another sip of his caffeine fix. "He showed me the bill of lading and *this* is the delivery address, including *my* name."

"Huh." Luna stood. "Curiouser and curiouser. All the more reason we should open it!" She clapped her hands and chanted, "Open it! Open it," as Wiley yapped in rhythm.

Cullen rolled his eyes and set his coffee cup down. "All right. All right. But not until I get a bite of this." He chomped down on the scone. "Delicious!"

"Come on! Come on! Let's get snappy!" She snapped her fingers in rhythm.

"Let me swallow, please." Cullen was always amused at his sister's exuberance. She was one of those people who could turn going to the mailbox into a party.

He wiped his fingers on the cloth napkin that always accompanied his morning ritual. "Grab me that crowbar." He pointed to the wall where he kept most of his tools.

"Aye, aye, Captain," Luna said, saluting as she brought him the implement he needed. "Any note come with that thing?"

"Not that I can tell from the outside. I am hoping there will be an explanation once we unpack it." He gently wedged the tool between two pieces of wood and pried the first slat off. He worked his way around the crate until the trunk was completely exposed.

"Wow. How old do you think this thing is?" Luna moved in a little closer.

"It looks like something from an old steamship. Maybe 1920s." He brushed a finger along the worn leather straps and took a whiff. "Smoke damage for sure."

"Smells like it was in or near a fire," Luna observed. "Check it out." She pointed to a small plastic pouch affixed to the trunk. It contained a folded piece of paper. "Maybe this will solve your mystery."

Cullen gingerly removed the envelope taped to the lock, being careful not to ruin the leather any further. The lock itself was in desperate need of repair.

He read it out loud:

Dear Mr. Bodman,
    Please pardon my lack of correspondence prior to the delivery, but time was of the essence and your reputation for restoration is impeccable. This trunk is what is left of my family's estate and it had to be

removed from storage. As you can tell, it was in a fire. Unfortunately, no one can locate the key, and the local locksmith could not guarantee opening it without further damaging the trunk and its contents. It is my hope you will find time to clean and restore it to the best of your ability.

Should you find the contents in good order, I would appreciate your holding them until the restoration process is complete, at which time I will have someone retrieve it. There is no particular rush as I have now removed it from where it had been stored for many years. Enclosed you will find a money order in the amount of $1000 as a deposit. Should you require more money up front, please send an e-mail to myfamilyheritage@ymail.com, and I will have funds transferred to you as per your instructions. My gratitude in advance.

Cullen looked blankly at his sister. "What?"

"There's no name or signature." Cullen passed her the note and the money order.

When she touched the letter, a slight shiver went up her spine. "There is something amiss."

"Uh-oh. Here we go." Cullen let out a big sigh and shook his head.

"Well, now, don't you think it's rather odd?" Luna asked calmly. She ticked off her fingers. "One. You get a mysterious delivery. Two. The trunk has been in or near a fire. Three. The note has no signature. And a big number four, there's a one-thousand-dollar money order. Come on, Cul. You don't have to be psychic to feel as if something is a bit strange here."

"Well, you're right about that. The strange part. But why do you think something is amiss?"

Luna gave him her impatient sideways look. Not quite an eye roll, but close. "Brother, dear brother. When will you ever learn?" She gave him a "tsk-tsk" and retreated to her café.

The Bodman siblings had grown up around antiques, and Cullen had taken over the family business when their father retired. Cullen would provide consulting and procurement for certain clients who were shopping for specific pieces or redecorating. But Cullen was more interested in bringing things back to life and took great pleasure in restoration.

Cullen was the strait-laced, Ralph Lauren

type. He stood around six feet and, at thirty-six, still had a full head of sandy hair, with just a few strands of gray at the temples. He had a good head for business and handled the finances for both his shop and the café.

Luna was clearly the ethereal one. They made an interesting pair. That was one of the reasons why Ellie Stillwell granted them one of the corners of the art center. In the beginning, Luna was concerned that Ellie would not approve of her paranormal abilities so she kept it on the down-low, only doing readings for people who were referred to her. She also had an overwhelming desire to help others by using it.

Just before the center had its grand opening, Luna sensed major anxiety coming from Ellie. Luna put her hand on Ellie's shoulder and told her to "have no fear." Ellie was stunned by the remark. It was something her late husband would say. Ellie was fascinated by this impish, perceptive young woman and asked for a little more, urging Luna to do an impromptu reading for her. Luna cited things from Ellie's childhood — something Luna could not possibly know about. After the brief exchange, Ellie felt a sense of relief and optimism, and she immediately took to the young woman.

Now they met every morning in the café for coffee and scones.

Before the siblings opened their shops in the Stillwell Art Center, Luna had been employed as a caseworker in Children's Services. Luna's extrasensory perception, together with her degree in psychology, created an odd yet interesting combination. Taking a night course in body language added to her professional toolbox. She drew upon all her skills when investigating a family issue, and they made her a remarkably successful advocate for kids.

Cullen, having been the traditional one of the two, was secretly thrilled to be out of the nine-to-five grind of working in an office. It was Cullen who had come up with the idea of the Namaste Café to be installed next to his workshop and showroom. Luna left Children's Services with the promise she would always make herself available if need be. She would also lend her skills to the U.S. Marshals Service when asked. Now Cullen and Luna were in their own element, surrounded by like-minded and talented souls.

Luna began to get ready for the day. She opened the sliding glass doors and placed

18

her NAMASTE CAFÉ sign next to the entrance. Scones, muffins, and croissants were displayed in large wicker baskets courtesy of Basket Case, another art stall at the center. She set up her easel in the far corner next to a table. It served as her medium for her readings; she sketched while using her ESP. Satisfied all was in good order, she looked across the atrium to see if her friend Lebici (Chi-Chi) had opened Silver & Stone, a one-of-a-kind jewelry shop.

Chi-Chi was from Nigeria and worked her own version of alchemy, creating beautiful pieces made from silver and stones from her homeland. Each morning, Luna, Chi-Chi, and Ellie Stillwell would have their morning coffee together before the center opened.

The light was almost blinding through the skylights and enormous sliding glass doors of the art center. One couldn't help but feel immersed in the heavenly warmth of the sun. At certain times of the day, there was a magical feel about it, as if you were part of something bigger. Something greater.

Chi-Chi was elegant in every respect. Her long box braids reached past her elbows, creating a wave with every movement. She wore a colorful caftan with one of her own pieces around her neck. It was in the shape of a snake with emerald stones for eyes. A matching bracelet adorned her wrist. Luna was always in awe of Chi-Chi's grace. She seemed to float a few inches above the ground. Stunning and mysterious. Her beautiful smile radiated affection. But don't cross her. She was kind and levelheaded. But also fierce and protective of those near and dear to her. She and Luna were kindred spirits, no pun intended.

The concept of the center was fashioned after the Torpedo Factory Art Center in Alexandria, Virginia. Literally, once a torpedo factory during World War I, the factory had evolved into the largest collection of working artists under one roof. Now, the Stillwell Art Center boasted a fine indoor collection of artists, sculptors, pottery throwers, birdhouse builders, wind chime makers, jewelers, basket weavers, furniture restorers, cheese artisans, and so much more.

One of the main attractions was the artwork of a welding sculptor named Jimmy Can-Do. No one ever saw him in person; the only evidence that he even existed was the finished work that showed up every day the center was open. His forte was peeling apart beer cans and turning them into statues, wall hangings, and mobiles. Each day they were on display in his open shop and sometimes in the atrium. The items held price tags with a notation:

PLEASE SEE HONOR SYSTEM BOX.

The box was placed just outside the glass doors of the stall. The sign on the box read:

WE RUN ON THE HONOR SYSTEM. IF YOU WANT TO PAY BY CREDIT, PLEASE LEAVE YOUR NAME AND CONTACT INFORMATION AND THE NUMBER OF THE ITEM YOU ARE TAKING. SOMEONE WILL CONTACT YOU. OTHERWISE, PLEASE DEPOSIT CASH OR CHECK. THANK YOU.

Patrons could take the piece and leave their name and phone number on a sheet of paper and place the paper in the box. He made everything from palm trees to baseball bats, all finished with polyurethane. Some people would hang around just before closing time, hoping to get a glimpse of the mysterious artist. But to no avail. Even Ellie Stillwell had never met him in person, and she respected his privacy. As long as he paid his rent and provided interesting pieces of his work, she didn't feel the need for a handshake.

The Stillwell Art Center was the culmination of two years of painstaking planning and development, including battling with local politicians. The same politicians were now among the center's biggest fans since no one in politics was going to pass up the opportunity to take credit for something that succeeded.

Ellie Stillwell had used her family money and resources to give creative hands a place and opportunity to work on their craft. She also wanted it to be an experience for those in search of inspiration, and sometimes a gourmet sandwich. Of course, there was always a fine bottle of wine to be procured at the Wine Cellar.

Ellie's vision had come to fruition, and now it was thriving. There was a five-year waiting list for a five-hundred-square-foot section of the glass-enclosed haven. Ellie wanted to provide a space where creativity could blossom and the community could gather. Every morning, she would arrive with her two German shepherds, Ziggy and Marley. And every morning she would marvel at the spectacular outcome of her wildest imaginings. Fundraisers were held at the center, with the artists donating their work for the local charity events. Stillwell Art Center was exactly what Ellie had envisioned. The humanities and humanity.

Ellie was in her early seventies, fit, and attractive. Her blunt, chin-length white hair gave her an air of sophistication. It was a very "artsy" look. She had earned her Ph.D. in art history from Duke University, where she had also met her husband, Richard. They led a simple life. She had taught at the local college, and he had practiced law. It wasn't until after Richard had died of a massive heart attack that Ellie discovered how much money she was really worth — $50 million. Richard had been a brilliant investor, and Ellie owned acres of farmland and commercial properties. She could afford to drop half of that into the humanities and animal causes, leaving plenty for a very comfortable life. She had no other plans for big changes. The art center was enough.

Arriving early before the center opened to the public, Ellie walked the dogs to the rear of the atrium, where it connected to a covered patio and several large, landscaped acres. To one side was a dog park. All well-behaved canines were welcome and were supervised by Alex, the dog handler. Visitors could comfortably leave their fur babies in the care of Alex, who would throw Frisbees, balls, or whatever the owner would bring for their pooch's pleasure. Alex was also in charge of keeping the place in super-pooper-scooper condition. Ellie was pleased to have someone who was trustworthy on the payroll, especially someone who loved animals. She let the dogs run to their favorite playmate, and Alex squatted to give them both big hugs. Ellie gave a thumbs-up and headed into the center. She spotted Luna and Chi-Chi and waved.

Wiley was the first to notice Ziggy and Marley bounding out the back. He lay down prone and covered his eyes with his paws. "Oh, do you want to play, too?" Luna scratched his ears. Wiley immediately perked up. She grabbed the walkie-talkie. They were required and provided by Ellie. Just in case. After the crazy incident with Rowena Millstone and the hillbillies from West Virginia, Ellie insisted everyone have a means of communicating with each other. Especially security.

Several months earlier — shortly after the center's grand opening — Luna had found herself face-to-face with a couple of intruders in Cullen's shop. Cullen was horribly late getting back and the only thing Luna had at her disposal was a fire extinguisher. Fortunately, the intruders were unarmed amateurs and she was able to keep them at bay until help arrived.

After that evening, Ellie purchased two-way radios for everyone to carry when they were on-site, and everyone was tuned to the same channel. Rather than using data on their cell phones, most of the tenants often used them to connect with each other.

Luna pressed the button on her handheld. "Alex?"

"Yup!"

"Luna here. Incoming!" She unhooked Wiley's lead and he made a beeline to the automatic sliding doors.

"Roger that!" Alex responded.

Ellie made her way to Luna and Chi-Chi, who were standing inside the atrium just outside the café. Ellie made a habit of stopping to greet the occupants of each stall she passed. She finally arrived where the two women waited.

"*E kaaro.*" Chi-Chi offered Ellie a slight bow with her morning greeting.

Ellie responded in kind. "*E kaaro.*"

"Namaste, Ellie." Luna gave Ellie her version of a welcome.

"Look at us. Multilingual!" Ellie showed delight as the others smiled.

25

"Come. We have scones with your names on them." Luna linked arms with Ellie.

"I am going to get fat," Ellie chided.

"Not if you keep to only one per day," Chi-Chi encouraged Ellie. "Moderation is important, yes. But one scone is important, too." The women chuckled as Luna handed each of them a plate with a scone and a napkin.

"Having your regular?" Luna walked over to the coffee machine.

"Yes, please," Ellie replied.

"Me as well. Thank you," Chi-Chi echoed.

The three women took seats at one of the café tables.

Ellie leaned in. "So, Luna, what's the latest with the handsome U.S. marshal?" Ellie was referring to Christopher Gaines, who worked for the service in the missing child unit.

Luna's mind wandered. She had met him several months before the center opened when an AMBER alert was issued. She was still working in child services at the time. She and her dog, Wiley, joined the search party, and not surprisingly, Luna had a "feeling" about where the child might be. It took little convincing for the marshal to follow her lead. He understood the concept of having a "gut feeling" about things. In less

26

than an hour, they found the missing little girl stuck in a large, felled tree trunk. She was unhurt except for a few scratches from trying to follow a bunny. The next day, Luna went to the hospital to visit the little girl and give her a stuffed bunny.

When Luna arrived at the hospital, she saw Marshal Gaines several yards ahead with a similar plush rabbit under his arm. It was at that moment that Luna wanted to swoon. The practical side of Luna told her not to even think about it. But several weeks after the missing child situation had been resolved, Gaines asked her to come to Charlotte to assist in a family emergency and a missing teenager. The service would pay her per day and her expenses, including a hotel. It was a two-hour drive in each direction, and the busy interstate was no place for a woman alone. Her boss let her use a couple of vacation days, insisting she not "make a habit out of it." But it was an opportunity she couldn't resist, in more ways than one. After it happened several times, her boss finally acquiesced to the needs of the U.S. Marshals Service.

Once they wrapped up for the day, Gaines, Luna, and one or two others from the field office would go out to dinner. It wasn't easy for her to keep her giddiness in check, but

Gaines was getting used to her zany but endearing personality.

She wanted to keep the communications open with him, but he lived two hours away. She didn't know how many more times her boss would bow to the feds and let her go to Charlotte and she had no idea if there would ever be a reason for him to come to Asheville. Then it hit her. The grand opening of the center was a good opportunity for her to invite him back to Buncombe County. She wasn't counting on his showing up, but for her own peace of mind she had to take the shot. What was the worst thing that could happen? Luna decided to pull up her big-girl pants and mailed him an invitation to the grand opening of the center. He hadn't responded, which was rather disappointing. She told herself that maybe he didn't get it. Or maybe he was on a case. Or maybe he just wasn't interested. But a half hour before the event ended, he walked in with a bouquet of sunflowers. He had remembered. Luna was thoroughly impressed. During one of their earlier dinner conversations, everyone was talking about their favorite places on Earth. Luna mentioned Tuscany because of all the sunflowers. When she saw him enter her café, sunflowers in hand, she almost fainted.

When Gaines arrived at the gala, he and Cullen immediately clicked. Luna was beginning to feel like the "little sister" until she pulled Gaines into helping solve the mystery of a will that was lodged in one of Cullen's salvaged pieces. As they pried into the origin of the will, they began to uncover a web of deceit. Between Luna's "vibes" and Gaines's resources, they were able to rectify a very bad situation. Since then, the three of them, together with Chi-Chi, had formed a comfortable bond.

Ellie cleared her throat. "Well?" Ellie pushed again. Luna started to blush. Thoughts of Gaines made her feel like a teenager.

"Wellll, I don't know." Luna fiddled with her coffee mug.

Chi-Chi put her hand on Ellie's arm. "Do not believe the words that are coming out of her mouth." Her voice had a lilting rhythm. No doubt, she could recite a passage from a poem by Edgar Allan Poe and make it sound like a nursery rhyme.

Luna blinked several times. "What are you talking about?" she replied, protesting just a little too much.

Chi-Chi then placed her other hand on Luna's. "Luna, owon okan. You can be honest with us. We are your friends." Chi-Chi knew very well how much of a crush Luna had on the marshal, but she wanted Luna to feel comfortable discussing it in front of Ellie. Ellie had become the matriarch of the group, and Luna and Chi-Chi welcomed her advice eagerly. Chi-Chi hoped Ellie could share some with her romantically reluctant friend.

"OK. OK." Luna took a sip of her coffee. "We've had dinner a couple of times."

"And?" both Chi-Chi and Ellie pursued in unison.

Luna shrugged. "*And,* nothing." She knew neither of her friends was buying her nonchalant attitude.

"Pul-lease, woman. You have been smitten since the very first day you met him. And I, for one, have been around you and that fine man." Chi-Chi tuned to Ellie. "I believe what we have here are two adults pretending there is no attraction. I have seen it. I have *felt* it." Chi-Chi sat back in her chair and crossed her arms. Nigerians were known for telling the truth. Except when it's someone calling or e-mailing you telling you that your uncle wants to wire $3 million into your bank account if you would just give them all your banking information.

Luna looked over at her friend. "Are you finished?" It was a rhetorical question. Luna knew by her body language that Chi-Chi had said what she had to say and was done. Not in a mean way. She was merely punctuating her sentence with her posture.

Ellie smiled at Luna. "I have to agree with Chi-Chi. I've seen the two of you together. There is definitely chemistry there. So, I repeat. What is the latest?"

"We haven't spoken since last week. He's been busy with a case. Apparently, a child went missing from Raleigh, and there were several sightings between there and Louisville, Kentucky. He's been working out of the Kentucky field office." She broke apart the brioche and slathered some butter on it. She let out a big sigh. "Speaking of getting fat . . ." Luna shoved half the brioche into her mouth, hoping it would end the conversation.

"I knew there was a reason I liked you." Ellie chuckled. "But you're not getting off that easy. You must be very fond of him."

"Yes. As in really-*really*. I feel like I'm back in high school." Luna swallowed in a big gulp, then pouted.

"But isn't that a wonderful feeling?" Chi-Chi's smile was ear to ear.

"Yes, and no." Luna licked the butter off her fingers.

"Yes, because it gives me a warm and

31

fuzzy feeling, and no, because it scares the bejeezus out of me. I'm afraid if I make a move, as in big move, I'll make a fool of myself."

"I am surmising you haven't done *it* yet." Ellie went for the deep dive.

"What? No!" Luna was emphatic.

"But do you *want* to?" Chi-Chi poked her with an elbow.

Luna slouched. "OK. I'd be lying if I said I didn't have fantasies about being with him. Yes, as in *being* with him. Sometimes I think the fantasy is enough. What if we did, and I was disappointed?"

Chi-Chi and Ellie almost doubled over. "I seriously doubt he would disappoint you." Chi-Chi grinned.

Luna looked up at her friends. "I am sure you are correct. But, what if *he* doesn't want to?"

"He is a man," Chi-Chi said plainly, causing everyone to howl. "And I have seen the way he looks at you. His eyes smile."

"Do you know when you'll see him again?" Ellie asked.

"No idea. Once the case is closed, he'll have to make up time with his son. Plus, he's still working on renovating his house. Plus he lives a hundred and twenty miles away."

"Sounds like a good situation. What I mean is, it could be promising. For the future." Ellie was trying to be reassuring. "Eventually, he'll finish his house, and his son will be in high school with plenty of things to do."

"And, from what I've noticed, in America, teenagers want little to do with family. They don't have many rules." Chi-Chi had been raised in a strict but loving household. Family first, which meant chores, church, school, and more chores.

"That's true. Even Cullen and I had certain responsibilities. Then again, we didn't have all the technology either. Twenty years ago, there wasn't an iPhone to drain your brain, and social media was in its infancy."

Luna thought for a minute. "Too bad it grew into the monster it is now."

"Just like so many teenagers." Chi-Chi laughed.

"I think you're changing the subject." Ellie sat up taller. "So you haven't done the thing yet. Has he kissed you?"

Luna's eyes went wide. "Why, Ellie Stillwell. How bold of you," she joked.

"Answer her question." Chi-Chi resumed the position with her arms folded, knowing the answer.

Luna was full-on blushing at this point. "Yes. And yes, it was won-der-ful. Sweet. Tender." Her eyes glazed at the memory of the first kiss, the first *real* kiss in his truck. "But that was the second kiss. The first one was a nose-knock." She shook her head. "You know the kind when you both go in for it and miss?"

"Do I ever!" Ellie was laughing. "That happened to me and Richard. More than once. The first time we were in a movie theater. I had a bin of popcorn in my lap. He turned sideways. I thought he was reaching for the popcorn and I leaned back. He lost his balance, and our heads banged into each other's. Popcorn went everywhere." Ellie smiled at the funny memory.

"Now, that's funny." Luna chuckled.

"I have also had a mishap," Chi-Chi offered. "One time when I was on a date, we were slow dancing. When he tried to kiss me, his hands got tangled in my braids. The more he tried to unravel them the more tangled he became. He spun me around and we almost fell on the floor." Chi-Chi demonstrated by pulling on several of her two dozen braids, yanking her head from side to side.

At this point, the women were doubled over. "What's all the hilarity?" Cullen's

34

voice was heard coming through the adjoining door.

"Nothing." Luna was trying to keep her equanimity, but her latest sip of coffee went up her nose. Cullen stood stoically. Luna tried to look up at her brother, but the coffee was now running from her nose and down her chin. She couldn't stop laughing.

"I'll come back later." Cullen began to turn away.

"No. No. Please." Chi-Chi beckoned him with a graceful wave.

Luna finally regained some poise. "What can I do for you, my brother?"

"I was wondering about that trunk."

"Oh. And so you've been bitten by the mystery bug, eh?"

"I don't know if I should deposit the money order or not."

"Why not?"

"Because I don't want to start something I can't finish."

"Now, that has never, ever happened. What's bugging you, bro?"

"The whole thing. The more I thought about it, and what you said, the creepier I felt."

All eyes went around the table. "What is making you feel creepy?" Chi-Chi asked.

Luna and Cullen explained about the

mysterious, smoke-laden steamer trunk, letter, and money order that had been delivered anonymously that morning.

"I really don't have time to start the project right now, but I am curious about all of it," Cullen added.

Ellie looked at her watch. "It's almost time to open the center. Why don't we reconvene later and we can have a group think about it?"

"I like that idea." Luna shot up from her seat. "We can make it a group project. I'm sure there are a few things we can do to help." She looked at her brother.

He smirked. "Not sure what I'm getting myself into, but yes, let's meet up later. Say five thirty?"

"Works for me," Luna said.

"We close at five today, so that is fine with me, too," Chi-Chi answered.

"You've got yourself a deal, young man." Ellie stood and patted him on the shoulder.

Cullen chuckled. "I hope I won't regret this."

Luna flicked him on the back of his head.

CHAPTER TWO

Thirty miles from Stillwell Art Center
Present day

Tori was just leaving her doctor's office. Her hands were still shaking from the news. She was pregnant. Again. Sure, lots of women have babies at thirty-eight. But those are normally planned. True, she had missed her last period; but she was never "regular." She suspected it was a result of a not-so-romantic situation with her husband.

Their first child was also unplanned, but she had been nineteen back then. Nineteen. She thought she was in love and that everything was going to work out fine. Work out fine in spite of the rocky beginning they had had. Not a chance. But she had believed. She believed that people could live "happily ever after." She *had* to believe it because that's exactly what he promised when he convinced her to run away with him the night of the party. "No strings to people who don't give a crap." She thought they would conquer the world. He had $5,000 in cash. Back then, it seemed like a lot of money. How naïve she had been.

The initial shock came when they realized that a month's rent and security deposit took a chunk out of his loot. Tori had wasted no time looking for a job. She scoured the papers every day. Google was barely up and running at the time, and websites like Indeed and ZipRecruiter hadn't been created yet. She finally landed a job as a hostess in a local restaurant. Her experience? Busing tables at the local pancake shop. With her pretty, youthful looks, it was enough for the proprietor to hire her. The pay wasn't great, but she treated it as an opportunity to hone her organizational skills, anticipating that she would eventually get a better job. The restaurant business was not where she wanted to spend her career, such as it was.

He, on the other hand, took a little longer to find something he thought was "suitable," but after another three months went by, he knew he had to do something. It was embarrassing to have your wife be the breadwinner, so he took a job at a local distribution center working in a warehouse. After a few months, he was done with forklifts and applied to the police academy. Decent pay, benefits, good retirement plan. Tori couldn't really argue with that. But being married to a cop? She had heard hair-raising stories, and a lot of it wasn't work related. But it was something.

Within the year, she got pregnant. They hadn't planned on it, but there it was. She worked up until a few days before she delivered a baby boy. And voila! They were a family.

She thought about her estranged family. It had been two decades since she had last seen them. She heard that her mother had been in and out of rehab and eventually died of liver failure. As far as she knew, her father had moved to Alabama to retire. When she was a kid, he would often say how he couldn't wait until he could "just hunt 'n' fish all day." She hardly ever saw him. He had been a long-haul trucker. He would be gone for weeks at a time. Tori sometimes wondered if he had a secret family stashed somewhere. And her brother? Nothing since the incident. She thought he might have gone into foster care.

Tears streamed down her face. Her guilt was multilayered. Her life at Casa Aluminum had faded into the dust. The night of the incident, she had fled the scene and sneaked a note into the mailbox. The last thing she wanted was a search party looking for her. The letter was short. She wasn't sure either of her parents would bother to read it, but she wrote it just in case anyone asked where she was.

Dear Mom and Dad,
  I'm sorry for all the trouble I caused and I won't be coming back. Don't worry about me. I'm fine. Really. And please, please do not try to look for me. That would only make it worse. I love you.

She had only been eighteen at the time, but the memories lurked in the shadows of her mind. She was horrified at what she had done, even if it was an accident. Looking back, she knew she had made a mistake. One of the first of many. With each bad decision, she fell deeper and deeper into the dark hole that had become her life. She wondered when the cycle would end.

And now? Now she had a new challenge. She knew she needed a miracle. But she seriously doubted that she deserved one.

It was that fateful event that crippled her thinking. Paralyzed her judgment. She didn't have the courage to face the consequences, so they fled. And he certainly

40

didn't want to have to answer questions either. He convinced her it was better this way. A clean break. They would be on their own. Together. It was a wild, romantic fantasy. They would find a place of their own. Get jobs. Together, they would dream about what they would do with their lives. *Yeah, dream, not do.*

Tori shook her head. Had she given more thought about what she wanted when she was a teenager, she wouldn't be in the situation she was in now. Yes, thinking things through should always be the first step. Sadly, she was finding that out the hard way.

She placed a hand on her belly. She didn't know how to tell him he was going to be a father again. Not that he was a terrible father. He had done all the father-son things over the years. Baseball, camping, fishing. But her son showed much more sensitivity than his father ever had. Brendon refused to go hunting, which sparked his father's ire.

No, Brendon was kind. Compassionate. Plus, he had a goal. She supposed he was making up for her failings in having a plan. He wanted to join the military. Army Cyber. He had been playing video games since he was nine. He had a knack for it. Now he was eighteen, the same age she had been when she ran away. But the military would be good for him. He would have a career, and with some luck, he wouldn't be in harm's way. She couldn't blame him either. Hadn't she run from a miserable upbringing? The only difference was that she had a bond with *her* child. Her mother had not.

But the idea of another child with him meant she would be tied to him for another eighteen years. That thought gave her pause. It's not as if she had seriously considered divorce. She rarely considered anything when it came to her own interests and needs. Thank goodness for George Layton. Even though he had helped steer her away from her job, it was in a better direction than the course she had been on. But now there was a big issue to consider.

For years, it had never occurred to her that her husband was controlling. After all, she never took control of her own life. But now she realized that her lack of control was the core of her problem. She simply went about her life as she always had, letting things happen *to* her instead of making them happen *for* her. She had not been fully aware of his passive-aggressive behavior until now.

In the beginning, he had insisted she dye her hair blond. She would be his own personal Barbie doll. He told her he was very disappointed in her when she chopped it off à la Jamie Lee Curtis. She told him it was easier for her with the baby and all. He sulked for days. That also reminded her of all the comments he made when she was pregnant. Once, when they were at a party, he kept remarking about another pregnant woman and how great she looked compared to Tori. He said she looked fat and bloated. It only fueled her insecurity further.

Over the course of time, his moods became darker. And it had been escalating lately, especially since Brendon had left. Going cold-turkey from coming off the Percocet hadn't helped. Several years before, he had been in a motorcycle accident and needed surgery. And just like every other doctor at the time, his surgeon had put him on pain meds. For a bit too long. After six months, amid the national surge and outrage about opiate addiction, the department's on-call surgeon would no longer refill his script. He had given up the motorcycle when he was told it had been totaled and didn't want to spend the money on a new one. "Those days are over," he had barked at her. And he had never been the same since.

Tori was aware that there were genetic ties

to addiction so she limited her alcohol consumption to one glass of wine. She didn't want to turn out like her mother. But her husband's family was a hot mess. All of his relatives had one issue or another. She kept that in the back of her mind and worked hard to keep their household as peaceful as possible. Reliability. Consistency. Argument avoidance. Life was just easier that way.

They lived in a small town. The crime rate was high, but it was mostly auto thefts, so his hours were relatively normal. Which meant that when he wasn't at work, he would be out with his pals.

She checked the bruises on her arm. It was partially her fault. When the doctor asked about them, Tori told her she fell carrying a load of laundry. It was half true. She had brought the laundry basket up from the basement when he grabbed her and started kissing her hard. It had been a while since they made love. He never seemed interested, but that night he was in the mood, and she was happy to oblige his desire. She hoped it would bring back some kind of spark to their relationship, but it had been rough and not very romantic.

Tori wished she had a best friend. Someone she could confide in. But there wasn't anyone, and even if there were, she didn't know if she should or could talk about it. For one thing, she was embarrassed. The other was that her husband was a cop. It was an unspoken rule. You didn't discuss your personal life with others.

Tori sighed and rested her head on the steering wheel. She was proof you shouldn't run off and marry the first boy you kiss.

CHAPTER THREE

Namaste Café
Present day

Luna looked at the clock. It was almost noon. She was happy Cullen had interrupted the morning's conversation. The subject of U.S. Marshal Christopher Gaines always unnerved her. When it came to men, she was skittish. Especially the ones she liked. Any woman with a brain should be skittish around men. But Gaines was different. He had an easy way about him. He was patient, charming, and had a good sense of humor. She didn't have to explain her "gift," and he showed tremendous respect for her work with children. They shared the same quick wit and dry sense of humor although Luna knew she could be a handful. Not that she was a flake, but when she zeroed in on something or someone, it was like trying to wrestle a sock out of a dog's mouth.

Weeks after the gala, Gaines had business

in the area and invited her to dinner. She wasn't sure if it was a date but when they knocked heads as he tried to kiss her, she figured that perhaps it was. It was awkward and funny at the same time.

Whenever Gaines was in the area, they would meet for dinner. Once they took a long hike in the mountains, and she went to Charlotte twice to help on a case. When they were alone, they would walk arm in arm as if they had been doing it for years. But they never held hands. It was OK if you were eight years old, but as an adult, holding hands was a sign of something more intimate. But she was comfortable and felt safe with him. He was always the perfect gentleman, never asking or pushing for her to bed down with him. He would kiss her softly at the end of the night, and Luna could feel the chemistry flowing between them. It was all she could do to maintain her balance. They were developing a bond. Something deeper. But it hadn't gone any further between them. Truth be told, she wished it had, but she wasn't going to push it. It had been sweet and lovely. Why mess with that? Which is exactly why she avoided discussing it with Ellie and Chi-Chi.

Luna pulled out her two-way radio and called Sabrina, one of the local college art students who volunteered at the center. "Bri? Can you hold the fort for me for a few minutes? I want to grab a sandwich and check on Wiley."

A scratchy noise came through, then Sabrina's voice.

"Sure. No problem. Be there in five. I'm upstairs at Hands of Time." Hands of Time specialized in vintage watches, all refurbished to their original condition, and many fetching prices well into the thousands.

Luna then signaled Alex. "Hey, Alex. How's my guy doing?"

Another scratchy sound before she heard his reply. "He's napping under the tree. He got a pretty good workout with the Frisbee this morning."

"Excellent. Thanks. I'll be over in a few. I'm going to grab a sandwich and swing on by. Do you want anything?"

More clicks and scratches. "If they have one of those roast beef and brie, I'll take it!"

"Roger that!" Luna waited a few minutes until Sabrina arrived.

"Thanks. I'll be back in about ten minutes."

"No problem." That seemed to be her answer for most things.

Luna bounced her way to the Blonde

Shallot, arriving just ahead of the lunch crowd. She checked the long wooden table for Alex's favorite. Luna would often buy Alex a sandwich for watching Wiley. Even though Alex was on the payroll, Luna wanted to show her appreciation for the extra time and energy he spent doggie-sitting. He would reach for his wallet until one day Luna proclaimed, "You do that one more time, mister, I'm going to smack you on the back of the head!"

Alex was grateful for the kind gesture. After his gig at the center, he would go to work at one of the big-box stores for another six-hour shift. He was paying off a student loan to learn how to be a veterinarian technician. After getting his degree, he started working at a local clinic, but within a few months he wanted to be on the playful side of animals, not holding them down to draw blood, take an X-ray, or trim someone's paws. Ellie paid him well, but he still had $30,000 of student loan payments to make. Alex was only twenty-five, but he didn't want to cross into his next decade with a huge amount of debt. If he kept up the pace, he'd achieve his goal in the next three years.

Luna delivered the sandwich while Wiley looked on with anticipation. "And what do you think you're getting?" She gave her pooch a big hug. He nuzzled her arm, waiting for the treat she was about to serve. That, too, had become a routine between them. After Wiley's nap, his mom would bring him a dog chew. "Such a nice day." She breathed in the fresh air.

"It is. If you want to leave Wiley here for the afternoon, that's fine with me. The only other two are Ziggy and Marley."

"Sure you don't mind?" Luna asked, knowing the answer.

Alex laughed. "Don't make me smack you on the back of the head!"

Luna chuckled and scratched Wiley's ears. "You be a good boy now." She turned and headed back to her café, stopping briefly to give Cullen his lunch. When it was available, his choice was the special smoked turkey, muenster, and coleslaw with Russian dressing. Delicious but messy.

From the back of the workshop, Cullen heard the automatic bell signaling someone had entered the showroom.

"Hey there! Oh, do I smell smoked turkey?"

"Your fave." Luna handed him the sandwich and a handful of napkins. "Any progress on the trunk situation?"

"Oh boy. I should know better than to get

you involved." He smiled at his sister.

"As if you could avoid it." She snickered in return.

"Gotta run. Sabrina is covering for me. See you later." She gave him a wave and a raised eyebrow.

Cullen sat at his workbench and unwrapped his sloppy lunch. He reread the letter. Why was the sender being so secretive as to his or her identity? Could the trunk hold something of value? Perhaps stolen? He was getting almost as impatient as his sister. He wondered how long it would take for Luna to use this mystery as an excuse to contact Gaines. Cullen was well aware of their flirtation as well as the mutual respect they shared.

Cullen liked U.S. Marshal Christopher Gaines. If they lived closer, they might even be friends. Not that he didn't think of Gaines as a friend, but a pal. Someone he could hang out with. He loved his sister, but they had different interests outside of work. He liked to watch sports, play golf, and fish. Maybe shoot a little pool now and again. Luna liked to watch comedies or thrillers and do yoga or take a walk in the park. Reading books was another one of Luna's favorite pastimes when she wasn't reading a person. She enjoyed the outdoors but not in the same way as her brother. But they had a pact promising to have dinner together at least one night a week. Lately, they had been inviting Chi-Chi to join them, an invitation she gladly accepted, and Cullen was equally glad she did.

Cullen was growing fond of Chi-Chi. She had a beguiling way about her. She was exotic, intelligent, and laughed at his jokes. Not even his sister thought Cullen had much of a sense of humor. She would say that while he "appreciated humor," he was "no Jerry Seinfeld."

Cullen secretly hoped he might get the courage to invite Chi-Chi out on a date. A real date. He hadn't discussed it with Luna, but *he* knew *she* knew. It was just a matter of time before Luna started poking at him. He chuckled at the irony. Luna would be the one to push him to take that leap, yet she was too chicken to do the same with Gaines. *Must be in our DNA,* he mused.

He looked down at the money order for $1000. Later that afternoon, he knew he would get some feedback from "the crew." Luna decided their little pack of friends needed to be called something. "The Squad" was already taken by a few in Washington, D.C., and they wanted to stay away from anything that had a hint of politics.

He thought about something Chi-Chi once said. "People who have made a difference in the world were not politicians." That comment spurred a lively debate one evening when Gaines was in town and the four of them went to dinner. She emphasized her point by mentioning Jonas Salk, Mother Teresa, Gandhi, Marie Curie. Gaines was stumped unless he went back to the Founding Fathers. Even now, some of their motives could be considered suspect.

Cullen smiled to himself. The four of them seemed to fit well together. He heaved a sigh and began to clear the debris that began as his lunch. Good thing Luna had brought him enough napkins.

Luna was pacing her shop. She was feeling restless about the trunk. It had been a quiet day at the art center. She had some time on her hands. She quickly ran back to Cullen's showroom, where he was talking to a couple about one of the brass light fixtures he had recently refurbished. He gave her a quizzical look.

She nodded in the direction of the workshop and continued toward the back. Cullen excused himself and came up behind her.

"Everything all right?"

"May I have one of the slats from the crate the trunk came in? And another look at the letter?" She was almost out of breath.

"I thought we were going to . . . never mind." Cullen knew that when Luna got a bee in her bonnet, there was no stopping the buzzing. He walked toward a wall where he kept packing materials and handed her a slat from the crate that had encased the trunk. "Letter is on the workbench. Now scram." He gave her a gentle, brotherly shove.

As Luna strode past the couple, she smiled. "Sorry. Sibling stuff." They smiled back at her.

Luna placed the letter and the piece of wood on the table next to her easel. She sat down, closed her eyes, and placed a hand on the two items. Luna had a particular interest in psychometry. It was the ability to feel vibrations emitted by an object. The laws of physics assert that everything is made up of energy, with subatomic particles moving at different rates of speed, regardless of whether it is a solid, liquid, or gas. She would argue the scientific aspects whenever she was questioned. Most people got the science part; it was the reading part that left them somewhat skeptical. That is,

54

until she would ask to hold something that belonged to them and would proceed to tell them things there was no way she could have known. Just like with Ellie when she told her about the coffee cake. The coffee cake that Ellie's mother would make for their birthdays when she was a child. And the darkroom in the basement of Ellie's childhood home. It took a lot of concentration to do it with a modicum of accuracy. It was like unraveling the molecular structure of an item and reading the energy. Crazy stuff. She wished there was a simple description or clarification.

When she was really pushed for an explanation as to why she believed that what she did was possible, Luna would discuss electromagnetic fields. "Take photons, for example. Light. You can't touch it, but you can see it." If that didn't shut them up, she would continue with the Hadron Collider and the Higgs boson particle theory. Eventually, their facial expressions would go blank. They either pretended they understood by nodding like a bobble-head, or they were genuinely interested. It was more often the former than the latter.

She sniffed at the wood. Nothing. She hadn't been expecting to get anything from it, but it was worth a try. Perhaps the owner of the trunk also owned the wood. She set it aside and placed her hand on the letter. She felt a rush of heat as her face became flushed. She felt a short spark of terror. It was followed by abandonment, then loneliness. Whoever wrote the letter had been through something horrifying and was now feeling abandoned and alone. She shot up from the chair and began to draw. She closed her eyes while her hands made a dozen pointed marks in the shape of an upside down *v* on the page. Then she drew a stick figure of a boy. She got a shiver, opened her eyes, and took a step back. She had no difficulty interpreting the marks on the paper as flames, based on the burnt smell of the trunk. You didn't need to be a genius or a psychic to figure that one out. The stick figure had to be the person who wrote the letter, no? Or could it be their son?

Luna checked the clock again. It was almost four. The center was closing in an hour, and they would have their brainstorming session. Luna felt a burst of energy. She knew in her gut this had to do with a young boy. She wasn't sure his age, but she believed she was on the right track. But right track to where? It all remained to be seen.

Luna began to clean up the café, washing

the porcelain cups and plates and emptying the coffee grinds into a bin.

She took what was left of the pastries and crumbled them up for the birds. Alex was bringing Wiley inside, Ziggy and Marley strutting behind.

Luna watched Chi-Chi glide across the landscaped interior of the atrium. She looked like a beautiful lotus flower floating on a pond. Luna wished she could move with such grace. But no. Even though she could recover a stumble with ease, Luna could be a bit of a klutz at times. Maybe it was from when she was a kid. Hanging around with her slightly older brother carved an easy path to become a tomboy. She still had a bit of that in her.

When they were young, Luna and Cullen would spend endless afternoons scouring the woods for the perfect tree to climb. She and Cullen would sit for hours playing I-Spy games. It wasn't unusual for Luna to have several conversations with the wildlife, too. Those were wonderful, peaceful, beautiful days. Not that her life wasn't wonderful, peaceful, and beautiful, but there was an innocence back then. Innocence. Once it's gone, it's gone. Luna sighed. She was very happy that she and Cullen remained close.

Luna continued to watch her graceful

friend move closer. Luna couldn't imagine Chi-Chi tripping or stumbling over anything. Instead, she envisioned Chi-Chi gliding over any obstacles in her path. It wasn't surprising that Cullen was rather taken with her, even if he wouldn't dare admit it out loud.

"E ka san." Chi-Chi addressed Luna with the usual Yoruba Nigerian afternoon greeting. Luna replied in kind. She enjoyed exchanging salutations in other languages, and often used "Ciao," the Italian greeting, when ending a phone call.

As Alex and Wiley approached, Luna squatted to greet her pooch. "Hey, pal!" She gave Wiley a big hug. He nuzzled her in return. "Thanks, Alex. You are a gem!"

"Any time. He's such a good dog," Alex replied. "See you tomorrow."

Chi-Chi squatted and spoke to Wiley in Yoruba. *"Ti o dara aja."* Luna swore he understood what she was saying as he nuzzled Chi-Chi in return.

"Even Wiley is multilingual." Luna snickered and scanned the café to be sure everything was in place. She snatched the drawing from the easel, the letter, and the wooden slat, then shut and locked the sliding front doors. The three of them entered Cullen's showroom from the adjoining entry. "Hi-di-ho!" Luna's voice sang through the showroom as Cullen greeted them with a big smile.

Ellie was coming through the main entrance of Cullen's place with Ziggy and Marley wagging their tails behind her. "Hi-di-ho to you," Ellie chimed back. "So where is this mystery project?"

"This way." Cullen turned toward the workshop with Luna, Chi-Chi, Ellie, Wiley, Ziggy, and Marley in tow. For their size, Ziggy and Marley easily maneuvered between the refurbished pieces of furniture and antiques without thumping their tails on anything.

In the workshop, Ziggy, Marley, and Wiley spotted the plush blanket Cullen kept for Wiley. After circling the blanket several times, the three dogs chose their spots and made themselves comfortable in a big doggie heap. Chi-Chi couldn't help but repeat what she had said a few minutes ago. *Ti o dara ajas.* Ellie looked at her quizzically.

"It means 'good dogs,' " Chi-Chi explained.

"Wiley already knows how to speak Yoruba," Luna said with a straight face.

Earlier that afternoon, Cullen had moved the trunk away from the wall and made enough room for everyone to circle it.

"That surely has a distinct odor," Ellie noted.

"It must have been very close to a fire," Luna said. "Close enough to pick up the smell but far enough to survive it."

"And you don't know where it came from?" Ellie knew she was asking a rhetorical question.

"No. Luna, you have the letter?" Cullen asked.

"Yep. I also tried to get some vibrations off it." She handed Cullen the roughly drawn sketch. "I believe those pointy objects represent the fire. The stick figure seems to be a young boy, but I couldn't zero in on the age. I also got a sense of terror, abandonment, loneliness." She shrugged.

"Maybe it was someone's son who died in the fire?" Ellie suggested.

"Oh, that would be a most terrible thing." Chi-Chi folded her arms and shook her head.

"That's just it. I didn't get a vibration that the person had crossed over. It was much more a sense of abandonment." She paused for a moment.

Chi-Chi asked softly, "But who? The person in the drawing or the person who wrote the letter?"

Luna thought hard. She placed her hands

on the trunk. A swarm of images swirled through her head. Like a movie in fast-forward. She steadied herself.

"Are you all right?" Chi-Chi unfolded her arms and placed a hand on Luna's shoulder.

"Yes. Wow. That was weird, even for me." Luna sucked in a big gulp of air through her nose and took a step back, away from the trunk.

"What was it?" Chi-Chi gently urged.

"They were flashes of an old swing, tickets, and something like a county fair. Maybe a carnival. You know, the ones that have a midway with games." Luna took another deep breath. "It went by so fast. It wasn't creepy or anything. I felt like I was spinning really fast on a carousel."

"Have you been able to open it?" Ellie motioned to the trunk.

"I was waiting for all of you. The lock is jammed. I'm going to have to use jeweler's tools. Plus, I want witnesses."

"Witnesses? Why?" Ellie asked.

"The letter said there might be contents and if I could set them aside and return them with the trunk. Since this whole situation is rather unusual, who knows what is in there and what the person might do." Cullen leaned against his workbench.

"I'm not following you, Cullen," Ellie said.

"Like if there was something valuable in there and it turned up missing?" Luna asked.

"Exactly." Cullen pushed himself off the bench and grabbed his tools. "Everyone ready?"

"What are you waiting for?" Luna cried out in excitement.

"Let's lay it down horizontally first." Cullen motioned everyone to help him tilt the trunk so the top was facing upward.

Cullen squatted and sat on his heels. He opened a small pouch and pulled out two small tools: a needle file and utility tweezers. He then wiped the old lock and hardware with a polishing cloth and some lubricant.

Luna folded her arms and was tapping her foot in anticipation. Cullen looked over his shoulder, put up his hands, and said in mock distress, "If you don't mind. I am trying to perform a very delicate operation here."

Luna cackled. Her brother was trying to be funny and succeeded. Maybe there was hope for his sense of humor.

Chi-Chi tried to stifle a laugh. "Apologies, Dr. Locksmith."

Cullen snapped his head around and looked at Chi-Chi. Was she flirting with him? He exaggerated clearing his throat.

"A-hem."

Ellie, Luna, and Chi-Chi moved in closer to watch. Chi-Chi's face was inches from Cullen's. He could feel her breath on his neck. He almost dropped the tweezers. "Room, please. This is a very delicate procedure." He waited for everyone to give him some space. And for his silliness to subside.

"Aye-aye, sir!" Luna gave him a tap on his shoe. She knew exactly what was happening and couldn't be more delighted. She actually got goose bumps. It reminded her of when she was with Chris Gaines. That awkward feeling.

It took a few minutes, then Cullen proclaimed, "Success!" He gingerly removed the hardware. "OK, before I open it, everyone should put on a mask in case there's ash or dust. Luna, can you grab them and some disposable gloves, please?"

Luna opened one of the storage cabinets and pulled out four surgical-looking masks and the gloves. "Boy, I thought I'd never have to wear these again." She thought about the nearly two years when everyone had been encouraged to wear a mask in public. "Gives me the willies just thinking about it." She handed the protective items to Ellie, Chi-Chi, and Cullen. Just before she was about to put her mask on, she suggested, "Maybe we should get the dogs out of here."

"Good idea." Cullen nodded at Ellie to round up the pooches and put them in the showroom. "They can't do too much damage."

Ellie motioned for the dogs to follow her. Wiley looked up at Luna. "It's OK. You can go with your buddies."

Wiley obediently followed his pals, and Ellie shut the door.

"Everyone ready?"

A resounding "yes" came from the group.

Cullen cautiously lifted the top of the trunk. There was a folded blanket that smelled worse than the trunk. The odor came right through their masks.

"Whoa!" Luna exclaimed. "It's amazing it's not in cinders."

Cullen gently removed the blanket and placed it on the floor. Luna began to unfold it. Wrapped within the blanket was an old diary. The edges of the pages had turned brown. It, too, had a lock. "Cul, take a look at this. See if you can unlock it." As she was about to hand it to him, she got another flash. Someone was running.

"What?" Cullen asked.

"Another flicker. People running." Luna

shook her head in an effort to clear it. She turned the secret book over to her brother. Another fold in the blanket revealed a small wooden box about ten inches long by twelve inches wide and five inches deep. She lifted the lid. It contained ticket stubs, a flyer, and fake coins. The kind you would use at an amusement park. Just like the vision she had experienced. She sat on the floor and scrutinized each piece. "Wow. This is someone's history."

"But whose?" Cullen was leaning over Luna's shoulder at this point.

Luna placed the items back in the box. It would be a tricky process to make any sense out of it. And the diary? That would require some time. It looked as if this was going to be a bigger project then Cullen had imagined. Not that he would try to figure out the puzzle of ownership, but now his sister was going to be immersed in it. He knew all too well that Luna would make every effort to piece it together. She was unstoppable.

Cullen checked the rest of the trunk. "Well, I feel like Geraldo Rivera when he opened a vault that belonged to Al Capone. All the hype and only dust."

"Well, now you just wait a darn second, mister," Luna objected. "We have the remnants of someone's life here. And I'm willing to bet *that* someone has something to do with whoever wrote that letter. That seems rather apparent to me. No?"

Chi-Chi offered support. "Luna has a very good point. Perhaps the owner was hoping you would find something. They implied that in the letter, correct?"

"Correct," Cullen answered. "But it doesn't necessarily seem to have any value."

"Ah," Chi-Chi replied. "People have value. I am in agreement with your sister. This person who sent this to you is looking for someone."

"But I am not in the missing persons business," Cullen protested.

"That is true. But you know someone who is. And your sister knows things. Even when she doesn't know what she knows." Chi-Chi gave a little chuckle.

"OK. But how would the person who sent this know we have connections with people who look for missing people?" Cullen asked.

"Now, *that* is a good question," Ellie replied.

"But Chris works with missing children," Luna pointed out.

"Yes, but he has access to vast amounts of information." Chi-Chi shrugged. "It might be a coincidence." She looked at Luna. "What do you think?"

"I don't believe in coincidences." Luna stared blankly at the trunk. "But that doesn't mean it was intentional either."

Ellie looked perplexed. "I don't understand. What do you mean it wasn't intentional?"

"I mean the person who sent it was hoping Cullen could get it open and return the contents, so that same person could use whatever *we* find to find who *they* are looking for. It just so happens we know someone in the business of finding people." Luna looked at Ellie. "Am I making sense now?"

"So you don't think the sender knows about Gaines or your particular talents?" Ellie asked.

"Not necessarily. But for whatever reason, the universe brought all of this, and us, together. It's called synchronicity. Simultaneous events with meaningful connections. And, together, we are going to figure it out." Luna placed her hands on her hips, signaling she was on a mission, and that was that.

CHAPTER FOUR

Present day

Tori sat in her car for a good long while and hadn't yet started the engine. She jumped when a woman knocked on the driver's-side window. "You OK?" It was the nurse from Tori's doctor's office.

"Yeah. I mean yes. I'm good. Thank you." She tilted her head slightly just enough to be convincing, without revealing her tear-stained face.

"You sure?" the nurse pressed. "You look a little pale."

"I'm fine. Really." She gave a slight wave and switched on the ignition, signaling she was fine. As she backed out of the parking space, the nurse continued to watch. Tori had a sinking feeling that the nurse had reservations about how "good" Tori was really feeling.

The nurse was surprised that Tori seemed overwrought about her pregnancy. But sometimes that happens, especially if it's not planned and if you're in your late thirties.

How did we get to this point? Tori wondered.

She wasn't ready to go home. She needed time to think. She couldn't have another baby. Not with him. Her job at the law firm paid well but not well enough for her to be on her own. Plus, he would never let her leave. Not without a fight. It would be ugly. His ego would not be able to take it.

Tori had been driving for almost an hour. She had no particular destination in mind. She was deep in thought, recalling the past twenty years, looking for the tipping point, the point at which things started to go south.

As expected, after they ran away, no one came looking for her. Them. His family was even worse than hers. Maybe that's why they connected at such a young age. They commiserated. His father was a drunk. Her mother was a drunk. They would often joke that their parents should get divorced and marry each other. They were going to rescue each other from their lives in "Casa Aluminum."

Dusk was setting in. The sudden ring from her cell phone caused her to swerve. Fortunately, no one else was on the road. She hit the Bluetooth button. Before she had a chance to say hello, the taut voice of her husband came through the speaker. "Where are you?"

"Running some errands. Sorry, hon." Tori steadied her voice. "Everything OK?"

"Yeah. Fine. Just wondering where you're at." He softened a bit.

"Like I said, running errands. You need anything while I'm out?"

"Nah. I'm going to meet the guys at Ringo's. Shoot some pool." He was referring to the watering hole the local boys in blue frequented. That was one place where he could let loose and know his fellow officers had his back. It was understood. No one let anyone drive if they were trashed. They'd try to sober up whoever was "overserved," at least to the point where they could walk, then someone would drive them home with another "brother" following in the sloshed person's car. It wasn't that often, but everyone seemed to bring some personal drama at one point or another. Cheating. Divorce. Loss of a loved one. Or it could be a cause for celebration. A "good collar," getting engaged, having a kid.

Tori wasn't about to give him a reason to celebrate. Not yet. Not tonight. She still had a lot of thinking to do. At that moment, she had to come up with an idea of what she was bringing home from her "errands." She knew he would eventually ask. Such a control freak. *Aha. There it was again.*

"You gonna grab something to eat at Ringo's?" Tori hoped he'd say yes.

"Probably. When do you think you'll be back?"

If she pushed the speed limit, she could be home in an hour. She would also have to stop at a grocery store or a drugstore to have a bag with something in it when she returned.

"About forty-five minutes." Tori knew he was not going to wait more than a half hour, so forty-five minutes was a safe time frame. If he was still home, she could always say she had gotten stuck behind a slow-moving vehicle. They had a lot of them where she lived. Tractors, mobile homes, wide loads. All common in that area.

"OK. If you're gonna be that long, I'll head over to Ringo's now," he said, his tone of voice signaling his indifference.

"Have fun." Tori squeezed out her best attitude. She was truly relieved she could postpone the conversation, at least for a while. She showed no signs of being six weeks into her pregnancy, so she had a little time. Time to think. Something she had neglected to do a long time ago.

Tori took the next opportunity to make a U-turn and head home. She did a mental inventory of the refrigerator and the pantry. There were a few things she could use. Thirty minutes later, she was pulling into a supersized grocery store. It was three times the size of the one closest to home. She pulled into the massive parking lot and found a spot close to the entrance. It was nearly six. Dinnertime for most people, which meant the store wasn't crowded. She grabbed a shopping cart, walked through the automatic doors, and pulled a sanitary wipe from the large dispenser that held a sign that read:

SAFETY STARTS HERE

She wiped the handle of the cart and continued into the large, well-lit store. It was like being in an amusement park for foodies. She was dazed for a moment, not being able to remember what she actually needed. The place made you think you needed a whole lot of everything.

There were separate sections for gluten-free, vegan, international, organic this, organic that. Nuts and seeds by the pound.

As she made her way toward the dairy section, she was stunned by the selection of milk. At her neighborhood store they had skim, fat-free, whole, and one brand of soy milk. But here there were several brands of oatmeal, coconut, raw, goat, almond, cashew, soy, lactose-free, fat-free. *Too bad it isn't free milk.* She laughed to herself. Then she thought about almond milk and chuckled again to herself. *I wonder how you milk an almond?* It struck her this was the most relaxed she had been all day. She felt anonymous perusing the aisles of the megastore and imagining herself creating wonderful meals. But for whom? They rarely shared a real meal together. He'd come home and take his dinner — pizza, whatever — and plop in front of the television. Forget inviting friends over for dinner. They hardly socialized except for parties with his work buddies and their wives. Sure, every summer they would barbecue, but that, too, wasn't exactly an afternoon with Bobby Flay at the grill. Burgers, dogs, and sometimes sausage. She'd make a potato salad, and guests would bring other sides. Beans, macaroni salad, watermelon. Typical summer fare. The men would play horseshoes and drink beer, and the women would gab about their kids or the latest local gossip.

Her life was a cliché.

As she passed through the enormous produce section, she overheard three women talking in the next aisle about an event they had recently attended. It featured that psychic-medium guy who used to have the TV show. He talked to dead people. Actually, *they* talked to him, and he'd convey the message to their loved ones. She listened intently, making every effort to appear not to be eavesdropping. Then one of them said, "I hear there's a woman at the Stillwell Art Center who does readings. She runs a café or something."

Another remarked, "Yes, but it's only by referrals."

A third voice asked, "How do you get one?"

"I'm not sure, but I was thinking of taking the kids there next weekend. They have a place where you can watch them blow glass, make baskets, throw pottery."

"Oooh, artsy," one of the women said in a mocking tone.

"They also have a sandwich shop and an outdoor area for dogs."

"What about kids?"

"They say that the kids get a kick out of watching the artists at work. I dunno. But I thought I'd give it a shot."

"Let me know how it goes and if you get in to see that psychic person."

"Will do! See you at the soccer game."

Lots of "byes" and "see yas."

As the other women went their separate ways, Tori was staring into space. Maybe that's what she needed. A good psychic. A medium. Whatever they're called. She wondered how she could find out more about it. Her. Maybe she, too, would take a little trip to the center on her day off, which was Saturday and Sunday. She then realized she would have to explain to her husband why she was going to an art center. Too many questions. She could take a personal day during the week. Tori worked at a small law firm as an assistant. There were three partners in the firm, and they rotated taking Wednesdays off. She could coordinate with her boss.

Luckily for Tori, she was well organized. She had to be. At the age of ten, she was the adult on duty. If it weren't for Tori, her little brother J.T. wouldn't have a clean pair of pajamas. There would be no meals, no lunch to take to school. In spite of the lack of adult supervision, Tori ran an efficient household. Her father would hide cash in one of the hutches for food and supplies. Only Tori knew where the money was hid-

den. Her father made sure of that. He didn't
want Tori and J.T.'s mother spending it on
booze. Yes, Tori had the sense and organizational skills out of sheer survival. But planning ahead for herself? There was never any
time for that.

Tori thought about J.T. She wondered
where he was. How he was. It stunk, not
having a family. Even if she hadn't run away,
she still wouldn't have a family. Sure, she
had one parent and a brother. But that
didn't constitute a family. They were simply
human beings sharing some of the same
DNA, bound together legally, and existing
under the same roof. She really thought her
life would be different by now. Maybe it
wasn't too late. She *prayed* it wasn't too
late.

Tori took one more spin through the
bakery department. A woman was handing
out samples of something called rugelach.
It was a small crescent pastry swirled with a
cinnamon filling. The buttery flakes melted
in her mouth. The sign read:

$20.00 DOZEN

She hesitated, but then she decided she
was worth at least six little cakes. If he knew
she was spending ten bucks on what he

76

would consider cookies, he'd have a cow. But Tori had a flash of confidence. *So what. Too bad.* She marched up to the counter and placed her order. As she glanced at her reflection in the bakery case, she could have sworn she had grown a couple of inches taller. *Must be the sugar.* She smiled to herself. Things were going to be different. She wasn't sure how, but she was determined to fix her life. Then she remembered something someone had once said. "You can't fix people. You can only fix yourself."

Tori took the white paper bag from the woman behind the counter, thanked her, and smiled. *Who would have thought a small mixture of buttery dough and cinnamon could cause an epiphany?* She was going to approach things a little differently now. Sure, he'd think she was being the obedient wife, but two can play at the manipulation game.

She pushed her grocery cart toward the deli section and ordered a half pound of bologna and a half pound of American cheese. She never understood why that was her husband's favorite sandwich. He'd be thrilled. Frankly, she didn't care if he was thrilled or not, but this was the first step in taking back some of her own power. Since she had been a strong ten-year-old child, she could be a mighty thirty-eight-year-old adult. Tori could hear him bragging at work, "Hey, look what the old lady made for me." God, how she hated that expression. *Old lady, my ass.*

CHAPTER FIVE

Stillwell Art Center
The same day

Cullen placed the blanket and its contents on his long worktable. "I'll get to the diary lock tomorrow."

Luna frowned.

"Listen. I know that as soon as I get it open, you'll be digging into it like an archeologist. You'll be engrossed for hours. Days," Cullen said evenly. It wasn't the first time he had had to convince his sister to take it easy. Slow down. "Besides, I don't know about anyone else, but I could use some dinner. It's past six."

"And I have to get Marley and Ziggy home before my board meeting," Ellie said.

"I'd be available to get something to eat." Chi-Chi hoped she hadn't crossed a line. It wasn't unusual for all of them to share a meal, but when it came to Cullen, she always waited to be invited. She also had

79

her own crush going on.

Luna still stood with her arms akimbo. "Huh. Traitors."

Everyone chuckled as Chi-Chi linked her arm through Luna's. "Come, girl. You need to make sure you are robust for this new puzzle."

Luna shook her head and pulled Chi-Chi toward the café entrance. "Gotta lock up." Luna felt her cell phone vibrate in her apron pocket. When she reached in and saw the caller ID, she stopped in her tracks. "Whoa."

"Something good?" Chi-Chi asked with a playful grin.

"I . . . it's . . . him." Luna began to blush.

"Well, don't be stupid, girl. Answer it."

Luna took in a deep breath. "Well hello, Marshal Gaines. To what do I owe this pleasure?" Her eyes went wide at Chi-Chi, as if asking, "Did I do that all right?" Chi-Chi gave her an encouraging nod.

Gaines cleared his throat. "Hello, Lunatic." Luna could hear the smile in his voice. "How are you?"

"Very well, thank you. And yourself?" She was trying to keep the tremor out of her voice.

"Great. Listen, I know it's short notice, but I am heading back to Charlotte, and I have to pass through Asheville. Any chance you guys are free for dinner?"

"Funny you should ask. Cul, Chi-Chi, and I were about to head out for a bite to eat after we take Wiley home. Where are you now?"

"Just outside of Weaverville. I wasn't sure what time I would be nearby; otherwise, I would have phoned sooner." He paused. "Do you mind if I join you?"

"Of course not! *We* would be delighted." Emphasizing the "we." Her palms were getting sweaty.

"I'm about twenty minutes away. Should I meet you somewhere?"

"Sure." Luna walked toward the mirror over her small utility sink. She wasn't exactly spruced up, and gave Chi-Chi a look of horror. Chi-Chi waved her off and mouthed, "You look fine."

"Copper Crown OK with you?" Luna asked, as she fussed with her hair.

"Sounds good. See you there." Gaines clicked off the call, relieved that she was willing to meet. He had driven six hours before he had found the nerve to call her. After knowing Luna for almost a year, he still got all stupid. At least that was his own perception of things. Perhaps if they lived closer, their relationship, such as it was, would have blossomed faster. Sooner. On the other hand, they both had a lot going on in their lives. *Slow and steady,* he kept telling himself. At least he was able to kiss her good night now without getting a concussion. He never pushed it any further. Luna was going to have to be the one to take it to the next level.

Chi-Chi was beaming from ear to ear. "It appears the marshal has missed the 'Lunatic,' " she teased.

Luna was sputtering. "Look at me! I have smoky dust on me, my hair is a mess, and it looks like I slept in my clothes!"

Cullen walked into the café. "What's keeping you guys?"

Chi-Chi smiled. "Your sister received a phone call from the good marshal. He is going to meet us for dinner."

"Cool!" Cullen was almost as excited as his sister. "What brings him into town?"

Chi-Chi tilted her head in the direction of Luna.

"Stop!" Luna protested. "He is on his way back from Louisville. That's all."

Cullen chuckled. "So he decided to make a right turn off the interstate?"

"It would appear so." Chi-Chi nodded.

Luna let out a growl. "Oh, you guys!"

"Thou doth protest too much," Chi-Chi replied.

Luna stomped her way to the ladies' room to see what she could do to salvage her appearance. Chi-Chi followed her. Luna was splashing water on her face and glumly stared into the mirror.

"Now, listen to me, woman. You are beautiful. Inside and out. I don't think the marshal would go out of his way to see you if he didn't agree with me."

"Oh, Chi-Chi. I always feel like a schoolgirl around him. Awkward and clumsy." Luna kept fussing with her hair.

"You are none of those things. Here, let me help you. But first take that thing off." In her excitement, Luna had forgotten to remove the work apron. Thankfully, that got rid of most of the smell of smoky dust.

In less than a couple of minutes, Chi-Chi braided Luna's hair so it fell in front of her shoulder. Chi-Chi then pulled out a tube of coral lipstick and dabbed it on Luna's cheeks and blended it in. "Well, that's one thing I cannot do on my face, but it works for you." They both laughed. Chi-Chi handed the tube over to Luna. "Now, on your lips."

In less than ten minutes, Luna was transformed into what she considered presentable. She sniffed at her clothes. "I still smell like a day's work is all over me."

Chi-Chi reached for the lavender air freshener, sprayed a big cloud of it, and waved the mist in Luna's direction. "He'll never know it came from a can. Trust me."

Luna laughed and gave Chi-Chi a big hug. "I don't know what I would do without you."

There was a loud rapping at the door. "You ladies finished in there? I called the restaurant. They're expecting us. Move it!" Cullen feigned impatience.

Luna swung the large door open. "Wow. How in the heck did you do that?" Cullen was taken aback at the instantaneous makeover.

"Chi-Chi has magical skills." Luna breezed past him. "Let's go. What are you waiting for?" She was teasing, of course.

The three arrived at the restaurant as Gaines was getting out of his Jeep. He briskly walked toward them, trying to decide what to do first, shake Cullen's hand or give Luna a hug. "Heys" and "hellos" filled the air. He instinctively opened his arms, and it turned into a group hug. Cullen patted him on the back. "Good to see you, man."

"Likewise." Gaines put his hand on Cullen's shoulder, wrapped his other arm around Luna's shoulder, and gave her an exaggerated side squeeze. It was effortless considering it was almost two months since they had been in each other's company. Lots can change in a short amount of time. But it was if they had simply picked up where they left off. It had been that way from the start.

The hostess greeted the frequent diners, reminding Cullen she had an old china cabinet she wanted him to look at. Luna gave Chi-Chi an eye roll. Both women knew the perky hostess was always flirting with Cullen. But Cullen never took the bait. He had other interests, even if the "other" person didn't know it. Yet. Soon. Maybe.

As they settled in their seats, Gaines began the conversation. "So, what kind of trouble are you getting yourself into these days?" Everyone knew he was joking. It wasn't necessarily trouble, but there was always plenty of activity swirling around Luna. She was a force of nature. Yet she navigated through it with aplomb. She was the calming center when things got a bit lively.

All eyes went to Luna. "What?" She slumped back in her seat, faking a pout.

"Well, that certainly tells me there is something afoot."

"Says Sherlock Holmes," Luna teased back.

Cullen jumped in. "Yes, there is something very puzzling going on. I received a very old trunk. A steamer. I'm thinking maybe 1920s. There was no return name or address, but there was a letter and a money order."

Luna couldn't contain herself and sat upright. "And it had been near a fire!"

Cullen leaned in toward the others and described the mysterious delivery. He went on to describe the contents, what little there was of them, and Gaines immediately knew what was going to come next. Luna was going to try to solve the puzzle. Who sent it? Who owned it?

"Of course, Luna has already tried to get a vibe off the wood and the letter." Now Cullen was being serious. They could tease her, but not question her.

"So what did you get?" Gaines turned his attention to her.

"I drew a sketch of peaks and a boy. He was unhappy. Abandoned. And at some point terrified."

"Could have something to do with the fire that the trunk was exposed to."

"Well, yeah, sure. But the kid. It was a very sad feeling. I didn't get a vibe that he had crossed over. So I'm thinking maybe he was around the fire?" Luna stared off in the distance, then shook it off. "No shoptalk."

"As if," Cullen joked. He turned to Gaines. "But I do happen to have a nice wardrobe closet that would be great for Carter's baseball equipment."

"That might work. Right now the laundry room looks like a grenade went off from a sporting goods shop."

Luna giggled. "No shoptalk."

"For now." Cullen began pouring everyone a glass of wine, starting with Chi-Chi. Cullen had called earlier and asked for a bottle of La Crema Pinot Noir to be opened and left on the table. It would give the wine a little time to "breathe." Not that Cullen was a wine expert. Far from it. But he knew the basics. And the La Crema was reasonably priced at around $25 a bottle. No sticker shock there. He knew not to commit that faux pas again.

After they toasted seeing each other, Cullen told them the story of when he was just out of college and on a date with a debutante. He wanted to impress her. He ordered a bottle of Châteauneuf-du-Pape, not realizing the price could range anywhere from $30 to $900 per bottle depending on the vintage. Luckily, that particular restaurant's highest priced bottle was $135. Still, he almost vomited when he got the check.

Everyone roared with laughter.

"Boy, do I know that feeling." Gaines added his own story about the time he was best man at a wedding. After the festivities, the wedding party went to the hotel where many of the guests were staying. They had congregated in the lounge area when he told the waiter to "bring the most expensive bottle of champagne you have! That's when I was introduced to Dom. Dom Pérignon. I had to call my credit card company and ask them to raise my limit. I think I'm still paying it off!"

Cullen was almost in tears. "Men can do some very stupid things to puff up their egos."

Luna and Chi-Chi looked at each other and nodded in agreement.

"Oh, and I don't suppose either of you have done anything stupid?" Cullen mocked back.

"Nothing like that." Luna smiled.

"Oh, I can think of . . . ouch!" Cullen was stopped short by Luna's foot on top of his under the table.

"Something wrong?" Chi-Chi asked innocently.

"Nah. Just a little charley horse." Cullen

replied by kicking his sister in return. But this time it shook the table.

Chi-Chi placed both hands on the table. "I do hope we are not having an earthquake," she said with a straight face.

"I think it's called a sibling seismic situation." Gaines chuckled.

Both Cullen and Luna sat up straight. It was reminiscent of when they were kids, after their parents would scold them during a squabble at the dinner table.

Then Luna got a flash. "Hey, Christopher, based on the letter, it seems as if the person who sent the trunk is looking for someone."

Cullen interrupted. "Weren't you the one who said, 'no shoptalk'?" Luna tapped his foot again, to which he responded, "Continue. Please."

Gaines smiled at both of them. "And you surmised there is a missing person involved? How?" He stopped and reversed his approach. "Why do I ask? I should know better by now." He laughed quietly.

"It was something in the letter. Something about the contents, and if they were in good order to please return them," Luna said. "I would think that was a given. You return items contained within. But he made a point of it, so it had to be on his mind."

"OK. But how do you know it's a he?"

Gaines mused. "Never mind. Dumb question."

"And, so, maybe you could help us find the missing person?" Luna spoke in an innocent, childlike fashion.

"We don't know if it has anything to do with a missing person." Cullen jumped in, hoping to save Gaines the headache he was about to inherit.

Gaines leaned back in his chair. "As much as I would love to join the Jessica Fletcher Committee, I have to get back to Charlotte."

"Tonight? But it's getting late," Luna said, disappointed. Disappointed for a couple of reasons.

Cullen decided to take a flying leap. "Hey, man, why don't you crash at my place tonight? I have a foldout in my den. Then you can get a fresh start in the morning."

Luna almost choked on her drink. Gaines staying at her brother's house. That could go in many different directions. She wished she had the guts to ask him to stay in her spare room, but she still wasn't ready for the totally awkward moment. If there would ever be one.

Gaines perked up. "Sure you don't mind?"

"Not at all. Give us a chance to catch up.

I have a few new fishing flies I'd like to show you."

"You tie them yourself?" Gaines was truly interested.

"I wish I could take the credit, but I'm learning."

"I've taken Carter fishing a few times, but I'd like to get him into fly-fishing. Something we can keep doing as I get older." He snickered. "Touch football is going to be out of my range soon enough."

Luna jumped in. "Don't be ridiculous! You're in great shape!"

"Yeah, now. But in twenty, thirty years, I'd still like to have something in common with my son."

"Christopher makes a very good point," Chi-Chi added to the conversation. "It is important to have strong roots and bonds at an early age. Too often children grow up and grow out of the family unit. Even if they move away, it's important to have something in common that can keep the threads of the family fabric strong." Everyone stopped for a moment to digest what Chi-Chi had imparted. "Take the two of you, for example. You have restoration and design in common, as well as the soul of an artist."

Luna was thoughtful. "True, but he still thinks I'm zany."

Gaines laughed. "I don't think that is something you can learn, or teach, for that matter."

"I know I've said this before, but you should think about being a comedian if this marshal thing doesn't work out." Luna wrinkled her nose at him.

"Well, if I'm not intruding, that would be great. I am a little beat, and two more hours on the road would probably finish me off."

"Good. Then it's settled." Cullen poured another round of wine. "Cheers!"

Luna tried to keep her thoughts under control. *What would they talk about? Me? Him? Would Cullen be audacious enough to ask Gaines how he felt about their "relationship"?*

She smiled in agreement. "Brilliant idea. You can stop by the center in the morning for a scone and cappuccino."

"Oh, but you wouldn't think of asking me to look at the letter, now would you?" Gaines teased.

"Only if you have time." Luna was being sincere. She could try to lure him back to Asheville once she got the project underway.

"Let's see how the morning unfolds. As long as I can be back in my office by one. I have a debriefing about the case in Louisville."

The rest of the evening passed by with anecdotal stories, jokes, and laughs. The four of them got along like old friends. Luna once joked that maybe they all knew each other from a previous life. But when Gaines gave her a sideways look, she decided to zip it. It was enough he had accepted her intuitive skills. She didn't want to ruin it by going all weirdo on him.

When the check came, Cullen immediately grabbed for it but Gaines protested. "Oh, no you don't. You're giving me a place to stay. Please let me take care of dinner."

Luna thought it was rather chivalrous of the two men to argue about who would pick up the tab. She was absolutely all in with equal rights, equal pay, equal everything, but if someone was going to be generous, she was not about to take that feeling of goodwill away from them. It took her a long time to accept a compliment with a simple thank-you, rather than an offhanded statement such as "This old thing?" Or gratefully accept a gesture with "I appreciate this very much" instead of answering with "You didn't have to do that." Using positive words in response to a positive word or deed elevates the intention even further. Luna was all about "living in the light."

"Thank you, Christopher. It is always a

delight to spend time with you. This was lovely." Chi-Chi placed her hands in a prayer position and bowed her head in respect.

Luna mimicked Chi-Chi's acknowledgment. "Yes, Marshal, always a pleasure. Thank you."

Gaines smiled, stood, and pulled out Luna's chair. Cullen did the same for Chi-Chi. It was a traditional courtesy that was always appreciated.

As they headed toward the parking lot, they had to decide who was going to drive whom and where. Gaines strained his brain to figure out how he could get Luna in his Jeep alone, not for nefarious reasons, but simply to spend some time with just her. Fortunately, Cullen made a suggestion. "Chris, why don't you drop Luna at her house, and I'll bring Chi-Chi back to her car. We can pick Luna up in the morning on the way to the center. You know how to get to my place, right? It shouldn't take more than twenty minutes to jockey everyone around."

"No problem. Give me your address again, and I'll put it in my GPS." Cullen gave him the info and Gaines punched it into his phone. He would transfer the information when he got in his vehicle.

"Cool. See you in a few, bro." Cullen did a slight jog to the passenger side of his SUV to assist Chi-Chi. Gaines did the same with Luna, who was now shivering. And it was seventy-eight degrees outside.

When Gaines touched her elbow, he could feel her trembling. "You OK?"

"Yes. Just got a little chill."

He took off his jacket and placed it over her shoulders. Luna relaxed into his powerful yet gentle hands as he massaged her arms. "Better?" he asked.

"Much." She hoisted herself into the Jeep. Funny how a simple touch could warm one's entire body. As Gaines moved to the other side of the Jeep, she tucked her head inside the flap of the jacket. She inhaled his masculine scent. She rested her head back and closed her eyes, immersed in the touch and fragrance of him. It wasn't cologne. It was simply him.

He jaunted over to the driver's side and bounded in. "Should I turn up the heat?" he asked innocently.

Oh, if he only knew how much he already had. Without thinking, Luna easily rested her hand on his thigh. "I'm good. Thanks."

Gaines was pleasantly surprised by the gesture and did nothing to dissuade her. It felt natural to him. He would have preferred if the invitation had been to stay at her place, but he knew she wasn't ready yet. To break the silence, Luna asked, "So how much *was* that bottle of champagne?"

"It was $299," Gaines said sheepishly.

"Wow! How long ago was that?"

"About twenty-four, twenty-five years ago. I was young and stupid. Sophistication was not in my wheelhouse."

"Well, you've come a long way, Marshal Gaines." Luna smiled.

"Me? Sophisticated? Hardly."

"I beg to differ. And you know better not to differ with me." Luna gave him one of her brightest smiles.

"Yes, I am a quick study. Or so I've been told."

They drove in silence for the next few minutes. When they pulled into her driveway, she said, "If you weren't meeting up with Cullen, I'd invite you in for a drink, coffee, whatever." She knew it was safe to say it because Gaines had to get over to Cullen's place. But it opened a door for a future opportunity.

"Rain check?" Gaines asked.

"Absolutely." She leaned over and gave him a peck on the cheek.

He took her face in his hands and brushed the few strands of hair from her cheek. "You are one special lady. Woman. Luna-tic. By the way, you look lovely tonight."

Then he kissed her softly. She felt the heat rising in her chest until she was completely flushed. It was all she could do to break free of the magical spell. But this was not the time or place for a tryst. She wanted it to be special. Secretly, so did he. He kissed her on the forehead and unlocked both their seat belts. He went to the other side of the vehicle and opened the door and walked her to the front porch. He took her hand and gently brushed his lips across the back of her fingers. "Good night. Sweet dreams."

Luna was dumbfounded. Speechless. She simply stood there, immersed in the pools of his deep blue eyes. No other words needed to be said. When she unlocked her front door, she glanced in the hallway mirror. "Lovely? If he only knew! Thank goodness for Chi-Chi!" Inside, Wiley was patiently waiting for a hug, his tail wagging to beat the band.

Several miles away, Cullen was transporting Chi-Chi to her car when it occurred to him that they were rarely alone together. He strained his brain to think of the last time it had happened. He drew a blank. The ride back to the center was about ten minutes.

He had to fill up the air with something. Sitting next to her in silence was unnerving.

Chi-Chi broke the ice. "I think your sister is sweet on Marshal Gaines. Do you not agree?"

"And vice versa." Cullen nodded as he kept his eyes on the road.

"So what do you think they should do about it?" Chi-Chi was as baffled as anyone as to why the relationship between Luna and the fine marshal hadn't moved ahead.

Cullen thought it was ironic that he should have to answer that question since he was in a very similar situation. At least on his end. "Huh. In today's world, men have to be very careful with their approach."

"Please explain." Chi-Chi was highly aware about the growing number of sexual harassment claims. Chi-Chi was also curious about Cullen's take on American male-female interaction. Where she came from, many marriages were arranged. And under Sharia law in the Zamfara State, a man could take up to four wives provided he treated them equally. Thankfully, her father had had the presence of mind and a decent enough education to know that was not what he wanted for his daughter.

"Ha. Where do I begin?" Cullen laughed nervously. "Over the years, there has been a tremendous amount of sexual harassment. Probably since the beginning of time, actually. But only recently has it become major news, with a deluge of lawsuits. Major executives losing their jobs, celebrities, you name it. And I can't blame the women for blowing the whistle on them." Cullen paused at a STOP sign to check the traffic. "Now men are overly cautious to approach a woman in any way so as not to offend them or have their intentions misconstrued."

"I understand. So if a woman wants a man to kiss her, she needs to invite him to do so?" Chi-Chi was playing coy with him.

Cullen chuckled nervously. "Pretty much. Sorta takes the romance out of it, though."

"So you cannot 'make a move,' as they say, without permission?" Chi-Chi asked.

Cullen let out a guffaw. "I know it sounds crazy, but this is what it has come down to."

Chi-Chi sat back, pondering this new information. She had dated several men, but the relationships never moved forward enough to the point of sex. Likewise, her religious beliefs forbade premarital sex regardless where you lived. That was one of the few moral imperatives that her family had instilled in her. At thirty-four, she was still a virgin. She often wondered if she would ever fall in love, but she knew she liked Cullen very much. Maybe that was what love was supposed to be about. Liking someone very much.

As they pulled into the parking lot of the center, Chi-Chi kept her focus straight ahead. "So if I wanted someone to kiss me, I would have to ask them to?"

"Awkward, huh?" Cullen was expressing his own feelings at the moment.

"Indeed." Chi-Chi thought about every-thing Cullen had said. She would save the invitation for another time. Someplace a little more romantic than a parking lot. She hoped that when she did ask, he would be happy to oblige. In the meantime, she would find out what kind of invitation was neces-sary.

CHAPTER SIX

Marion, NC
That evening

Tori was relieved to see that her husband's pickup was not in the driveway. She knew he wouldn't wait for her, but she was relieved nonetheless. She removed the small bag of groceries and entered the house through the side door. It occurred to her that no one ever used the front door. So strange. It wasn't as if it was a big walk from the gravel driveway to the front of the house.

They lived in a small ranch. It had been built in the 1950s under the G.I. Bill. A number of similar developments throughout North Carolina had been built at the same time. The tobacco industry and furniture manufacturing had enticed many looking for a decent wage and a safe place to raise a family. Tori and her husband had bought the place from the son of the original owner. After his folks died, he decided to move his family to a less rural part of the state. It was a quaint, historic town, named for Brigadier General Francis Marion, a Revolutionary War hero who earned the nickname "Swamp Fox."

Located in the Blue Ridge Mountains, it was also in the middle of nowhere and somewhere else. The scenery was beautiful, with the backdrop of the Pisgah National Forest, the highest point east of the Mississippi. For people who loved the outdoors, the hiking trails were magnificent.

It was a relatively quiet, historical town with fewer than eight thousand residents. As far as the crime rate, drunk and disorderly was commonplace, as well as domestic disturbances. When there were serious crimes, the FBI or the U.S. Marshal Service usually stepped in. For the most part, her husband's job wasn't dangerous. Almost boring. And so was her life. The only excitement for her was her job. Except for the occasional domestic quarrel during a divorce action, it was a relatively quiet and predictable job. For that she was thankful.

Tori put the groceries away and snatched her white bag of pastry pleasure. She clicked on the TV to watch the last of the news. Not much new. She thought they should rename it S.O.S. for "same old stuff." She licked her fingers, savoring the buttery morsels of delight. It dawned on her that if something so small could make her feel this good, imagine how good she would feel if she could sweeten the rest of her life. She giggled. Yes, it was a pastry epiphany. Or a sugar high. She was going to be on top of her game even if she didn't know what the game was. Yet. But she had hope. Faith. She had to remind herself that in spite of fleeing from home right after high school and having a baby at nineteen, she had a good job at a respectable law firm.

She finished off the final piece and tried to shake the crumbs into her mouth. Instead, they got all over her shirt. She giggled again. Time to take a long hot bath and begin to discover who she was.

Tori ran the tub, sprinkling Epsom salts under the spigot. Her doctor told her it was safe to use it in a warm bath and it would help with any stress. She thought about it. Stress. It was odd that she didn't feel it. Not at that moment. She felt invigorated. Maybe it was her hormones. She slid farther down into the cozy water and propped a rubber pillow under her neck. She strained her mind, trying to remember the last time she had treated herself to this kind of relaxation.

She thought about the past twenty years. How had they gone by so quickly? Retracing her life, she remembered the excitement of their first year of marriage. Sure, there were ups and downs, but they kept, or maybe *she* kept believing they would have a good, solid, happy life together. For the most part, it was solid. Financially comfortable. He was paid well and had benefits. Good? Yes, when her son was growing up. Happy? Not so much anymore. It was the same old adage about growing apart.

After Brendon was born, she went back to work at the restaurant, but the hours were tough. She managed to juggle her schedule for several years until her son was in grammar school. With Brendon being involved in a lot of activities, doing the chores, shopping, and working, Tori was beginning to feel weary. And she was only twenty-six at the time.

One of the restaurant's frequent customers owned a small law practice in town. He was several years her senior. Maybe the age her father might be now. He was a kind man who usually ate alone. If it was a slow night, she would stop by his table and chat. He seemed to appreciate the company. They would talk about her son mostly. How fast kids grow up. Over the years, she discovered he was a widower and had a couple of grandchildren. One evening, he told her his receptionist-assistant was going to retire and he needed to replace her. Much to her surprise, and out of the blue, he offered Tori the job. "Why don't you come and work for me?"

Tori was dumbstruck. "Mr. Layton, I don't know anything about the law."

"You seem like a quick study, and I'll pay you double what you're making here."

"But you don't even know what that is!" Tori smiled.

"I can guess." He paused. "I've seen how you manage the crowd here. I know you're in charge of ordering supplies and making the schedules. You're a bright young woman. I think you'll do fine."

"Seriously, Mr. Layton. I am truly speechless."

Tori could not believe her luck. A regular job in a regular office, with regular people.

"I've been coming here every Friday night for years. You are always kind and efficient. With Dorothy leaving, I really need someone to keep me and Robert in line. We can't be trusted on our own." He let out a guffaw.

"I don't know anything about working in an office," Tori responded.

"You'll learn. Besides, most of our clients are regular people who need wills drawn, real-estate closings, a few divorces, and a little estate planning. And I use that term lightly. It's not as if we have a lot of estates in this area. The bigger money is closer to Asheville, but it's a good, decent practice, and I'm sure you'll get the hang of it soon enough."

Tori was truly taken aback by his offer. "Can I talk it over with my husband?"

"Of course. The hours are ten to four Monday through Friday. No weekends, no evenings. The salary is twenty dollars per hour."

"Are you sure you're not a salesman?" Tori joked.

George Layton laughed. "I was when I was in law school! You think about it and give me a call. The sooner the better. Dorothy is leaving at the end of the month, and I'd like her to be able to show you the ropes." He handed her his business card. "Please. Think about your little boy. You'll have more time with him. My only concern is that if I steal you from this place, they may start spitting in my food!" Both let out a big cackle, causing other guests to turn their heads.

Tori took the card and tapped it in her

hand. "I will certainly think about it." But she knew she was going to accept. She just had to run it past her husband first. Heaven forbid she make a decision without him.

It had been a no-brainer. The money and the hours were so much better than the grind of being a mom and housewife all day, then being a hostess at the busiest restaurant four nights a week. When she told her husband about the offer, he had a mixed reaction. The money was a great incentive, but it would put Tori in front of an entirely different situation. He liked the way things were. Predictable. It was a reaction from when he was in his teens and his entire life was chaos.

Tori remembered the feeling she had when she accepted the job. Elation. And for some odd reason, she was feeling that same emotion now. She rested a hand on her belly. Maybe it *was* her hormones.

As the water became tepid, she decided it was time to dry off and make a cup of tea. She wondered how long she could keep her pregnancy a secret. Another month, perhaps.

Over the past twelve years, she had learned a lot at Layton and Bellows, Attorneys-at-Law. If the office was quiet, she would read articles from various law journals. Some of it was way over her head, but she never hesitated to ask questions. Both partners appreciated her interest and encouraged her. Even though she had no illusion of going to college, let alone law school, she was a quick study and was especially interested in family law. One particular article about grandparents' visitation rights was startling. She couldn't imagine having to go to a lawyer to see your own grandchild. Not that it mattered in her life. Brendon would never know his maternal grandmother or grandfather, and his paternal grandparents were MIA. For two people to have so much in common, it was a mystery how they had grown so far apart. She would feel bad for Brendon not having grandparents, but in the case of her parents and her in-laws, he was much better off.

She also felt bad that he had no siblings. Not yet anyway. But it would have been nice if he had a family unit he could be a part of. Maybe that's why she was so close to him. She tried to protect him from loneliness and any feelings of abandonment without being a helicopter mom. All in all, Brendon was a well-adjusted, responsible young man. He had a good head on his shoulders. She sighed. She missed his humor and his attention.

She wrapped herself in a long, plush robe, made some chamomile tea, and settled into bed with a book. Around eleven, she saw the headlights of the pickup pull into the driveway. Normally, she would be half asleep, and he would fall into bed. Sometimes he would kiss her on the head. But tonight was different. She wanted to see what it was like to have a conversation with him at the end of his day and an evening of bacchanalian behavior.

She heard him rattle around the kitchen for a few minutes, opening and closing the refrigerator door. "Whoa! Check it out!" She surmised that he had found the bologna and cheese.

Tori called out to him. "That's for lunch tomorrow, hon."

He came sauntering into the bedroom. "Well lookie here. You're awake!"

She smiled up at him. "I am." He bent over to give her a kiss, his breath smelling of sour beer. She kept smiling. "So you found your surprise?"

He plopped down on the side of the bed and took off his boots and tossed them toward the closet. Tori suppressed a cringe. She had asked him repeatedly to leave them in the laundry room over the years. She realized the shoe thing and the socks-on-the-floor thing were inherent in males.

"Whacha readin'?" he asked, as if he were interested. Tori thought maybe it was his idea of foreplay.

"Just another mystery novel."

He started rubbing her leg. Even though it had been several weeks, she had no interest in sex that night but didn't want to get into a squabble with him. Instead, she hopped out of bed. "I have an idea." She quickly moved toward the kitchen. "Let's have lunch now!"

He groaned. "Are you serious? It's almost midnight."

"That's why they call it a midnight snack. Come on!"

She pulled out the packaged cold cuts, mayonnaise for him and mustard for her, lettuce, and a loaf of white bread.

He shuffled in a few minutes later. "You really *are* serious."

She pulled out a can of beer and poured it in a glass and handed it to him. He pulled out a chair and sat at the dining-room table. "You're in quite a mood tonight."

"I took a hot bath. It helped me unwind. I should do it more often." She brought the plates of sandwiches to the table, skipping the bologna on hers. "So, how was Ringo's tonight?"

"The usual. I won ten bucks shooting pool. That Larry Norton thinks he's Minnesota Fats, and I kick his butt every time."

"Maybe you should let him win once in a while. Then he'll have more confidence and raise the ante," she said with a devilish grin.

"Boy, you really are in some kind of mood. I like it." He chomped down on his sandwich, squirting mayo out of the sides and all over his hands. His demeanor suddenly became dark. "Damn. Can you please go easy on this stuff?"

"Sorry, hon. Here, let me take care of that." Tori got up and grabbed a paper towel, reached in the fridge, and pulled out another beer. He had downed half of the first one before his first bite. She was determined to help him pass out. She wasn't in the mood for anything except peace and quiet. She topped off his glass and handed him the paper towel. His attitude shifted back to being less surly.

"Got enough for tomorrow?" He spoke with a mouthful of food. She tried not to look at him gnashing his teeth on the artery-clogging combination.

"Yes. I can make you two sandwiches if you'd like." She was still being perky. Not for his sake, but for her own sanity. "And I'll even throw in a few pickles. How does

111

that sound?"

"Sounds good to me." He wiped his mouth, crumpled the napkin, and tossed it onto the plate. He pushed back his chair and guzzled the rest of the beer, draining what was left in the can. "I'm bushed."

Mission accomplished, Tori thought to herself. "Go on to bed. I'm going to clean up in here."

Without a word, he stood and shuffled toward the bedroom. If she had played it right, he would be snoring in less than ten minutes.

Tori slowly wiped off the dishes, removing the crumbs one at a time. After rinsing the plates and glasses, she looked around the kitchen for something else to occupy herself. When she heard the first snore emanating from down the hall, she knew it was safe to go to bed — except for the peace and quiet part.

CHAPTER SEVEN

Buncombe County
Later that evening

Luna could not settle down. Wiley's eyes kept following her walking back and forth. He sighed several times. "What?" Luna squatted and looked at him. He nudged her arm. "What?" He let out another sound, but this time it was almost a groan. She sat down next to him.

"Yeah, I know, pal. Something's gotta give with me and the marshal. But I don't know what to do." His ears perked up. "Sure, he's kissed me several times, but as soon as I feel the heat and the sexual tension, I freeze up."

Wiley got up and went for one of his tennis balls and brought it over to her. "You want to play while we're having this important discussion?" She talked as if he were a person. To her way of thinking, they were on the same wavelength but spoke different languages. He let out a soft yelp. Then it hit her. "Play." She needed to be more playful with Gaines. Sure, she flirted, but obviously not enough. Not enough for him to make the big move. Even a small move. They had been in each other's "personal space" many times, feeling each other's breath on their neck. Just thinking about it made her giddy. But tonight — the brush of his lips on her fingers — that was much more intimate than any of the kisses they had exchanged in the past. Too bad he had to get over to Cullen's. But maybe it was better this way. She vowed she was not going to let him leave the county again without a big make-out session with her. "What do you think about that? Big make-out session next time?" Wiley gave an affirmative woof.

Now that she had made that decision, she was confident she could finally go to bed and fall asleep. Maybe even do a little soul traveling in her dreams. Some people called it astral projection. An out-of-body experience. This area of metaphysics fascinated Luna — she often felt as if she were hovering over someone when she would do a reading. It was a sense of floating.

She once had a dream about Cullen when he was on a camping trip. She was "viewing" it as if she were in one of the trees

114

when she saw Cullen's sleeve get singed on the campfire. It startled her to the point where she shot up in bed. She checked the clock. It was only a quarter after eleven. Maybe he was still awake. She had to call to see if he was all right. She hoped there was cell service where he was doing his rugged man thing.

An alarmed voice answered. "Luna? Is everything all right?" Cullen knew Luna wouldn't track him down unless it was an emergency.

"Cul, are *you* all right?" Luna asked in return.

"Yeah. Fine. What's going on?" he asked in a very heightened manner.

"I had a dream. You singed your sleeve on the fire. Are you OK?"

Cullen froze for a moment, then he looked at his sleeve. "Yes but, but, how? . . . how . . . did you know?"

"I told you, I had a dream." Luna gave a sigh of relief.

"I don't know what you're taking before you go to bed, but either figure out a way to make millions or stop doing it. You're freaking me out."

"You should be used to it by now." She snickered.

"Yeah, but it generally doesn't involve me."

"OK. What-ev. You be careful. I need to get a good night's sleep. Sweet dreams." Luna clicked off the phone.

Luna smiled, thinking about that incident. Maybe she would focus her thoughts on Gaines while drifting off to sleep. During one of her classes at the New School for Social Research, a discussion had come up about soul traveling. The professor explained they should think of it like Bluetooth or WiFi. You can't see it, but you know it's there, and you're sharing the same frequency. It sure sounded like an episode of *Star Trek,* but they used to think the world was flat at one time, too.

Luna realized that instead of relaxing, she was getting energized and knew she had to turn down the kilohertz.

She went to her bookshelf and rummaged through her collection of New Age books. She found the one she had used in her class from several years ago, written by Albert Taylor, a former NASA aeronautical engineer. *If he didn't give it creds, then who could?* She'd remember to quote him next time the subject came up. She laughed. *Uh, maybe not. Not quoting, just not ever bringing it up.* It was spooky even for her.

Before she settled down, she let Wiley out the kitchen door to the fenced-in yard so he could have his final outdoor break for the night. She peeled off her clothes, taking one last sniff before she tossed them in the laundry basket. It was a mix of smoke and lavender fields. She smiled, thinking about her makeover in the ladies' room. *God bless Chi-Chi.* She wrapped Chi-Chi's skillful braid around her head, covered it with a towel, and jumped into the shower. Satisfied she had managed to wash the dust and air freshener off her, she pulled on her favorite terry-cloth robe, then padded to the kitchen to let Wiley back in. She made a cup of hot chocolate, tucked the book under her arm, and headed to her bedroom, Wiley at her heels.

She thumbed through the well-worn pages, reading the notes she had scribbled in the margins. A sense of elation came over her. She might not skyrocket into the astral plane, but she was going to set her mind on dreaming about Marshal Gaines.

The next morning, Luna awoke refreshed and buoyant. She always kept a pad and pen next to her bed in case she had a dream she thought worth remembering and dissecting. In her dream, she was at Cullen's house with Chris Gaines. Cullen was showing Chris his new fly-fishing equipment. That was a given since they had discussed it over dinner. She hadn't seen any of Cullen's new gear yet, but in her dream, she watched Cullen show Gaines a spindly thing with orange and red spikes. The words "casaba melons" came to mind, so she wrote them down.

She bounced out of bed, and Wiley did the same. The two raced to the kitchen, Wiley yapping with excitement. His squirrel buddies were trying to get into the bird feeder again. It was their morning ritual. Squirrels, Wiley, and coffee.

Luna switched on the TV to see if anything had blown up while she was asleep. Just another politician hawking the latest book on "enough already." A few minutes later, Wiley was scratching at the door for his breakfast. Luna let him in while she was still clicking the remote when she came across a cooking show. Then it hit her. She would invite Gaines over for dinner the next time he was in town. Why hadn't she thought of that sooner? For someone with a good brain and instincts, hers did not seem to work on matters of the heart. *Her* heart. She shook her head. "What do you think of that idea, Wiley? Invite the marshal for dinner?" He woofed again. "Right, pal. If that doesn't start a fire between us, then I'm giving up!" Wiley made a grumbling sound before lying prone and pulling his paws over his eyes.

Luna finished her coffee and shuffled her way to the bathroom, where she gave herself a discerning check. Except for a few wayward wisps of hair, the braid was still intact. She studied her face closely in the all-too-powerful magnifying mirror. "Why did I buy this thing?" She moaned, eyeing the pores that appeared as craters. Then she reminded herself that it was better if she caught the flaws before anyone else did. Why she cared so much was because she was in her midthirties and still single. Not that she had any intention of letting herself go, but why not be at the top of your game for as long as possible, looks included?

She splashed cold water on her face, then applied a daily moisturizer and eye balm. That was followed by a light foundation, blush, a dusting of shimmery eye shadow, a sweep of mascara, and pale lipstick. Pretty, without looking like she was going to a gala. The next challenge was deciding what to wear. She was standing in front of her open closet for what seemed like an eternity when her phone rang. It was Cullen. "We'll be there in about ten minutes." Luna was caught off guard. She *had* been staring at her closet for an eternity. Now she had to hustle. What hadn't she worn in front of Gaines before? She racked her brain. A blue silk tunic at the far end of the closet caught her eye. She had been saving it for a special occasion and decided every day is a special occasion if you're healthy. Today was as special as any other. Even more. A pair of slim white pants and a pair of metallic flats finished off her outfit. She grabbed her collection of bangle bracelets and hoop earrings just as Cullen's SUV was pulling into her driveway. Wiley was already pacing the floor, his tail wagging a mile a minute.

"Come on, boy!" Luna grabbed her backpack, thinking maybe it was time to retire the hippie-dippie thing. She flung the coat closet door open and pulled out a decent-looking tote bag and quickly transferred her stuff. She let out a big breath of air as she unlocked the front door and stepped outside. "OK. Here we go," she muttered under her breath. Wiley was already at the rear passenger door, barking his "hellos" to the men in the vehicle.

Gaines jumped out and opened the door for her and her pooch. "Your chariot awaits."

Playing along, Luna put out her hand so he could assist her into the cab. "Why, thank you, kind sir." He made an exaggerated bow.

"Please be sure to buckle up," he instructed her. "And Lord Wiley as well."

"But of course." Luna enjoyed the little play they were performing for each other. Wiley sat next to her in anticipation of getting himself buckled in as well.

Gaines returned to his seat. "Tallyho, old man." He quipped at Cullen.

Cullen groaned. "Thank goodness it's not a long ride."

"Party pooper," Luna joked. She couldn't hold her curiosity. "So how was the rest of your evening?"

"I'm going to be about three grand in the hole by the time your brother finishes with me," Gaines said wryly.

"What do you mean?" Luna was surprised.

"He has a few very nice pieces of furniture that would look great in my place."

"Cul? You're going to sell him stuff from your house?" Luna was even more surprised.

"He was digging the dining-room table. If you recall, he wanted the table from the Millstone estate, but you commandeered it. I thought it would only be fair if I sold him the one I found. They're very similar."

"And what else are you going to try to fob off on him?" Luna poked at her brother.

"The wardrobe I'm working on. But that's in the shop. It's for Carter's athletic equipment."

"What else?"

"A dresser. The midcentury oak piece that's in my dining room."

"I don't want to clean you out, man," Gaines responded to Cullen's inventory.

"That is a very nice piece. Are you sure you want to give it up?" Luna asked. "You spent a lot of time on it."

"Shush. I have this guy on a hook. Let me reel him in," Cullen said conspiratorially.

"Right. Sorry," Luna whispered. "Speaking of hooks, did you guys discuss flies?"

"Since when were you ever interested in fly-fishing?"

"Just curious." Luna wondered about her dream.

"He showed me his new Cabela's Adams," Gaines said over his shoulder.

"Did you say 'casaba melons'?" She got a bit of a chill and sank back into the seat.

Both men laughed. "This is why I don't bring her fishing with me." Cullen glanced over in Gaines's direction.

"I don't like worms," Luna retorted.

"See? She doesn't know the difference between a worm and a fly." Cullen chuckled.

Luna was still reeling from the casaba melons. Had she really intruded on their energy the night before? It had only happened when she was in the same room with someone and that one time when Cullen was camping. And it was always planned. Never from miles away. For the first time in a long time, she spooked herself.

"Next time you're out this way, we should take in some trout fishing," Cullen offered.

Now Luna was beginning to feel like the little sister again. But then she remarked, "And I'll cook whatever you guys catch for dinner."

"Now, that sounds like an invitation I can't resist," Gaines said cheerfully.

Luna tried to avoid pouting. Well, she was halfway there about making dinner. Now she had to figure out how to get her brother out of the way. She'd cross that bridge when she came to it. Meanwhile, she was happy there would be a next time.

They pulled into the back of the art center and Cullen parked the SUV. Luna waited for her prince to open the door for her. She was not disappointed. Gaines put out his hand, which she gladly grasped and gracefully exited the vehicle. Cullen was on the other side freeing Wiley from his halter.

Gaines made a crook in his arm and threaded Luna's arm through it. "If there were a puddle, I would gladly lay my coat before you."

"Well, ah do declare," Luna said in her most convincing Southern drawl. "For a Yankee, you are quite the gentleman, Marshal Gaines."

The two walked in step to the back of Cullen's workshop and entered the building. "You two done playing Rhett and Scarlett?"

"Oh dear brothuh, why must you be so crass?" The accent continued.

"And I thought the ride here was going to be long." Cullen shook his head, but he was secretly enjoying the playfulness between the marshal and his sister. Now, if only he could get in some kind of rhythm with Chi-Chi.

As they made their way through the workshop, Luna reluctantly disengaged her arm from Gaines and pointed to the mysterious trunk and the contents. "There it is. And over there is the diary and the box of memorabilia."

Gaines looked over at Cullen. "Mind if I take a look?"

Cullen laughed. "I'm willing to bet that if

124

you don't, you will be incurring the wrath of Luna."

Luna made a snarky face. "I'm going to pick up my order at the Flakey Tart. See you in the café in a few minutes. Come on, Wiley." Wiley eagerly followed Luna to the massive sliding doors that led to the patio and park. Alex gave a wave, and Wiley bounded in his direction. "See you in a bit," Luna called out. Alex gave her the thumbs-up.

Luna crossed the large indoor landscaped atrium and saw Chi-Chi opening her shop. Jimmy Can-Do had been there at the crack of dawn to place his work around the atrium. To that day, no one had ever caught a glimpse of him. Such an odd thing.

Luna gave morning greetings to everyone she saw, receiving the same in kind. The light coming through the glass ceiling made for a beautiful sunny mood. It didn't hurt that her crush was in town either. She hurried to the pastry shop, where they had her morning order ready. "Thanks, Heidi! Have a good day!"

"Hey, Luna! Got a sec?" Luna heard Rita from the Blonde Shallot call out.

Any other morning would have been fine, but today she didn't want to miss a minute of Gaines's time to brief him on the trunk.

"If you walk with me."

Luna guessed Rita was perhaps a couple of years older than she. Maybe thirty-eight or nine. Luna knew she was married to a teacher and had two teenagers in high school. Luna had met the family at the grand opening and they often stopped by on the weekends.

It wasn't often the other tenants would hang out with each other. With the exception of Chi-Chi, Cullen, and Luna, most would go their separate ways at the end of the day.

Rita lowered her voice. "Can I ask you something?" Rita spoke with a bit of hesitation.

"Shoot!" Luna said as she walked briskly back to the café.

"I heard you are into psychic stuff."

Luna looked around. A lot of people knew, but to what extent she wasn't sure since most of her clients were supposed to be on the down-low. She didn't want visitors who loathed the idea of the paranormal to be insulted or put off by her presence. Luna was in protection mode when it came to Ellie and the center.

"I've been known to do readings if that's what you mean."

"Yeah. That."

126

"Why do you ask?"

"It's about a friend of mine," Rita said.

"Does she want a reading?" Luna asked hurriedly.

"No, it's for me."

"Sure. No problem." Luna set the boxes down and pulled out the wicker baskets. "How about later? Around five?"

"Great! I'll buzz you on the squawk box." Rita waved, and Luna continued to get the café ready.

Ellie and Chi-Chi started in her direction. Ziggy and Marley were already in the dog park with Alex and Wiley.

"E kaaro." Chi-Chi bowed in respect.

"E kaaro," Luna replied. "Namaste."

Ellie always got a kick out of their morning greetings. "It's such a nice way to start the day. It gives it a fresh feeling."

"And that is exactly what it is supposed to do," Chi-Chi said in her beautiful, articulate, singsong voice. Her enunciation was impeccable.

"So what do you fine women have on your agenda today?" Ellie asked.

"Cullen managed to talk Chris into crashing at his place last night," Luna said mildly.

"And why not yours, young lady?" Ellie gave her a suspicious look.

"It wasn't the right time," Luna defended herself.

"It was Cullen who offered first," Chi-Chi backed up her friend.

"Well, that's too bad. I was hoping for a little dish," Ellie teased.

"Dish?" Even though Chi-Chi had a marvelous grasp of the English language, some slang made no sense to her.

"Gab. Gossip," Luna informed her.

"Oh, I see. But what does the word 'dish' have to do with anything?"

"Dish it out. Serve it up," Luna explained as she placed the scones, muffins, and croissants in the baskets.

"It also means an attractive person, especially a woman," Ellie added to the urban dictionary.

Chi-Chi sighed. "I have been here for many years, and I still do not understand your language."

Ellie and Luna laughed. "Don't feel bad. I had to figure out that the word 'dope' meant good or cool and not just drugs or someone who is stupid," Luna said.

"Then there's 'doping,' " Ellie added.

Chi-Chi closed her eyes. "Please, no more."

Luna began to make their usual coffee when Gaines came into the café.

"Marshal! So nice to see you!" Ellie went over and gave him a kiss on the cheek.

"Likewise." Gaines smiled.

"Please, everyone grab a seat." Luna gestured toward one of the café tables.

"Cullen said he'd be by in a few minutes. He had to get an invoice ready for a customer who will be here in an hour."

"Speaking of invoices. Are you really going to clean out Cullen's house?" Luna asked, as she was frothing the last cappuccino.

Gaines laughed as the other two women looked on in surprise. "No. Just a couple of things. I also want to take a look at what he's done lately."

"I would be happy to advise you, but I have never been invited to your place, so it's difficult to make recommendations." Luna was feeling a little brazen this morning as she carried the tray of coffee over to the table.

"Well, we're going to have to fix that. I can use all the help I can get." Gaines stood up and took the tray from her.

Was that a real invitation? She wanted to kick herself for even putting a negative spin on his words. *Practice what you preach, girlie.* She puffed up her chest. "Well, you let me know, and I will bring my sketch pad."

129

It dawned on her that she might get some crazy vibes from his place. *Let's not get ahead of ourselves.* She walked over to the counter, where she had prepared a basket of everyone's breakfast favorites.

Ellie groaned and gleefully snatched a raspberry scone.

"You've been working on your place for quite a while, haven't you?" Ellie asked.

"Yes, it's been over eight months. I don't have a lot of spare time these days."

"Then you surely need Luna's expert eye," Ellie said coyly.

"Really. I would be happy to. Any particular color palette you have in mind?" Luna was quite sincere.

Gaines thought a minute. "Is brown a palette?"

"I do believe you need serious assistance," Chi-Chi said thoughtfully. "Brown is not a color."

"Not to you. You are a walking rainbow!" Ellie smiled.

"Every color has a vibration," Chi-Chi explained.

"Doesn't brown vibrate?" Gaines asked.

"What do you think of when you hear the color brown?" Chi-Chi asked Gaines. "Shoes? Dirt?"

Gaines flashed a big smile. "I see your

130

point. OK, how about blue? Navy?"

"What colors do you have in your house now?" Luna asked.

"Brown sofa. Brown floors. Brown kitchen cabinets. Brown wall paneling."

"So you were serious?" Chi-Chi seemed surprised.

"I was. But that doesn't mean I like it." Gaines clarified his earlier statement. "It's the original stuff that was in the house when I bought it. Except for the couch. That was from my basement."

"I think someone should declare a state of renovation emergency." Ellie clapped her hands together with delight.

There was a moment of awkward silence when Gaines took the next step. "I have Carter this weekend, and the following I have a seminar. How is three weeks from now?"

"I'll need someone to cover for me here." Luna was between elation and panic.

"I'll get Sabrina or one of the other pages," Ellie offered right away. She was not going to let Luna squirm her way out of spending time with Gaines.

All eyes were on Luna. "I guess it's a plan, then."

She was just about to add, "Should we ask Cullen," but bit her lip. *What about sleeping arrangements?* she thought.

As if he read her mind, Gaines immediately offered, "You can stay in Carter's room. He'll be at his mom's."

"How old is your son now?" Ellie asked.

"He'll be thirteen in a couple of months."

"That's a very active age."

"You're telling me. Between his studies, his sports, his dog, and puberty, I have my hands full!"

"Especially the puberty part!" Ellie joshed.

"You bet. That's the worst of it!" Everyone broke out into cackles and guffaws.

"What's all the hilarity?" Cullen came bounding in.

"Teenage talk." Gaines dragged another chair over to the small table. Normally, they were arranged to accommodate two or three people, but that morning five were huddled in the corner.

"Christopher was telling us about his son and his many activities," Chi-Chi replied.

"A teenager? I can only imagine!" Cullen pulled the chair so he could be closer to Chi-Chi.

"You have some very strange customs," Chi-Chi said matter-of-factly.

"But you've been here for years!" Luna exclaimed.

"That does not mean I understand any of

it." Chi-Chi smiled. "We had a very strict upbringing. There was a lot of love, but also a lot of discipline."

"Sometimes I wonder who is in charge nowadays," Ellie mused. "I see some of the kids who come in here and I want to smack the parents! They let them run wild."

"You should direct them outside," Cullen chimed in.

"I wish I could, but it's starting to become a problem. Some of the mothers think this is a babysitting service while they guzzle wine and eat their gourmet salads."

"I noticed that, too," Luna added. "They buy a bottle of wine at the Wine Cellar and salads at the Blonde Shallot, sit at a table on the patio, and set their screaming kids loose."

Ellie had a bit of a troubled look on her face.

"Maybe you should hire a security guard for the atrium," Gaines suggested.

"But we have excellent security surveillance."

"There is nothing like a man with a badge to terrify rambunctious children." Gaines winked at Ellie. "He doesn't have to carry a gun. Just a shiny badge and a uniform. He simply needs to look intimidating."

"That is a brilliant idea." Ellie perked up.

"I know just the person for the job. He used to help manage the farm. He's retired but still spry. He wanted to retire while he still had some good years in his bones, is what he said. He also said if I ever needed any help to call him."

"That's great, Ellie. How old a man is he?" Luna asked.

"Around sixty. He was in very good shape when I last saw him. Just under a year ago. At the grand opening. So, unless he's gone all flabby in the past twelve months, he might fit the bill." Ellie leaned back in her chair.

"I think the meeting of the round table has been productive." Cullen took the last sip of his coffee. "I need to get to work."

"And you, sir," Luna pointed to Gaines, "have to review our puzzle before you leave."

Cullen got up and brushed against Chi-Chi accidentally. He was mortified. "I am so terribly sorry." Cullen spewed an apology.

Chi-Chi was happy her honey-toned skin didn't reveal the blush in her cheeks. "It is not a problem."

Luna piled the dishes, cups, and the basket onto the tray and placed it on the counter. Ellie said her goodbyes and

134

thanked Gaines for his superb suggestion.

"If it doesn't work out, let me know. I might have a few contacts of retired law enforcement in the area."

"Thanks again." Ellie gave him a hug.

"I must get to my shop," Chi-Chi said to the group. "Enjoy the rest of the morning. Have a safe trip home." She waved to Gaines as she turned to leave.

Luna could barely contain her excitement. She, Cullen, and Gaines were on another "assignment" together. She put the sign on her door that said:

PLEASE GO NEXT DOOR FOR SERVICE

Even though the sensor would trigger a bell in Cullen's workshop, a sign was helpful.

"Let's do this," Luna said playfully, as she bounced toward the rear of Cullen's showroom and into the workshop. She was as excited as a child would be going to an amusement park.

Gaines paused for a moment to enjoy her boundless enthusiasm. She was part nymph and part woman. Luna stopped in her tracks and turned to him. "Everything all right?" She cocked her head.

Gaines's smile was from ear to ear. "Everything is just fine."

"What's so funny?" she asked.

"Your excitement to solve a puzzle," Gaines replied.

"Well, isn't that what you do at your job? Solve puzzles? You just call them cases." She smirked at him.

Gaines nodded as he continued to smile. "I guess you are absolutely correct. I never thought of it that way."

"Stick with me, Marshal. I'll have you thinking things you never thought before." She raised her eyebrows with a devilish smile.

If she *only knew,* he thought.

If he *only knew,* she thought, as they caught each other's eye. She felt her face get a bit flushed.

"Is it getting hot in here?" Cullen opened the rear door. He wasn't being facetious, but he was right on the money.

Gaines tried to keep his cool. No pun intended. Luna started fanning her face with her hand and began her speaking with a Southern drawl again. "Ah do declare, I have the vapors!"

Cullen turned back in their direction when the double entendre occurred to him. *Well, good. It's about time these two got down to business.* Cullen was well aware of the

136

fondness between his sister and the good marshal. He also knew Gaines was sweet on Luna. The night before, after the fly-fishing show-and-tell, the two shared a beer before they turned in. Gaines tried to be subtle, but the more questions he asked Cullen about Luna's social life, the more Cullen realized Gaines had real feelings for his sister. During their conversation, Gaines asked Cullen about his social life as well. Girlfriend? Clubs? Activities?

Cullen explained he had been through a few relationships and made a conscious choice to focus on himself and his work, and when the right person came along, he would be happy to pursue it. He explained he thought there was too much pressure to be "paired up with someone." He wasn't far from wrong. Dinner invitations at people's homes seemed limited to couples. He also made a point to tell Gaines that Luna was usually his plus one, including the fact she didn't have a boyfriend. He was subtle about it, but he knew that Gaines wanted that particular piece of information and was happy to oblige. When Gaines and Luna spoke on the phone, neither one ever brought up the subject of dating anyone so neither of them knew about the other's social life.

Cullen gestured toward the trunk. "And there it is."

The three of them gathered around the smoky wood. "There was no return address?" Gaines said rhetorically. He already knew the answer. "Let's have a look at the letter."

The three walked to the large worktable where the contents were laid out. Cullen handed Gaines the letter.

"Curiouser and curiouser," Luna chirped. "Check this out." She pulled on a plastic glove and gently lifted the diary from the table. "Cullen is going to pick the lock." Luna handed it to Gaines, folded her arms, and started tapping her foot.

"OK. OK. I'll do it this afternoon. I know it looks simple, but I don't want to break it or ruin the flap. This is sensitive work, my dear."

"You'd think he was performing surgery," Luna joked.

"It's *my* kind of surgery." Cullen made a face.

"What-ev." Luna rolled her eyes. "Here, take a look at this." She opened the wooden box. "It has some flyers, ticket stubs, and coins that look like they came from a carnival or something."

Gaines peered into the box and moved a

few of the memorabilia around with his pen. "I don't suppose you used gloves when you opened the letter?"

Cullen's face dropped. "It hadn't occurred to me because I didn't know it was going to be anonymous."

"Good point," Gaines replied.

"Do you think you can lift some prints off any of this?" Luna pointed to the contents.

"I could," Gaines said. "But why? Do you want me to run them through AIFIS?" He was half joking, referring to the fingerprint data system.

"Could you?" Luna's eyes widened.

"Not unless we believe a crime has been committed," Gaines informed her.

"But what if there was but we don't know it yet?" Luna asked, hoping he would oblige.

"I'll tell you what. You put the pieces of this puzzle together, and we'll review it."

"Are you pulling my leg?" Luna asked.

"I wouldn't dream of it. I'm serious. I know how your mind works and the rest of that woo-woo stuff." He made a circular gesture in front of her.

"Deal?" Luna put out her hand for him to shake.

"Deal." Gaines shook her hand. "Maybe you'll have some info when you come out to Charlotte."

Luna thought carefully. "We'll have a lot of ground to cover between this and your renovation. Besides, I don't know how much info I'll have by then."

"Well, we'll just save your project until after you're done with mine. How's that?" Gaines asked.

"Sounds like a *very* good plan." Luna was elated. They now had two projects to work on together. *Any excuse to spend time with him.* And Gaines felt the same way about her.

Gaines looked at his watch. "I've got to hit the road." He turned to Cullen. "Thanks again, man, for putting me up at your place last night."

"Any time," Cullen replied, but Luna had her own ideas about future sleepovers. She was going to have one at Gaines's house in a couple of weeks. She got all goofy thinking about it.

CHAPTER EIGHT

The next day
Tori got up before her husband and made him two of his favorite sandwiches, being mindful to go easy on the mayo. Heaven forbid he make a mess in front of his coworkers, or even worse, in the squad car. She put on a pot of coffee, took a quick shower, and got ready for work.

He came ambling out of the bedroom looking like his hair had gotten caught in an eggbeater. She smiled. It reminded her of when they were younger, would make love in the morning, and she would ruffle his hair. She missed those days of feeling free and having a future ahead. It hadn't turned out exactly as she had hoped. Not even close. Once Brendon had been born, everything changed. She was more or less tied to the house except when she was working, and her husband kept to his routine and his social life. She didn't think it was reasonable that he could hang out with his friends and she was stuck at home. Not that she had many friends, but there didn't seem to be a fair division of child-rearing, diaper changing, laundry, shopping, cooking, and cleaning. It was as if she was stuck in the 1950s. *But even June Cleaver had the garden club.*

She thought about being pregnant and having a baby at thirty-eight. It wouldn't be easy. By the time the kid was twelve, she would be fifty, and most likely, she would be the oldest member of the PTA. She reminded herself that many women were having children later in life, so maybe, just maybe, she wouldn't feel like an old lady. But that was years ahead.

Her thoughts ran back to when she was younger and imagining things were "years ahead." But years fly by, and before you know it, you're stretching your arms in order to read the instructions on a bottle of aspirin. She wasn't quite there yet, but she had a few acquaintances slightly older than she was who were carrying around "cheaters." She did a little research and discovered it usually starts to happen around age forty. She sighed. *Great. I'll be squinting to read the labels on the jars of baby food.* If only she had family to help out. Someone to talk to.

The law firm was a comfortable environment, but as of now, she wasn't sure if she could discuss her deepest personal matters. She also knew that her pregnancy would become obvious. Her reverie was interrupted by her husband scraping the chair along the floor. "You're up early."

"I made you lunch." She handed him the brown bag that contained two sandwiches, a bottle of water, an apple, and two oatmeal cookies.

He peeked inside. "Wow. Thanks for lunch, Mommy."

She caught her breath. *How could he know?* She quickly regrouped and chuckled. "I'm sure your mommy never made lunch for you."

"You got that right. I think she made me a cheese sandwich once. Probably something left over from the roadhouse where she worked."

"Well, you enjoy your lunch, sonny," she teased him.

"You're in a good mood this morning. You were in a good mood last night, too. What gives?" he asked casually.

"Maybe it's a residual reaction to that bath." She poured coffee for both of them, pulled out a chair, and sat at the table. "What's your shift this week?"

143

"Probably the usual, but I may swap with Dexter on Wednesday. He wants to take his kid to a ball game."

"What time does he work?"

"Four to midnight."

"That's not too bad if you can get enough sleep when you get home."

"I might take off Thursday to go fishing with Jack."

Tori's mind raced. She wanted to plan a day to get to the art center where that psychic woman was supposed to work. This was throwing a monkey wrench into it.

She held her breath for a moment, hoping her next sentence wouldn't start an argument. "I was thinking about taking Wednesday off."

"What for?" He slurped his coffee.

"I heard there is an interesting art center near Asheville."

"Since when are you interested in art?" He looked up from his mug.

"It's not just art. There are other people who do pottery, glassblowing. Stuff like that." She sighed. "I'm thinking about getting a hobby now that Brendon is gone."

"Well, you go do that artsy thing on your own. Count me out." He guzzled the rest of his coffee, pushed his chair back, and headed toward the bathroom.

144

Tori was relieved that it was an easy conversation. It hadn't occurred to her that he wouldn't be interested in the artsy part of it. Of course, she purposely left out the psychic part. The more she thought about it, it was a good idea to find a hobby. Wednesday was shaping up nicely. With him having a later shift, she wouldn't have to worry about getting home in time to make dinner. She'd make him a snack before she left for Stillwell. Now she just needed to clear it with Mr. Layton.

Tori put the cups in the dishwasher and tossed out the coffee grounds. She usually had toast for breakfast, but she was feeling a little queasy that morning. Nerves? Baby? Both probably. She decided to grab a roll and butter on her way into the office. Too bad she had stuffed her face with all that rugelach the night before. She should have saved one piece for the morning. She called out, "I'm heading out. See you tonight." He grumbled something in return. She grabbed her purse, jacket, and keys and moved swiftly out the door. She wasn't sure if she was going to be sick, and she didn't want to answer any questions if she barfed in front of him.

As soon as she got in her car her stomach calmed down. She pulled down the visor and took a peek at herself in the mirror. At least she didn't look pale, or on the verge of turning green.

Tori drove the fifteen minutes it took to get to the local coffee shop. She'd get a donut for Mr. Layton while she was there. While she was waiting for her order to come, she saw a woman behind the counter give her a strange look. Tori thought she looked familiar but couldn't place her. She'd paid for her bag of carbohydrates and started toward the door when she heard her name being called. She stopped and turned. It was the same woman who had been looking at her a few minutes earlier. "Yes? Do I know you?"

"I know you." The gray-haired woman gestured for Tori to come closer to the counter.

"What can I do for you?" Tori was puzzled.

The woman leaned closer. "It's more like what I can do for you," she said with an odd expression.

"I don't understand."

"Yeah, but you will. Stop by Ringo's on Thursday night."

"What is this about?" Tori was baffled.

"Honey, I seen you come in here a lot. You're married to that cop, right?"

"Well, yes, but . . ."

"Ringo's. Thursday. Around nine."

"But . . ." Tori stammered, but the woman turned away and moved toward the back, into the kitchen.

Tori got into her car. She was mystified. Why on earth would a stranger approach her and tell her to be at Ringo's on Thursday? Sure, that was her husband's usual night out with the guys. It was a bar and pool hall. She had been there less than a half dozen times. It wasn't the kind of place you'd take the family for dinner, nor was it a place for any respectable woman to be hanging around.

She shrugged and drove the last five minutes of her commute to the office. When she arrived, she noticed that Mr. Layton was already at his desk. She stuck her head inside his door. "Good morning!" She jiggled the bag.

"Oh dear, you didn't." He groaned.

"Oh, but I did." Tori smiled. "Got a minute?"

"Of course. Especially after you brought me a donut." Mr. Layton motioned for her to take a seat. "You know my doctor would give you an ear thrashing if he knew."

"And give you a bigger one knowing you ate it!" Tori joked. It struck her that she felt more comfortable in her work environment than she did in her own home. Maybe because it no longer felt like a home without her son around. It was just a house with furniture that she shared with someone.

"Mr. Layton, would you mind if I took the day off on Wednesday? I have some important errands I have to run."

"That's fine. It's my week to frustrate myself on the golf course." He bit into the sugary dough.

"Thank you. I appreciate it." Tori smiled.

"Everything OK?" he asked.

"Yep. Everything is fine." She was about to get up from her chair when she decided to share her situation with her boss. She knew it was rather soon, but it was going to happen eventually. The idea she hadn't shared it with her husband yet was odd, but in order for her to make a sound plan for herself, it was imperative for her to inform her boss. "Mr. Layton. There is something I need to tell you."

Layton's face went grim. "Please don't tell me you're leaving?"

"No. Nothing like that." She sucked in a huge gulp of air. "I'm pregnant."

Layton looked startled. He didn't know how to react to that news. Was this a good thing or a bad thing? He knew life wasn't paradise for Tori, but a child? At thirty-eight?

"Yes, I am just as surprised as you are. It wasn't planned." Tori started twisting her napkin on her lap. "I intend on having the baby, but to be completely honest with you, I haven't told my husband yet."

Layton looked even more perplexed. "How far along are you?"

"A little over six weeks." Her eyes welled up. "Mr. Layton, I love working here. Ever since Brendon joined the army, well, it's usually the best part of my day."

Layton clasped his hands and tapped his nose with his two forefingers, something he would do when he had to think. "I'm flattered you feel that way, Tori. I don't mean to pry, but are things bad at home? You hardly ever speak about it."

She sighed again and unfurled her napkin, trying to catch the tears before they streaked her makeup. "Mr. Layton, from the outside, my marriage may look, well, I can't even say happy, but it seems to be OK. We have a routine. We make a decent living. But it's empty."

"I see." Layton sat up in his chair. "You left home at a very young age. You thought you knew everything there was to know about life." He gave her an understanding

149

smile. "That expression, 'If I only knew then what I know now,' has probably been said hundreds of thousands of times throughout the ages."

"You're right about that." Tori felt as if someone understood her. "I was only eighteen when I left. Had a baby when I was nineteen. Then the next nineteen years flew past me. I was busy raising a son, working, and taking care of the house. There hardly seemed to be time to think about anything except what was coming next. Soccer. Baseball. Camp. Baking cupcakes for the PTA."

"And now you have a very big something to think about." Layton nodded. "I want you to know we will help you in any way we can."

"I appreciate that very much. You have been so kind to me. You plucked me out of a grueling job at the restaurant and gave me an opportunity to learn and grow. You encouraged me to take an online course to become a certified paralegal. I could never thank you enough for what you've done for me."

"And you have never disappointed me, Tori." Layton thought for a minute, calculating when she would be due.

"I want to continue working here, Mr.

Layton." Tori had a pleading expression on her face.

"Well of course you will continue to work here. And we'll make sure there are accommodations for the baby after he or she arrives. We have the break room you can use. Set up a crib, playpen. Babies don't do much in the beginning. Eat, sleep, poop." He chuckled, trying to ease Tori's angst.

"Once the child is old enough for day care, we can work on that together. As you know, the local day care is one of our clients," Layton offered. "Tori, I do not want to lose the best paralegal I've ever had. But don't tell Dorothy." He smiled again.

Tori got up from where she was sitting. "Thank you, Mr. Layton. You cannot imagine how relieved I am." Tears streamed down her face. This time she didn't care. It was worth getting the mascara smeared under her eyes.

"Tori, I think of you like family. Anything I can do, just let me know. I won't mention it to Robert until you're ready for everyone else to know."

Layton got up from his chair and walked to where Tori was standing. She threw her arms around him like he was a giant teddy bear. "You have no idea how grateful I am."

"You can do something for me." He held

her at arm's length. "After all these years, will you please call me George?"

Tori burst into a big smile. "I don't know if I can, Mr. Layton."

"Well, you give it a try, or I'll tell my doctor about the donuts."

"I believe there is some culpability in that regard," Tori joked.

"See, I knew you were a smart woman. We'll make a pact. No mention of donuts. Not to anyone."

"You got it. George." She smiled as she punctuated his name.

Tori went to her desk feeling a lot lighter and more optimistic than she had just twenty-four hours earlier. *What a difference a day makes,* she thought to herself. Now that she was a bit more relaxed, she thought about that odd conversation at the coffee shop. Ringo's? Thursday? What would her husband say? Maybe she wouldn't tell him and surprise him. Maybe he wouldn't like that either. She would decide when the time came. For now, she was looking forward to her excursion to the Stillwell Art Center to see if she could find the psychic and maybe a hobby.

CHAPTER NINE

Stillwell Art Center
Later that day

Luna hovered over Cullen's shoulder as he gently disengaged the lock on the diary. "Do you mind?" He smirked. "Space. I need some."

Luna backed away a few inches. She made an attempt to move in again, but Cullen caught her standing on her tiptoes and peering at him. "Will you please stop?" For the first time in a long time, he was losing his patience with his sister.

"Jeez. Fine. What's gotten into you?" Luna took a huge step back.

"Sorry. Nothing really."

"Oh, that 'nothing really' does not sound very convincing," Luna taunted him.

Cullen set his fine tools down. "I need some advice."

"OK, but keep working." Luna was less interested in giving him advice than she was about what was in the diary. That wasn't the norm. She would be all up in his business on any day of the week if she had an inkling something was going on with him.

"Never mind." Cullen went back to disengaging the lock. He was about to hand it over to her. "You should probably wear gloves."

"Good point." Luna went to the drawer and pulled out a pair.

"Here. Happy now?" Cullen still had a grim look on his face.

"Ecstatic!" Luna hopped up and down. "Now, tell me what is it that requires my assistance?"

Cullen put his jewelry tools in their pouch and returned them to their drawer. "I think you know what I'm going to say."

"That you should ask Chi-Chi out on a real date?" Luna gave him a wide-eyed look.

Cullen started to sputter. "But . . . how . . . ?"

"You can't be serious. First of all, I am your sister. Second of all, I am a bit woowoo. Third, I've been around you when you're with her. Even Stevie Wonder could see it on your face."

"So what should I do?" Cullen laughed nervously.

"Well, duh. Ask her." Luna laid the diary

154

down on a piece of tissue paper on the table. She then folded her arms. "What are you waiting for?"

"Me? What are *you* waiting for?" Cullen snapped back.

"I don't know what you're talking about." She brooded. "Besides, this is a conversation about you, buster. Just ask her if she'd like to have dinner with you. How hard is that?"

"Last night, when I was driving her back here, we discussed certain protocols. I told her that because of all the sexual harassment going on, it's as if a woman has to invite a man to kiss her."

"Say what?" Luna knitted her eyebrows. "You said that?"

"Yeah. Kinda stupid, but it was the only way I could explain it."

"Jeez. So now you're waiting for *her* to make a move?"

"Yes. And if she was interested, why didn't she 'invite' me?" he asked, using air quotes.

"Well, I think that topic deserves a little more attention before you start making assumptions." Luna was being the thoughtful sister now. "I think you should 'invite' her to dinner." Luna returned the air-quote gesture. "By the end of the evening, I am sure she will give you the green light."

"And if she doesn't?" Cullen frowned.

"Then you keep being her friend. Listen, you don't have to make any decisions about what action needs to be taken. Invite her to dinner and play it by ear. She is probably just as nervous as you are."

"You think so?" Cullen looked a bit more uplifted.

"Oh, come on. The two of you are just as wacky as me and Chris. Speaking of whom, did he say anything about me last night? Huh? Huh? Huh?"

"Oh, now we're making this about you?"

"I thought we were finished talking about you," she teased. "I told you what to do. Next subject. Me."

Cullen gave her a wry grin. "Yes, the marshal asked about you." He paused deliberately. "Well, not exactly."

"What? What?" She was going to choke it out of him if he didn't answer soon.

"We talked about some personal stuff. I told him my theory about relationships and how people are almost forced to pair up so they'll be invited to things that only couples get invited to. Like dinner parties."

"So? Where does the stuff about me come in?"

"I said you were usually my plus-one

because you weren't involved with anyone either."

"And?"

"And that's it."

"That can't be it! Spill, brother, spill!"

"OK. If you must know, and I know you must, I wanted to let him know you were unattached; and no, I didn't tell him you were all googly-eyed over him."

"Thank goodness for some miracles." Luna smirked. "And what about him? Is he involved with anyone?"

Cullen paused again. "No. He said that after the divorce he had to rearrange his life so he could spend time with his son, plus his schedule is always up in the air. Most women don't like to be second or third on the list of priorities."

Luna bit her lip. "So I guess I'm not even on the list."

"I wouldn't go that far. He is genuinely interested in you."

"Did he say that? Did he?" Luna was looking for reassurance.

"He didn't have to. Jeez, sis, do you need a building to fall on top of you? For a psychic, you really stink at your own personal stuff."

"Hey, watch it. Listen, being skittish is in our DNA. Look at us. We are in our midthirties and acting like teenagers."

Cullen chuckled. "You have a very good point there, missy. So how about we encourage each other to make a move."

"Oooh, Cullen, that would be so out of character for you. And me," Luna said thoughtfully. "Not the encouragement part. I mean the make a move part."

"OK. So how do I get Chi-Chi to invite me to kiss her?" Cullen folded his arms and leaned against the worktable.

"Duh. Invite her to dinner. Someplace romantic. After a glass of wine, you'll both be relaxed. Then you can take her hand across the table and give her a wonderful compliment as you gaze into her eyes."

"I'm not Cary Grant or even *Hugh* Grant. That only works in the movies."

"Bull-oney! Instead of being cynical, how about trying a little positive thinking?" She cocked her head and gave him her sideways stare.

"What if she flinches?" Cullen whined.

"Oh my Lord! Can you just try it? If she pulls her hand away, then you'll know. You've got to get out of your own way, my brother."

"You should talk! I see you all gaga over Chris."

"Yeah, well if he's interested, why hasn't

he made a major move?"

"Did *you* give him the green light? I mean, have you ever leaned in?"

"What do you mean leaned in?"

"I know he's kissed you good night. Right? So, why didn't you just turn into a limp noodle and let the sparks fly?"

Luna burst out laughing. "Listen to us arguing over who is the bigger chicken." Luna walked over to her brother and gave him a big hug. "You know I'm your biggest cheerleader. Trust me on this one."

"And what about you? What's *your* next move?"

"I've been a little hesitant because, if you think about it, Chris and I haven't spent a lot of time together, as in the same space. Yes, we've known each other for a while, but that's different than being around each other. I actually had a plan to invite him to my place for dinner next time he's in town, but now that he's invited me, or should I say I volunteered to help him, I'll be going to Charlotte in a couple of weeks."

"Oh, that should be very interesting. Didn't he say you can stay in Carter's room?"

"Yes! With all the baseball memorabilia." She chuckled. "I'll bring a pair of pretty pajamas. Nothing too lingerie-ish. I don't

159

want to come off as a trollop."

She giggled. "Come to think of it, I don't have any bedclothes in either category. I've been sleeping in T-shirts and sweatpants. Yikes. That's kinda pathetic."

"From a man's point of view, I think a pair of silk pajamas with a matching robe would be elegant, classy, and a touch of . . ." His voice trailed off.

"Touch of?" she pushed.

"Sensuality. OK. I said it." Cullen ran his hands through his hair. "I have a hard time thinking about you in that way."

Luna guffawed. "That is hilarious. I am a woman, in case you hadn't noticed."

"Yes, but you are my sister first." Cullen grinned.

"Fair enough. And I appreciate your input. I'll have to take a ride and do some shopping." She nodded to herself. "I want to be appropriately dressed." She giggled. "And I am going to make a reservation for you at Bouchorelle for the weekend I'm away. It's a good excuse for you to ask Chi-Chi to go to dinner." She gave him a wink.

Cullen took in a big gulp of air. "Tell me it isn't going to be a full moon, please."

"Nope. A new moon, which is perfect for new beginnings. Speaking of dinner, I am famished. Should we go grab a bite?"

"Aren't you going to dig into that diary? You were so anxious for me to open it."

"Yes, but with fresh eyes. I'll call Chi-Chi and see if she wants to grab a pizza. I'll casually bring up my excursion to Charlotte and 'hey, why don't the two of you keep each other company while I'm gone?' or something like that."

"You crack me up. But, sure. Why not?"

"It will be the perfect segue." Luna grabbed Cullen's walkie-talkie and buzzed Chi-Chi. "In the mood for pizza with me and Cullen?"

"I was just thinking about pizza. How did you know?" Chi-Chi was half serious.

"Because I'm me, that's why." Luna laughed. "Fifteen minutes?"

"That should be fine. Thank you. I'll meet you at the café."

Luna had an impish look. "Yes, I know. I am a goddess."

"Let's not push it, OK?" Cullen gave her a big hug.

"I'll go clean up the café. Be back in a few. Ta-ta!" Luna went outside to fetch Wiley.

"Hey, Alex. Has he been a good boy?" She squatted down to scratch the dog's ears and give him a hug.

"Always. I swear, I wish some of these kids

161

would behave as well."

"I hear ya. I think Ellie has a plan to handle the little maniacs."

"Really? Like putting Valium in their milk?" Alex was teasing, but Luna knew the sentiment.

She laughed. "She is going to hire a security guard."

"But we have state-of-the-art security, right?" Alex looked confused.

"Yes, but a big man with a uniform and a badge is what will keep those hooligans in line," Luna explained.

"Huh. That never occurred to me."

"Me neither, but Marshal Gaines was here earlier and suggested it to Ellie. Kids under ten have a lot more respect for authority, especially when it isn't their parents."

"Good point."

"So the moms can sip their chardonnay and pick at their salads, and the kids won't be running around like a pack of squirrels looking for nuts to hide."

"What do you suppose they'll do to keep themselves entertained?"

"Not our problem." Luna chuckled. "Let the mommies figure it out. Maybe they'll bring them to day care or hire a babysitter or bring the nanny. They can certainly afford it."

"I could never understand why parents bring their children out in public, then ignore them," Alex wondered aloud.

"It's an accessory. Or a 'look what I did. I gave birth.' "

Both of them laughed out loud, and Wiley gave a woof.

"Right? You need to pass a test to deliver the mail, but you don't have to do anything to deliver a baby."

"Alex, that was quite an astute comment."

"Yeah, I have a few every once in a while."

Luna smiled. "Gotta run. Thanks again. See you tomorrow."

"Have a good night," Alex called out, as Luna and Wiley dashed to the café.

As everyone was closing up, Luna realized she had never pinged Rita. "Dang." She picked up her walkie-talkie. "Rita, I am so sorry. The day just got away from me."

"No problem." Rita sounded sincere.

"I have a busy day tomorrow, but how is Wednesday looking for you?"

"That should work fine. After we close?"

"You bet. I am marking it down on my calendar." Luna did exactly that. "Again, sorry."

"Again, no problem," Rita echoed.

Chi-Chi was crossing the atrium as Luna was closing up. "Good evening."

163

"English?" Luna was surprised that Chi-Chi did not greet her in her native tongue.

"I'm trying it on for size." Chi-Chi's face lit up with a big smile.

"How about *'Buona sera'* since we're having pizza?" Luna suggested.

"My, we are multilingual now." Chi-Chi smiled again.

Cullen met up with them in the café. "Should we take one car?"

"I have to drop Wiley off at home, so why don't you and Chi-Chi follow me there? Chi-Chi can ride with you, and you can bring her back to her car later."

Cullen's palms started to sweat as he recalled the conversation from the night before. "Uh, sure."

"If it is not an inconvenience for you," Chi-Chi offered.

"No, not at all. I have to come back this way."

"Are you sure of that?" Chi-Chi asked.

"That I have to come this way? Yeah. Pretty certain. I live a mile from here." Cullen was trying to add a little humor to the conversation.

Chi-Chi nodded and smiled. "Then I accept."

Luna averted her eyes to keep from looking at Cullen. The die was cast. Now for the invitation. To dinner. The other one would be up to Chi-Chi.

Cullen and Chi-Chi followed Luna to her house, where she dropped off Wiley. Then she piled into the back seat of Cullen's vehicle. Cullen seemed a bit nervous, so Luna suggested he turn on some music. "Cruisin' " by Smokey Robinson was playing, and everyone began to sing along.

Chi-Chi shocked both of them with her fine voice.

"Wow. Impressive." Cullen snapped his head in her direction.

Cullen and Luna stopped singing as Chi-Chi took the second verse, vocalizing like a pro.

When the song ended, Luna hooted and clapped as if she was at a concert. "Oh my goodness! How did we not know you had pipes like that?"

Chi-Chi was trying not to be self-conscious. "It is how I learned to speak English. I was very happy to hear it on a television commercial recently. It is what you call a feel-good song."

"What else do you have in your repertoire?" Luna asked.

"Almost every Motown song," Chi-Chi replied.

"Motown, eh?" Cullen asked. "That's a

bit before your time, isn't it?"

"It was my parents who introduced me to the music. Good music will always stand the test of time. The talent on those records was very different than what is coming out of recording companies today." Chi-Chi was surprising them with another side of her. "Remember, they did not have the technology at the time. Recording sessions were the test for talent. They could not doctor it." She let out a big sigh. "I suppose I am not the best consumer for today's entertainment."

"Neither am I," Cullen confessed. "I like music where I can understand the lyrics and which has a melody I can remember."

"I'm with you on that," Luna chimed in. "Hit the next song on your playlist."

Out from the speakers came the perky whistling of Bobby McFerrin singing "Don't Worry, Be Happy."

"Oh, I love this song!" Chi-Chi began to sing along. "*Ooh, ooh oo-ooh, ooh, oo-ooh.* You cannot help but be happy when you sing this. And did you know he is singing all the parts? The bass, the percussion, the background? And he has an album with Yo-Yo Ma."

"Such a talent," Cullen added. "It's in his DNA. His father was an opera singer, the first African-American male to perform at the Metropolitan Opera. He also dubbed the vocals for Sidney Poitier in *Porgy & Bess*."

"Really? I thought that was Sidney Poitier singing." Luna was truly surprised.

"I hate to break it to you, sis, but that wasn't Audrey Hepburn singing in *My Fair Lady* either."

Luna joined in with Chi-Chi and continued to sing until the song was over. "I like your taste in music." Chi-Chi was smiling from ear to ear.

"Thank you." He smiled back. "It's a bit eclectic. I don't think I own anything that was recorded after 1996."

"I understand," Chi-Chi assured him. "Either I cannot understand the lyrics or I feel as if they are yelling at me. Even ballads. And the language. *Ori mi o!* Shameful. Maybe I'm being fussy, but I prefer to sing something that has meaningful lyrics, not four-letter expletives."

"Well, *you* have a beautiful voice." Cullen was reassuring.

"Thank you. I wish I could do it more."

"Why don't you join a group?" Luna asked.

"I have thought about it, but I wanted to focus on my business before I got involved in other activities."

"Understandable." Cullen nodded as he continued to watch the road ahead.

"Well, the next time there is live music somewhere, we'll make sure you'll show off more of your talent," Luna said.

"I do not want to be a show-off," Chi-Chi said plainly.

"That's not what I meant." Luna gave her a pat on the shoulder.

"For now I must be satisfied with singing at home."

"Whatever you say, woman." Luna knew when the opportunity presented itself she would be dragging Chi-Chi up on a stage, platform, or bandstand.

They arrived at Three Brothers Pizzeria and were given the usual big hello greeting from Louie. He showed them to their regular table, where they could see the cooks prepare the pizza behind the cutout in the stone wall.

Halfway through her first slice, Luna brought up her forthcoming visit to Gaines's house. "It should be fun." She took another big chunk. "What are you guys going to do while I'm away?"

She thought Cullen was going to choke on his escarole.

"I have not thought that far ahead." Chi-

Chi shrugged.

Luna turned to Cullen. "What about you?"

He barely got the first forkful of escarole down before he came close to gagging again. "I hadn't given it much thought." He averted his sister's eyes.

"I have an idea. Why don't you try Bouchorelle?"

"I have not been there," Chi-Chi admitted. "I have not had the occasion to go."

"Well, how about a 'Luna is out of town' occasion?" Luna took another bite trying to be inconspicuous.

"Is that an occasion?" Chi-Chi raised her eyebrows in confusion.

"It could be." Luna wiped her lips, hoping Cullen would take the cue. But he didn't. She wanted to kick him under the table, but that would be too obvious. The three of them were sitting very close together. "Cul, I think you should take Chi-Chi to Bouchorelle. She's never been." *If he doesn't jump on this right now, I'm going to hit him with a meatball.*

"Well, sure." Cullen was just a decibel above muttering.

"Luna, you cannot tell your brother to ask me to dinner. It is not polite," Chi-Chi admonished her.

"Ha. We're all friends here, and he is my brother, so I can definitely boss him around." Luna chuckled.

Cullen finally got the guts to speak up. "Chi-Chi, I would be delighted if you would join me for dinner at Bouchorelle, when my pesky sister is out of town. That *is* an occasion I can celebrate."

Luna could barely hold in her excitement. "Now I won't worry about the two of you pining away while I'm gone."

"You're going for one night," Cullen reminded her.

"Yes, but you will miss me." Luna dug her fork into Cullen's escarole and shoved it in her mouth. "Mmm . . . garlicky." She stopped in her tracks. Her inclination was to say, "And be sure to skip the garlic when you're on your date," but she just let it float away in her thought balloons. She'd spare Cullen the further embarrassment.

They split the check three ways, which is what they normally did. As they were leaving, Luna whispered in Chi-Chi's ear, "Don't worry. Cullen will pick up the tab at Bouchorelle."

Chi-Chi stopped in her tracks, getting ready to protest, but Luna slipped her arm through Chi-Chi's and gave her a look that said, "Don't argue. Keep walking, girl-friend."

CHAPTER TEN

Stillwell Art Center
Monday

Normally the center was closed on Monday and Tuesday in order to give everyone time to do whatever personal things needed to be done, clean up their shops, order materials, or simply take the day off. But for Ellie there was no day off. She would do a walkabout on Monday morning with Ziggy and Marley, checking that everything was in its place.

A few artists worked on those two days, enabling them to tend to their shops. Jennine from Clay-More was one of them. It was alone time to make whatever she would put on display for the week. She would hold classes and give people an inside look at her workshop, but generally she was dressed to the nines, tens, and often over the top when the center was open to the public. Plus she had an apprentice who would throw clay on

Friday and Saturday when the center was bustling. Ellie never quite made the connection between someone who posed as a mature glamour girl and making pottery. Once Ellie made a comment about it, and Jennine's answer was, "I love to get my hands on things and mold them." Over time, watching Jennine pounce on men, the answer made a lot of sense.

Ellie went into her office on the second floor, which overlooked the atrium. From there she could see the front entrance and the rear glass doors to the patio. The only thing that hindered her view was the interior landscaping, but that was a very small inconvenience. Very small.

She pulled out her Rolodex. Yes, Ellie still used the same spinning wheel that held years of contact cards. She once tried to transfer all the information into an Excel spreadsheet, but flipping through the cards was a lot easier and for some odd reason, more satisfying. With technology dictating our lives, we've lost the use of a lot of our senses. Smell, for example. You can't smell anything over a phone or computer. Taste. Same thing. Touch? Keyboards or phone pads. *Would anyone know how to use a pencil?* she mused. Even our sense of hearing has been dampened by digital recordings and portable mediocre speakers. There is nothing like sitting in your home with a good sound system where you can hear all the parts. The violins, cellos, chimes, woodwinds. The fine points of music. Ellie sighed. *They call it progress. I call it unfortunate.* Unfortunate because people have become incapable of basic communication. Emojis, abbreviations. They don't even speak on the phone. Just a bunch of diodes and keystrokes.

Ellie flipped to the letter *B.* Nathan Belmont. She picked up the landline and dialed his number.

"Stillwell Art Center?" Nathan was surprised to see the caller ID. "Is this *thee,* Ellie Stillwell?"

"Nathan Belmont. How are you?" Ellie's smile could be heard through her voice.

"I'm doin' great. And you? Everything all right?"

"I'm doing great myself, and yes, everything is fine. But I need a little help."

"Shoot. What's up?"

"I know you've been here a couple of times."

"I have indeed. You created a masterpiece."

"Thanks, Nate. I am in awe every time I walk in here. I can't believe I've been able to pull it off!" Ellie chuckled.

"So what can I help you with? I'm not doing any more heavy lifting." He snickered.

"No. Nothing like that." Ellie went on to explain about the social-status mothers bringing their children to the center and letting them run wild.

"Oh, I know the type."

"Yes. They buy two bottles of chardonnay, salads, sit on the patio, and ignore their kids. They run all over the place. It's like Chuck E. Cheese."

Nathan let out a bellow. "And I imagine that's not too popular with visitors."

"Oh, you are not kidding. Last week one of the little brats practically knocked a woman over. She didn't get hurt but she was very annoyed. And I don't blame her."

"So what do you need from me?

"A good friend suggested I hire a security guard."

"But you have the most sophisticated system in the county."

"I do indeed. But it's not so much about security as it is about intimidation."

"Ho. Ho. Ho." Nathan's deep voice was reverberating in the way Ellie remembered. "If I am hearing you correctly, you want me to wear a uniform and look authoritative."

"Bingo. As U.S. Marshal Gaines pointed

out, there is nothing like a large man with a badge to keep the little rug rats from wreaking havoc. I don't want to keep anyone from enjoying the center, including the lushes, but they are very dismissive of their children."

"Don't they all have nannies?"

"Even a nanny needs a day off, so the mommies come here with their children and expect the center to be their nannies."

"Gotcha. So what do you want from me besides my brawn and good looks?" He snickered.

"Would you be interested in working here a few days a week? I'll pay you well, you'll get free lunches from the Blonde Shallot, and all the pastry you can eat from the Flakey Tart. Of course, the same goes for the Cheese Cave."

"Hmmm. I think you had me at Flakey Tart." Nate laughed.

"Can you come over and we can work out a plan?"

"You free today?" Nathan asked.

"For you? Absolutely." Ellie was elated. "We're closed to the public today so you'll be able to get a good walk-through."

"Sounds good. I can be there in an hour. Does that work for you?"

"Perfect. Just ring the front buzzer. I'll be

in my office or my cell will notify me that someone is at the door."

"You got it. See you shortly."

Ellie was delighted for a couple of reasons, not the least of which was seeing her loyal friend and farm supervisor again. The second was that she might have solved an annoying problem. And third, it would be nice to have Nathan around again. She missed seeing him every day.

It was coming up on the one-year anniversary of Stillwell Art Center. Even now, as she stood looking over the balcony down at the atrium and its dozens of artisan shops, she could easily well up in tears. She thought about her husband, Richard, who had passed away a few years earlier. How she wished he could be here to see it. Then Luna's words echoed in her ear. "He's always with you." Ellie truly believed it. When Luna did a cold reading for Ellie, she used a phrase often used by her deceased husband, "Have no fear, my dear." It didn't matter if it was making a dinner reservation or white-water rafting. Richard instilled a sense of confidence in her. He would often tell her that if she was fearful of something, she needed to ask herself, "What's the worst that can happen?" Then, after mulling it over, she should ask another question:

"What's worse than that?" It made a lot of sense if you boiled it down. Unless "death" or "illness" was the answer, then "just do it," as the commercial suggests.

When Ellie took on the multimillion-dollar project, the worst thing would be to lose most of her money. If that happened, she would still have a couple of million left over. *Everyone should be that lucky.* Ellie was truly grateful for her financial stability and having the resources to help fund other artists' goals. She felt that was one way of giving back. Paying it forward.

Like clockwork, Nathan arrived. Ellie appreciated Nathan's work ethic. She moved back behind her desk and buzzed him in. Her office was rigged with every electronic device for maximum security. She could do a major lockdown if it ever came to that. Heaven forbid.

Nathan opened the big glass doors and took long strides into the atrium. He still looked robust. Ellie squinted and blinked. *He looks better than I remember,* she thought to herself. A little grayer around the temples, but she could see the definition in his muscles pressing against his long-sleeved polo shirt. She leaned over the railing and called down, "Nathan! So good to see you! Wait there. I'll be right down."

Ellie checked herself in the reflection of the glass door. *Why?* She couldn't answer that. Not yet anyway. Was she ready to start dating? But who? Ellie was no shrinking violet by any stretch, and it wasn't that she fancied any kind of romance, but it would be nice to have a dependable man around even if they weren't each other's type.

Ellie bounded down the center staircase, Ziggy and Marley leading the way. Nathan immediately squatted to greet them. "How are my guys doing? Miss me?" Nathan nuzzled both of them as they nuzzled back. He stood and picked Ellie up off the ground and spun her around. "Woo-hoo! I've been waiting a looonnng time to do that!"

Ellie was nonplussed. Nathan had never manhandled her like that before. Sure a hug, but this?

Ellie faked anger and lightly pounded him on his chest. "Unhand me, you brute!"

Even the dogs knew he was simply having fun. Had it been anyone else, the dogs would have him pinned to the ground. As soon as he set her down, she gave him a long hug. "You are looking fit as a fiddle." She couldn't help noticing he must be doing something to keep himself in such good shape.

"I work out at the gym a few days a week.

179

Been doing a little volunteering with some of the yoots." He mimicked Joe Pesci from *My Cousin Vinny.*

"Then I have the perfect opportunity for you."

Ellie's eyes gleamed.

"Do tell, sweet lady. It's OK if I call you a lady?" Nathan asked cautiously.

"Of course. Why not?" Ellie seemed surprised by the question.

"Because everyone is so darn sensitive these days. You never know what is going to offend someone." Nathan gave a big sigh.

"Oh, for heaven's sake, Nathan. We've known each other far too long to even think about being offended."

"Glad to hear you say it. Makes me think everyone should wear a sign saying, 'Don't call me this,' or 'Don't call me that.' Or be sure to call me a list of things, but not this list." Nathan chuckled. "I understand it's important for people to be sensitive, but some take it to an extreme. I ought to know."

"I certainly agree. Everything is politicized and scrutinized. If people were just a little kinder and tolerant, we wouldn't be having this conversation."

"Ellie Stillwell, how I miss working for you," Nathan said with a warm smile.

"That's why I called you. Maybe we can fix that situation." Ellie was ever hopeful Nathan would consider the offer she was about to make. "But let's grab a sandwich first. The Blonde Shallot brings a dozen or so on Monday and Tuesday for the artists who are here on the days off."

"That's mighty nice of them." Nathan followed Ellie as she walked toward the sandwich shop.

Nathan looked around. A basket of sandwiches sat on the main counter with a glass jar beside it. There was no one else in the kiosk but the two of them. "Doesn't look like anyone is here."

"They're not. Rita drops off the sandwiches and leaves a jar for people to pay whatever they can."

"Say what?" Nathan looked baffled.

"The honor system. We have another person who operates the same way, but he does it every day." Ellie grabbed two roast beef sandwiches. "This OK with you?"

"Sure. But you need to explain further." Nathan watched as Ellie put a twenty-dollar bill in the jar.

"And they just leave the money and sandwiches out?"

"Yes. I know it's unusual, but we appreciate each other's efforts and try to support

181

each other in whatever way we can. That's how I charge rent, too."

The two walked toward the large sliding patio doors. Ellie motioned Nathan to sit at one of the café tables.

They sat quietly for a brief moment. "It really is good to see you, Nathan." Ellie smiled and touched his hand.

Nathan gave it a squeeze. "Likewise." They unwrapped their lunch, and Ellie began to explain her rental agreement with the artists.

"I charge them ten percent of their net business. That, too, is on the honor system."

"You mean you leave it to them to figure out how much rent to pay?"

"That's the system. It's been working so far."

"But how do you know if they're being honest?" Nathan had a very puzzled look on his face.

"I have to trust them. Of course, I could always ask for an audit of their books. It's in their lease agreement. But I can tell by foot traffic and just by looking at what they have in inventory. Besides, they will never get a better deal unless someone bankrolls them."

Nathan snickered. "Miss Ellie, you always had good instincts. This place is magnificent. Why would anyone want to screw it up for themselves?"

"That's what I am counting on. By the way, you're not going to keep calling me Miss Ellie, now are you?"

"Force of habit, I guess." Nathan gave her a knowing nod. "I'll do my best. So, tell me, what do you have in mind?"

"The Stepford wives come almost every Thursday. With their precious children. If you could be here Thursday through Sunday, that would be perfect. We're open from eleven until five on Wednesdays and Thursdays, from ten until eight Fridays and Saturdays, and from eleven to four on Sunday. If we are having an event, the times may change. Once a month we have a string quartet from six until eight on a Saturday."

"Would you want me here all four days?" Nathan was calculating in his head.

"That would be wonderful. Saturday can be a long haul. We get rather busy in the afternoon."

"What if I get one of my young adult fellows to pitch in for a few hours?" Nathan was thinking out loud. "I have a fine young man who would probably appreciate the apprenticeship. I'll train him to look mean." Nathan laughed.

"That could work," Ellie said. "As I said,

it's the physical presence of an authority figure. Does he look young or older? You know what I mean."

"He's Latin-American. About five-foot-ten-inches tall with a build that will make the women swoon. He can be intense, but a nice kid. Name's Mateo."

"Well, that sounds like a good plan." Ellie had already put pen to paper and wrote down the numbers as far as his salary and benefits. "I'll pay you thirty dollars per hour, plus health insurance. It's thirty-seven hours. You can pay Mateo from your salary. Would you be amenable to that?" Ellie slid the page over to him.

"Eleven hundred a week?" Nathan eyes widened.

"That's what I was paying you when you were at the farm."

"Yes, but this is a much easier gig."

"Wait until Chuck E. Cheese Thursday." Ellie cackled.

"Ellie Stillwell, it will be a pleasure doing business with you again." Nathan leaned back in his chair. "So what type of uniform do you want me to wear?"

"Go to Seigel's or Howard. They have very nice dress uniforms. Single- and double-breasted."

"You have done your homework, haven't

you? Why am I not surprised?" Nathan gave her a big grin.

"You know me well. You can have a badge embroidered, or something to pin on. I'll leave the authoritative visual aspects to you."

"Roger that."

"Which reminds me. Everyone has a walkie-talkie. We had an incident early on, and I wanted to be sure my people had easy access for communication."

"Is there anything you haven't thought of?" Nathan kept grinning.

"I guess I'll find out if and when the occasion arises." Ellie let out a huge sigh of relief. "I am so very happy you are willing to do this for me."

"Like I've said so many times, anything for you."

Ellie reached across the table and squeezed his hand. "Come, I'll show you around the place."

CHAPTER ELEVEN

Wednesday

Tori awoke with a sense of anticipation. She crawled out of bed so as not to wake her husband. She planned to fix something for him to eat later. Her mission was to keep him in a good mood for as long as she could.

The week before, she had frozen some beef stew, so she pulled it out to defrost. She boiled up some noodles that he could reheat. A big chunk of bread was wrapped in aluminum foil, which he could also warm. Satisfied that he would be satisfied, she started on her usual fare of toast with a little butter. She decided to trade off her coffee for herbal tea. Not that she was a fan of herbal tea, but she didn't think she needed the caffeine that morning. She was already juiced up. She had no idea if she would find the woman, nor did she know if the woman would spend any time with her. But it was worth taking the chance.

She heard her husband get out of bed and head toward the bathroom. She wasn't sure if she should bolt or wait. It was too early to head to the art center, but she didn't know what else to do with her time. Bake! She decided if she baked cookies, that would keep her busy and her husband satisfied his wife was doing something wifey.

About a half hour later, he came out of the bathroom with a towel wrapped around his waist. She knew what that meant, but not today. She was already showered and dressed.

He came up from behind and put his arms around her and pulled her close to him. She could feel him getting aroused. As if a guardian angel was watching over her, the timer rang on the oven. "Oops. Can't let these burn." She jiggled away from him and put on oven mitts.

"Well, maybe while they're cooling down before I do?" He sounded rebuffed.

"Oh, hon, not now, please." Tori was sweet, but she knew it didn't land well with him.

"Fine." He let out an exaggerated sigh and meandered out of the kitchen.

Tori looked up at the ceiling, mouthed the words, "thank you," and gave a sigh of relief.

She checked the digital clock on the stove. It wasn't even close to nine. She had to find something to do to keep herself occupied. Maybe she would stop in the office to check the mail. It would kill some time. She yelled down the hallway, "See you later, honey. There's food in the fridge for you to heat up later." She heard a grunt in the distance. His way of saying, "Have a nice day."

Tori realized she was very nervous. There was so much to think about. She also realized that once she thought about things, she would have to take action. If the past twenty years hadn't taught her a lesson, then she would never learn. She was happy she had chosen to tell her boss about her situation. It gave her enough confidence to get through another day. The pregnancy would be a challenge, but she was feeling better about it now that she knew her employer would be on her side. She didn't want to think about how her husband would react to the news. She also knew she might have to leave him at some point. As confused as she was, one thing was for certain — she was not going to spend her life having more regrets. She knew people stayed together "because of the kids," but kids are a lot smarter and much more in tune with what is going on around them than adults give them credit for. Kids can sense tension. Most people can. But kids internalize it more. They will blame themselves for the tension between their parents. She knew that firsthand. For years, she blamed herself for her mother's drinking and her father's absence. But by the time she was twelve and had to care for her little brother, she was aware enough to realize that her circumstances were not her fault. The sad part was that she never took care of herself. Sure, as far as hair, clothes, makeup as she got older, but mentally she was "on hold." She kept believing the answer was ahead, never thinking it was within her.

Since working at the law firm, she had witnessed a lot of reasons for the sort of domestic turmoil that led to divorce. Most of the time it was infidelity, but the infidelity was a result of someone's not feeling loved, not being emotionally supported, or just mutual disengagement. On countless occasions, she had heard the words "We drifted apart." It made her wonder about the word "drifted." Were they ever on course, or were they always adrift? Looking back, she realized that she and her husband had been adrift from the beginning. First it was being adrift from their families. Second, they were adrift from a purpose. A goal.

Consequently, they drifted away from each other, but neither one recognized it. At least neither admitted it. Now that she was finally aware of how her lack of a compass had gotten her into this boggy mess, she wasn't going to let her boat run aground again. Not if she could help it. *But enough of the metaphors,* she thought to herself. But they gave her a clear picture of her situation.

On her way to the office, she stopped at the diner to get a buttered roll for herself and a donut for Mr. Bellows. She would have picked up something for Arlene, the receptionist, but Arlene was gluten-free and there were few diners in the area that didn't specialize in high sugar and wheat content.

As she was paying the tab, the same woman gave her a knowing nod. It gave Tori a bit of the willies. Who was that woman and how did she know about her and her "cop" husband? In her excitement, and plans to get to the art center, she had almost forgotten about the foreboding message the woman gave her. "Thursday. Ringo's." Then she remembered he said he might go fishing on Thursday. *What's up with Thursday?* She shook it off for now. She had bigger things on her mind today.

When she entered the office, Arlene gave her a big hello. "Hey, thought you weren't

190

coming in today."

"Just wanted to check the mail," Tori said confidently. "Is Mr. Bellows in? I brought him a donut. Sorry, they didn't have any gluten-free goodies."

"It's OK. I bake my own." Arlene raised her ugly-looking muffin to show Tori. "He's not in yet," she said, with a longing glance at the donut bag. "Sure wish I could eat one of those, though, but if I do, well, you know what happens." Arlene pointed to her backside, referring to the gastrointestinal issues she experienced.

Tori smiled, thinking, *Too much information, thank you.* "I'll leave it on his desk." Tori walked into Robert Bellows's office and placed the donut on top of a napkin so the grease wouldn't get all over his desk blotter. Blotters were made to absorb ink, not necessarily an oily piece of fried dough. Tori looked around the office. It was as stereotypical as a lawyer's office could be. Big Brayton Manor executive desk with a large brown leather chair, matching barrister bookcases and credenzas. Two club chairs sat in front of the desk and a settee was in front of the large bay window. A small round table was on one side with four chairs. It was almost a duplicate of George Layton's with the exception of the window treatments, wall covering, and carpeting. Robert's office had a green palette while George's was deep burgundy. His wife wanted more warmth and did the decorating for her husband. It had remained that way since they opened the office thirty years before, but George hadn't had the heart to make any changes after his wife passed away.

Both men had family photos, awards, and various memorabilia on their shelves. Robert's were sports related, while George's were family and historical, with a large old-world globe on a stand in the corner. But both offices were comfortable and gave the client a sense of safety and security.

Tori tried to imagine how many people passed through the doors and what troubles they brought with them. But she knew that whatever the issue, George and Robert would find a solution. Just like George was helping her find hers.

After an hour of sorting through mail and e-mails, Tori went into George's office. She pulled out a law book that contained information about divorces in North Carolina. Even though she did most of the research for her boss, she wanted to look at the statutes from her own perspective. The most important detail was in order to file for an "absolute divorce," the couple must be separated for at least one year and one day. In many instances, couples signed a separation agreement, which covered terms and responsibilities. She knew he would never go for it. Another option was a DBB: Divorce from Bed & Board — a court-ordered separation due to abuse or adultery. It does not constitute an absolute divorce, but the court can intercede to resolve property issues. Tori's head was spinning. She knew she wasn't eligible for a DBB. Sure, he was sullen, but that didn't reach the level of abuse. It was more of emotional abandonment that pained her. The one bright spot was the issue of child support. That could be filed at any time.

She was sorry she had opened the book. Her elation about going to the art center was clouded by the reality of logistics. She folded her arms and rested her head on the table. A soft knock startled her.

"You OK?" Arlene asked.

"Yes, I'm fine. Just a little headache," she lied. It was a huge headache, literally and figuratively.

"Can I get you something for it?"

"Thanks, but I have some aspirin in my purse."

"Is there anything I can help you with? I thought you were taking the day off."

"No, but thanks. I was just looking up something for a friend." Tori checked her watch. "I'd better get going. I have a lot of errands to run." She waited for Arlene to leave the doorway so she could put the book back on the shelf. She didn't want Arlene to know what she had been reading about. Tori stood up, hoping it would give Arlene the hint to scram. It worked. She stretched and put her thoughts on pause. Maybe the psychic could steer her in the right direction. At least she knew Mr. Layton had her back, even if he wasn't yet aware he might be representing her at some point. She resigned herself that if she didn't face her issues head-on, she could be spinning in circles. Getting there was the big challenge.

She grabbed her purse, keys, and jacket and headed out the door. "See you tomorrow."

"Sure thing. Have a good one!" Arlene was still picking at that ugly muffin.

Luna, Ellie, and Chi-Chi got together for their usual morning coffee and delectable delights from the Flakey Tart.

"What's on your agenda today?" Ellie asked as she sipped her cappuccino.

"I have several clients." Luna broke off a piece of her brioche. "Word must be getting out. I hope you don't mind, Ellie."

"Why would I mind? It brings people into the center. Some of whom would most likely never come here. I look at you as a 'promotional item.' " Ellie smiled.

"Huh. I never thought of myself as that." Luna scrunched up her face. "But if it keeps the traffic flowing, then that's a good thing. I just don't want people to get all weirded out."

"Have you looked around?" Ellie chuckled. "We are surrounded by eccentric people."

Chi-Chi almost spit out her coffee. "I suppose I am one of them?"

"Of course you are. That's why we love you," Luna teased. "I think anyone who has any sort of an artistic streak is a bit eccentric."

"That's what makes them special." Ellie patted Chi-Chi's hand.

Chi-Chi smiled brightly. "I suppose you are correct. We are special."

"Yes indeedy!" Luna got up and rinsed her coffee cup. Chi-Chi and Ellie did the same.

"OK, you fine women. Y'all have yourselves a lovely day."

Chi-Chi folded her hands in prayer position. *"Oni a dara."*

"You have a nice day as well." Luna gave her a slight bow. "Namaste."

Luna made sure everything in the café was set up and ready for her influx of clients. She checked her schedule. Five. That's a lot of energy for one day.

Tori nervously began the thirty-mile drive to the center. So much was going on in her mind. The word "divorce" floated through her head a few times, but when it came to the actual act of it, well, that was a different story. After reading through the law books it hit her. There was a lot to do. Now, looking at it from a personal point of view, she had a much better appreciation for all the divorce cases she had worked on. She simply did the paperwork. This time it would be her doing the heavy lifting. How? That was a big question. How was she going to approach him? He would feel like he'd been blindsided. Not that it should come as any big surprise. Many marriages are mediocre or even bad, but no one has the wherewithal to make a move, so they suffer in silence. Then comes resentment. She thought of asking him to go to marriage counseling, but he would balk. He was perfectly fine with his situation. That was the problem. It was *his* situation. Not theirs, as a couple, or hers. She never had the strength to fight back. Stand her ground. Speak her mind. She feared his wrath, so she remained silent.

Tori thought about stopping somewhere to grab lunch but had heard there was a café in the center. She wondered if it was the same café the woman operated from. She wanted to give herself ample time to check out the situation before she approached the woman. If she was, in fact, approachable. She drove another twenty minutes until she came upon a lushly landscaped area with a sign that said:

WELCOME TO THE STILLWELL ART CENTER

She turned on to what appeared to be a private road that led to the massive structure. It was the size of a mini-mall. She found a place to park and sat in her car for a few minutes to gather her thoughts and fortitude. She had never done anything like this before. Venturing on her own. In search of answers. She checked the visor mirror. She looked respectable; her short-cropped blond hair framed her face. Her makeup stayed intact. She ran a stick of gloss over her lips, unbuckled her seat belt, and got out of the car. She steadied herself. She was embarking on a different course. One that hadn't been laid out for her. She was on her own today.

She entered through the massive glass doors and found herself amidst a lush garden with breathtaking skylights. The perimeter was marked with artists' shops and beautiful colors. It was a tsunami of visual stimulation. She didn't know where to begin. Then her eyes went immediately to the corner where pieces of sculpture sat alongside another glass door. They appeared to be made of metal. Her first inclination was to look. She slowly walked around one side of the atrium, glancing into the windows of ceramics, glass, birdhouses, and jewelry. It was a bit overwhelming. It could take all day to find the woman she was in search of. When she arrived at the front of the metal-sculpture kiosk, she got a shiver. She peered inside and saw that no one was on the premises. She saw the sign about the honor system but resisted touching any of the objects. After browsing through the shop, she turned and noticed a sign for the Blonde Shallot. She was getting hungry and decided to check it out. As she made her way toward the sandwich shop, her eyes darted around to see if she could find the mysterious woman's café. There it was. Namaste Café. She stopped in her tracks for a moment to peek into the shop. There was a woman around Tori's age with a very long braid, granny glasses, and bangle bracelets standing next to an easel. Tori thought perhaps it was the woman she was seeking. There was another woman seated at the adjacent table, and they were talking. By the expression on the braided woman's face, it was a serious discussion. She resisted the urge to go inside. She would check again after she had some lunch.

Tori entered the Blonde Shallot and decided to try something different and bought a caprese sandwich with fresh mozzarella, prosciutto, tomato, and pesto on a ciabatta roll. She grabbed a bottle of water and carried her lunch to one of the high-top tables in the atrium. She found a seat where she could keep an eye on the café, hoping the woman would be free to talk at some point. She watched the first woman leave. She was wearing a pair of dark sunglasses and had a large piece of paper rolled under her arm. Tori couldn't tell if she was crying or trying to be incognito. Within minutes, another woman walked into the café. She watched them shake hands, then the braided woman motioned toward the table next to the easel. Tori thought she might have the wrong person. Maybe she was simply a sketch artist. Then she saw the braided woman sit across from the customer, who took off a piece of jewelry and handed it to her. The braided woman clasped the piece and closed her eyes for several minutes. She began to write something. The customer kept nodding. Then the braided woman got up and went to the easel and began to sketch. It was a very odd interaction. At least from Tori's point of view. Several people stopped midway and blocked her from seeing what was happening next. Tori tried not to be conspicuous by craning her neck when the people finally moved away from her line of sight. At that point, the braided woman tore off the paper, rolled it up, and handed it to the customer. Both women nodded and shook hands again. Tori was now convinced that the braided woman was the one she needed to speak to and wondered if this would be a good time to approach her. But before Tori could wrap the remains of her sandwich, the braided woman slid the glass door shut, put up a sign, and disappeared through a connecting door into the restoration showroom. Tori sighed and decided she should finish her lunch and walk around the rest of the center. Maybe by the time she had completed her first lap, the woman would be returning to the café. A few minutes later, a young college-age woman entered the café and removed the sign. It became more confusing as the minutes went on. Maybe *she* was the person?

Luna entered Cullen's workshop and yawned. "I am exhausted, and I still have two more people to meet with today." She pulled up a chair and rested her head on the long worktable.

"Did you have any lunch?" Cullen asked.

"Not yet. I asked Sabrina to cover for me for a half hour. I needed a break."

"I'll go grab something and bring it back. You can hide out here for a while. Roast beef?"

"With cheddar please. Thanks."

"Be right back." Cullen grabbed his wallet and headed through the main door of his showroom.

Tori watched closely as a tall, nice-looking, clean-cut man with sandy brown hair appeared from the showroom. He was close in age to the woman from the café. Probably the same age as Tori, maybe a couple of years older. But not by much. Maybe forty, but it was hard to pinpoint. She eyed him walk toward the sandwich shop, nodding at each person passing by. His face lit up when he spotted a striking honey-toned woman with long dark braids, half of which were wrapped around her head. She wore a beautiful purple caftan with exquisite silver and stone jewelry. Tori noticed the woman was coming from a stall that said:

SILVER AND STONE

Probably the owner, Tori thought to herself. It occurred to her that there were several people close to her age who had businesses. Careers. Sure she had a good job, but she had never considered it a career. She couldn't complain, though. It was so much better than working as a hostess with ungodly hours.

Tori watched as the stunning woman gave a brief nod and smile to the tall, sandy-haired man. Tori thought they could be dating by the way they looked at each other. Something about the man's face. There was a special light in his eyes. The beautiful woman had a gentle but innocent, maybe even shy look about her. The two people caught up with each other. They were smiling and laughing. Tori tried to remember what that felt like. The man nodded toward the door of the shop he had just left. The woman nodded back in acknowledgment as she placed her hand on his arm. Tori's feeling was correct. There was some kind of spark.

She watched the woman walk to the corner where the man had come from and go inside. Several minutes later, the man exited the sandwich shop with a large bag and strode to the same door. *Must be having lunch together. But what happened to the hippie-looking woman?* Tori shrugged and finished her sandwich. Her eyes were fixed on the strange corner shop with the metal sculpture. Maybe she would take a look. She glanced in the direction of the café and calculated that she would be able to spot the woman if or when she returned.

Cullen strode into the workshop with three sandwiches. One for Luna, one for Chi-Chi, and his favorite sloppy lunch. "Did you bring enough napkins?" Luna teased.

"I'll have you know that I am not a messy eater," Cullen shot back.

"No, you are not. But the sandwich has different ideas," Chi-Chi said with a straight face.

Cullen chuckled. He was enjoying Chi-Chi's company and humor more each day. He calculated how many days it would be before they went to dinner without his sister. Two weeks and a few days. He didn't like to wish his life away, but in this case he was eager to be alone with Chi-Chi in a beautiful, romantic restaurant.

The three of them made small talk as they devoured their lunch. When they were finished, Luna and Chi-Chi helped clear the table of their bags and napkins. Luna announced she would take the diary back to her café and try to get something from it while waiting between clients. She was careful to be sure she wore latex gloves and handled it as if it were something fragile.

Chi-Chi had a box of amethyst she needed to peruse for the jewelry show coming up. Cullen was going to start to work on the trunk. Clean it up, fix the hinges and lock. The biggest obstacle was getting the smell out of it. For something that had survived a fire, it sure did stink. In the letter, the owner mentioned it being in storage. Maybe it was packed with other fire-related items.

Tori watched the tall, stunning, honey-toned woman exit the showroom through the main door. She thought she saw a shadowy figure move from the showroom into the café. Shortly, the younger twenty-something woman exited the café, and the hippie type returned to the corner table next to the easel. Tori made a mad dash across the atrium, but before she reached the café, another person walked in. She realized she had been stalking the woman for over two hours and hoped no one else had noticed her odd behavior. Tori decided to write a note and leave it on the counter inside the café. One way or another, Tori was going to connect with her.

She searched her tote bag and pulled out the small pad and pen she always carried with her. Many people use their phones to write lists and take notes, but ever since she was in school for her paralegal certification she discovered there was a lot of note-taking on paper. She printed her name and phone number and jotted, *If you have time today, can you please call me? You were highly recommended.* There. That made it sound like she knew what she was doing and that someone had referred her. Technically, someone had recommended her but not directly. That was a good enough argument in the legal sense.

Tori folded the piece of paper, made her way across the atrium, and entered the café. She nodded at the hippie and left the note next to the large coffeemaker. The hippie nodded back and smiled.

Tori felt a huge sigh of relief. She had made contact. Maybe the reading wouldn't be that day, but she had literally got her foot in the door. The tension in her shoulders relaxed. She hadn't realized how taut she was. Now she could browse around for real and look at the art displays and maybe, actually, find something she could turn into a hobby.

She walked over to Hot Sand and watched with fascination as someone blew glass into a colorful sphere. She noticed several of them hanging from the ceiling. The tag said:

WISHING BALL

How appropriate. Maybe she should buy one. She picked one with colors of turquoise and aqua. The price was $65. She stopped and decided it would be too much to spend and her husband would have a conniption fit. Another artist walked over to her, and said, "Hi. We're having a special today. Everything is twenty percent off."

Tori eyed the ball again. "It's beautiful."

"One of my faves, actually," the artist said.

Tori did the math in her head. Just a little over $52. She could fudge that in her weekly household allowance. Then she stopped herself. She didn't have to justify buying something beautiful and original. Sure, there would be a bit of a dust-up over it, but she didn't care. She contributed plenty to their overhead, including doing all the chores. "You've got a deal."

The artist pulled out a step stool and plucked it from the hook. "I just polished it this morning so it's good to go! Make a wish!"

Tori didn't know where to begin but then settled on "guidance." She closed her eyes and repeated it silently to herself. That was a lot easier than she thought.

The artist smiled. "Let me wrap that up for you." She took the glass ball and went into a back room. Tori watched with curiosity as the other artist continued spinning glass into an object of art. A few minutes later, the artist returned with a colorful shopping bag with the piece of blown glass carefully packed in a box surrounded by bright tissue. "I put some filament in an envelope for you for when you hang it."

"Thank you. I think it's the first real piece of original anything I've ever owned." Tori blushed with a slight bit of embarrassment.

"Well then, I am rightly pleased you chose one of my pieces to begin." The artist smiled brightly and handed the rainbow of colors to her. "Thank you very much and I hope to see you again. Good luck and enjoy your day."

Tori felt much lighter even though she knew she wouldn't be very light much longer. There was a spring in her step similar to the one after she told Mr. Layton, George, about her predicament. Maybe her life had turned a page. And if that were the case, Tori decided she was going to be the one writing and reading it.

After Luna's appointment left, she opened the note on the counter. She got a strange feeling from it. Not that strange feelings were uncommon for her, but this was a little different. There was something oddly famil-iar about the vibe she got from the paper. She shrugged and checked her schedule. The afternoon was whizzing by, but she had some time around four thirty. She wondered if the woman could wait until then. She had promised Rita she would talk to her just after five. Luna decided to dial the number.

A nervous voice answered. "Huh . . . hello?" Tori could barely choke out the words.

"Hi. This is Luna. I believe you left a note for me in my café?" Luna was bright and cheerful.

"Yes, this is Tori. Thank you for calling me."

"Nice to meet you, Tori. Are you still in the building?"

"Yes, I am on the second floor doing a little window-shopping." Tori knew that was about as close as she would ever come to owning a vintage Chanel bag. She was stunned at the prices. Even a used quilted bag fetched almost $2,000. She wondered what the original price was. Not that it mattered.

"I have some time between four thirty and five if you'll still be around."

Tori checked the many watches in the window at the Second Time Around shop. It was an hour and a half from now. But she was there, and she wasn't going to miss the opportunity. "I think I can keep myself busy until then," Tori replied.

"Great. See you later."

"Thank you very much." Tori clicked off her phone. She could not believe she was really going through with this. She had walked through the center twice already and wasn't sure what she would do for another ninety minutes. Then she remembered she had a couple of magazines in her car. She went back to the parking lot, retrieved the magazines, and returned to the center. This time she went out the large glass doors that led to a patio. Even the landscaping was a work of art, inside and out. She noticed a small brass plaque that read:

LANDSCAPING BY CALGO GARDENS

That explains it, she thought to herself. They were known throughout the state for their landscape architecture.

She walked through the garden, noticing wind chimes and birdhouses. Several other plaques indicated where they came from. Blowin' in the Wind was obviously the wind chime maker, and Tweety's Townhouse had to be the birdhouse guy. She had breezed past both of them when she was inside. She liked the sound of the chimes. Relaxing and melodious. *Maybe I should have purchased those instead,* she mused. But she was happy with her magic ball. After all, wasn't that the whole reason she was at the center? She needed some kind of magic in her life.

She saw a sign for the dog park and noticed three animals resting quietly under a tree. Two German shepherd adults and one she thought might be a collie. As she passed, the collie-looking dog lifted his head. It was almost as if he was saying hello. *Get a grip, Tori. You may be on a mission, but let's not blast into oblivion with imaginary conversations with dogs.* A man who looked like he was in his mid-to-late twenties gave her a wave. Tori waved back. *Everyone is so friendly,* she thought. Maybe it was the artwork. Creative people being creative. Enjoying what they are doing. She sighed. She still hadn't come up with something for a hobby. Glassblowing was surely out of the picture. Then she remembered passing a small shop with origami figures in the window. She turned and headed back to the interior of the center and walked toward Between the Folds.

When she entered the shop, she was mesmerized by all the different shapes of the origami. Most people are familiar with the crane, but it is an entire art form creating shapes out of one piece of paper. A petite Asian woman greeted Tori at the door. She was wearing a beautifully embroidered black kimono. She bowed slightly and spoke perfect English. "Good afternoon. My name is Suki. Welcome."

"Hello. I'm Tori." She took a breath. "Wow. This is amazing."

"Thank you. Are you familiar with origami?"

"Not really. I know it's a paper-folding art, but I have never seen anything like this."

211

She scanned the room.

"Yes, most people know about the crane, but as you can see, there are an infinite number of possibilities. Would you like me to show you?" The woman gestured toward a long table with various colors and sizes of paper.

Tori had some time to kill, so she thought it would be fun. "Sure! But I have to warn you; I am all thumbs," she said shyly.

"Not to worry. I can teach you to fold a crane in less than fifteen minutes."

"Seriously?" Tori sounded doubtful. "If you say so."

"Wonderful. Please take a seat."

Tori placed her special magic shopping bag and her tote on the seat next to her right. The woman sat on her left.

"What color would you like?" Suki asked.

"Purple?" Tori asked, wondering if the color mattered.

"Purple is a powerful color." Suki nodded and handed Tori a sheet and took one for herself.

The woman explained that most of the figures are from single sheets, but you can join them together. She motioned toward the small garden of paper flowers.

"That is incredible," Tori said in awe.

Step by step, Suki instructed Tori to make

the folds, turning the paper, and more folds. As promised, within fifteen minutes, Tori had a purple crane.

"You see? That wasn't very difficult." Suki smiled.

"Wow. I would never have guessed I could do this." She kept turning the once flat sheet of paper that had turned into a three-dimensional bird.

"I teach workshops once a month. Usually two hours. It is very relaxing." Tori realized that she had been so focused on folding the paper correctly that she had forgotten about pretty much everything for ten minutes. "Amazing." She looked at an origami mobile with baby animals. "How long would it take to make something like that?" She pointed.

"That would take many hours." Suki smiled.

"Like how many?" Tori asked.

"It would depend on how many animals you want," the woman said.

"What about a crane mobile?" Tori decided on something less challenging.

"You just made a crane in fifteen minutes, but I encourage people to take their time. Enjoy the process. That is part of the beauty of origami. It is not a race."

"Duh. You're right." She kept eyeing the

baby animal mobile. She thought she could make it for her baby. She had enough time. "Tell me more about your workshop."

"The first Saturday of the month. We have a 'work with an artist' day for many of the shops. Of course, space is limited. Let me get you a brochure." Suki walked over to the front counter and pulled out a glossy booklet.

"Here. This tells you about the center, the artists, shops, and activities for the month. I have a workshop in two weeks if you are interested."

Tori hesitated. "How much is it?"

"We like to encourage people to get involved. You only pay for supplies. For here, it's about eight dollars."

"Really?" Tori thought for a quick minute. "Can I sign up?" She realized this was something she could pull off without a lot of pushback from her husband. She was going to be playing with paper. He could go play with his friends, which is what he usually did anyway.

"Oh yes. You are the first one for that weekend. I only take three people at a time in case each wants to make something different." Suki handed Tori a clipboard with a sign-up sheet.

"Great." Tori filled out her name, address,

phone number, and e-mail. On the line that said "Experience," she wrote *1 crane.* Suki laughed as Tori handed back the clipboard.

"In the meantime, go to the website and take a look. This isn't all of it."

Tori blinked in wonder. "I hope I can make up my mind by the time I get back."

Suki walked Tori to the door and handed her the purple crane. "For good luck."

"Thank you." Tori's eyes welled up. That was the second time that day someone had wished her good luck. Coming to the center was the best thing she could have done for herself, even if she hadn't met yet with the woman whose name was Luna.

Tori placed the purple crane on top of the box in her shopping bag. It was getting close to her appointment time. She wandered toward the ladies' room to freshen up. She checked her profile in the mirror. Nothing yet. Not that she expected any change from that morning, but now she felt she was gaining momentum for the momentous task of moving forward with her life.

Tori entered the café at 4:30 sharp. "Hi. I'm Tori."

"Yes, hello, Tori." Luna held out her hand. "Nice to meet you."

"Thank you for taking the time to see me. I know you have a busy schedule."

"Well, let's see what we can do in the short amount of time we have. We can always reschedule, and I'll work out the fee depending on how much time we have. Is that all right with you?"

Fee. Tori hadn't thought about how much it would cost. *How stupid of me.*

"Shhh ssshure." Tori's word stumbled out of her mouth.

"I forgot to ask, do you take debit cards?"

"Sure. Cash. Check. Sometimes I even barter with the other artists." Luna tried to make Tori feel comfortable. She could sense the woman was tense. Her energy was all over the place.

Tori thought about the small origami crane. She jokingly pulled it out of her bag. "Will this do?" She laughed nervously. "Just kidding."

"My fee is one hundred dollars for an hour's reading. But right now we have about twenty-five minutes. I really don't like to rush these things so how about this. You and I chat for a bit, then we'll make an appointment for a full hour, and I won't charge you for today. Would that work for you?"

Tori thought it was more than fair. After all, she was the one who barged in. "That is very kind of you."

Luna gestured toward the easel and table.

"Take a seat. Would you like coffee? Tea? A scone?"

"Oh, I don't want to impose," Tori replied.

"It's a café, darlin'." Luna chuckled.

Tori giggled nervously. "Decaf?"

"Coming right up." Luna went to the large coffee machine and popped in a decaffeinated capsule. "Cream? Milk? Skim? Almond? Oat?"

Tori remembered the variety at the super supermarket.

"Cream is fine." Tori stifled a giggle.

"I'm with you." Luna made a cup for each of them. "I really don't get the other stuff. But I guess it's an industry now." Luna brought the coffee cups over to the table.

"I was wondering, how does one milk an almond?" Tori had to share that with someone, and she felt that Luna might appreciate the humor.

"That is a very good question. I've often asked myself the same thing. Or an oat. Or a cashew. They're so small." Luna pinched her thumb and forefinger together.

Tori felt very comfortable in this kooky woman's company.

Luna took a sip and nodded toward the easel. "Do you mind? I like to draw when I'm doing a reading although this is really just a preliminary getting to know you.

Now, I don't want you to think I am going to go online and do a background check. I simply want to get a sense of you. No pun intended."

"The thought never occurred to me. I mean your checking me out. I know they've said that about a lot of famous psychics, but I know there is something to it."

"Exactomundo," Luna replied. "So, tell me, Tori. What brings you here? I should probably know that, right?" Luna chuckled. "Let me know if there is anything you don't want me to tell you. I can get very personal."

Tori thought for a moment. *Isn't that why I'm here? Guidance? Information?*

"Fire away!" Tori said with confidence.

"First, I need something of yours. A piece of jewelry. Don't worry, I am not going to keep it. I just want to hold it for a few minutes. And it won't leave your sight."

Tori had a cheap pair of earrings that she had bought days before. The only other thing she was wearing was her wedding band. If Luna was as good as those women said she was, Luna was going to get some serious vibrations.

Luna placed the band in her palm and closed her eyes. She held it for several minutes. Luna hesitated a moment before she spoke. Did she want to open the conversation with pregnancy? Might as well get the hard part over first. "Did you recently discover you were going to have another child?"

Tori almost fell over. She, her doctor, the nurse, and her boss were the only other people on the planet who knew.

"Another child?" Tori responded.

"Yes. I feel two energies around you. I also see a young man wearing a uniform."

"That's my son. He's in the army. Tech stuff." Tori was shaking. "Is he going to be all right?"

"Yes. He is going to do very well." Luna hesitated again. She handed Tori the ring, stood, and went behind the easel. "This second child was not planned, correct?"

"Yes. That is correct."

Luna kept looking at Tori while her hand scribbled on the tablet. "You and your husband aren't quite aligned. It's as if you've grown apart."

"Correct again."

"I'll be honest. It doesn't take a psychic to figure that out. Most people come to me because of relationship issues. People even grow apart from friends. From goals. From ideas. We are in perpetual motion, but some people are stuck in a hamster wheel."

Tori giggled nervously. "Here's the thing.

I am not happy. Sometimes I think I'm clinically depressed, but when I get to my workplace, I feel fine. But there is a high ratio of unhappiness and being home. I haven't told my husband about the baby yet because the idea of raising another child with him is crushing." She twisted her napkin on her lap, a habit she noticed she had been cultivating when she was nervous. "It's as if we live separate lives, but I'm responsible for everything that has to do with running the household. Being with him and another child would be like raising two kids at the same time. Believe me. I did it for eighteen years."

"Is he in the service as well? I see a uniform with a badge."

"He's a cop."

"Huh. I see a very long, narrow road. Have you been with him for a really long time?"

"Yes. Right after high school. I mean right after as in the day after graduation. We ran off together."

Luna nodded when her cell phone buzzed. It was Cullen.

"I'm sorry. I have to take it. It's my brother."

Tori nodded.

"What's up, Cul? Now? But. OK. OK. I'll

220

be right there." She looked at Tori and frowned. "I'm sorry. My brother is expecting a delivery and he's tied up with a client. I have to sign for it. You have my number. Call me, and we'll set up a real meeting. Is that OK with you?"

Tori was more than willing to come back. "Yes. Yes, that's fine."

"You have my number in your caller ID, but just in case, here's my card." Luna handed her a card that simply said:

NAMASTE CAFÉ—GOOD VIBES ONLY
— LUNA BODHI —
828-555-1920

"Thank you for your time today." Tori smiled. "I plan on coming back in two weeks for the origami workshop."

Luna thought for a moment. "Dang. I will be away that weekend." She had a fleeting thought about meeting Tori before she left for Charlotte, but that would be too much pressure. She wanted the day to be all about Marshal Gaines. "We'll figure it out. Just give me a call when you can, and we'll set something up." Luna was getting antsy. She didn't want Cullen calling her again and telling her to move her butt. "I really have to run."

"Sure. Sorry." Tori gathered her things and moved toward the door.

Luna scurried to the back of Cullen's workshop, where a truck was delivering an old sideboard. It looked mid-century and was covered in layers of paint. *I guess back then people couldn't afford to keep replacing furniture so they painted it. Now you can buy the cheapest stuff and replace it in a few years.* She didn't know which was worse: scarring a great piece of furniture with spray paint, or just tossing something out. We had become a disposable society. On so many levels. She was glad Cullen was in the restoration business. Everything he touched had once been a quality piece of something and he returned it to its pristine beginnings. Well, maybe not entirely. Some things were beyond repair, but for the most part, Cullen was a wizard when it came to dilapidated furniture.

Luna instructed the driver where to deposit the sideboard, signed the electronic box with her finger, and handed him twenty dollars with her other hand. "Thanks, ma'am."

"You're welcome, but please don't call me ma'am." Luna gave him a sideways look.

"Oh, no disrespect, *miss.*" The driver winked, nodded, and tucked the bill into his vest pocket.

"Southern men." She shook her head and smiled.

Luna briskly walked through the showroom, where Cullen was going over sketches with a client. Luna gave him the thumbs-up and went back to the café, where Rita was waiting for her.

"Hey there. Sorry I'm a few minutes late. I had to help Cullen with a delivery."

"No problem," Rita said in earnest.

"So what's up? By the way, my brother loves that smoked turkey thing that requires a bib!" She laughed. "Where did you learn those combinations? You make great sandwiches!"

"I used to be a waitress at a diner and got sick of the food, so I started experimenting. One day my boss got a little miffed because I brought my own lunch. I cut him a piece and he went bananas. It has now become my roast beef and brie. He put it on his menu and asked me to keep coming up with new ideas. Then people started asking me if I did parties. I said yes even though I had no experience!" She chuckled. "And now here I am!"

"I wondered how you got started. I would never have thought of mixing some of those ingredients together. Kudos to you!"

"It makes dinner easy. I bring home the leftovers!" Rita laughed.

"But you seem to be selling out almost every day," Luna noted.

"I always keep a stash of extras," Rita whispered.

"Oh. Good to know." Luna smiled. "And your secret is safe with me."

"So what brings you to our corner of the world?"

"Can I ask you something?" Rita spoke with a bit of hesitation.

"That's what I thought we were doing." Luna laughed. "Let's take a seat and you can tell me what's on your mind."

Rita took a long, deep breath. "I had a friend a long time ago who ran off with her boyfriend, and I never heard from her again. It's bugged me to this day. I still keep a photo of us on a shelf at home."

"I'm not necessarily good at missing persons, but I know someone who is."

"Uh, no. It's not like that. I mean it's not a *real* missing persons thing. I kept hoping I'd hear from her, but I never did. It makes me sad when I think about it. I can't believe she would do that. Go off without a word. We were BFFs except for the 'forever' part. We practically grew up together."

Luna thought about it for a moment.

"Sure. I'll do a reading, but I don't know if it'll be much help."

"I'd appreciate it. If I only knew what happened to her. She had kind of a crummy family life, so my mom and grandma would do something special for her on her birthday. I wonder how she might be spending her birthdays now. If she's still with us, if you know what I mean."

"How long has it been?" Luna asked.

"I think twenty years."

It was Luna's turn to take in a long breath. "Wow. That *is* a long time, but then again, time seems to fly, too. You don't really think about it until you think about the number. I recently asked a friend how old her grandson was. I thought maybe he was three. Turns out he's seven! I almost fainted. Anyway, so tell me more."

"She's been on my mind a lot lately. I can't quite put my finger on it."

"You're preaching to the choir. I totally get it. I'm grateful I have people around me who know about my woo-woo side and don't judge." Luna shrugged and chuckled. "Or maybe they do behind my back."

"I doubt it. You are very well liked," Rita stated.

"So, your friend just up and left? No note?"

"She ran off with her boyfriend. There was an accident, and they skipped town."

"What about her parents? Didn't they go looking for her?"

"Like I said, she had a crummy upbringing. Her parents were away when she skipped town, but she left a note saying not to look for her. I went to the house every day for weeks, hoping she would show up, but her mother said I was being a nuisance and to leave her alone. So I did. I went to college, then I got married, had kids, yada, yada, yada."

Luna stepped up to the easel and was taken aback when she saw the drawing. In her haste to help Cullen with the delivery, she hadn't had time to look at the sketch she drew when she was talking to the woman named Tori. Luna rarely watched what she was scribbling. To her, it was like automatic handwriting. She tore the sheet off the pad and rolled it up. She couldn't wait to show it to Cullen and Chi-Chi. But that would have to wait. She had promised Rita she'd read her.

Luna refocused on the person at hand. "Before your friend left, did she give you any indication she was going away? I know I sound like a detective, but any clues could help me get a sense of something. Anything.

Like I said, I am not in the missing persons business, but sometimes it's helpful to talk things through regardless of whether or not they are psychic impressions or just facts."

"We grew up in the same town, went to the same school, belonged to the same Brownie troop. I remember a big fight she had with her mother about the fee. I think it was like ten dollars at the time. My mom felt sorry for her, so she paid for it."

"Sounds like your mother was a second mother to your friend."

"More like a first mother, but my friend became more of a mother to her little brother. Her father would leave money for groceries and she would go to the store with us and shop."

"Sounds like a troubling situation," Luna said sympathetically.

"When we got into high school, she started dating a guy. I guess it was dating at the time, you know, making out behind the bleachers at school, maybe a movie. School dances. That kind of stuff."

"Was she in love with him, or should I say did she think she was in love with him?"

"I never got the impression she was truly, madly, deeply in love. We only think we are at that age."

Luna chuckled. "And sometimes it carries

over through adulthood."

"Yes, I suppose it can. I'm lucky. My husband and I met in college. We were in a study group together my junior year. Then, after several months, we started going out without a crowd of people around us. By the time we graduated, we knew we were right for each other."

"When did you learn to make those sandwiches?" Luna's mind went for the food.

"I worked part-time during college and the first few summers when I was teaching. Then I got pregnant. After the kids were born, I wanted to spend more time with them and started building my catering business. It was something I could do from home, and events were usually on the weekends, when my husband was home."

"And now you are the queen of gourmet delights!"

"Hardly." Rita laughed. "But I really enjoy it, especially when I know someone is enjoying what I make."

"Do the kids help you?"

"Melissa seems to have an interest, but Brian grew up watching Food Network and he only cares about eating, not cooking or preparing."

Turning the focus back to Rita's friend, Luna continued, "Did your friend have any interests? Anything she ever talked about wanting to do with her life?"

"Not really. The older we got, the more responsibility she took on at home. Her boyfriend, well, I wouldn't call him a loser, but he was aimless, too. I think because they both had depressing upbringings all they thought about was getting as far away from home as possible."

Luna sighed. "And now kids are living with their parents until they're in their late twenties, if they ever leave at all."

"Funny how the world has changed so much in twenty years."

"Technology thrusts us forward before we have a chance to get our balance. I just saw a woman a little while ago and said we are in perpetual motion." Luna sighed. "People need downtime. Even if it's just for a few minutes a day. Clear your head. Hit the reset button."

"I agree, but I'm also guilty of never stopping to catch my breath."

Luna smiled. "One of the basic precepts of Zen is breath. Through deep breathing, one can clear the mind of anxiety, stress, anger." Luna looked at Rita, hoping she didn't lose her with the Zen thing.

"I totally understand the idea. It's putting

it into practice that seems to be the challenge."

"Ah. There's a word: challenge. Challenge is only our perception of the level of difficulty."

Rita gave Luna a quizzical look.

"It's a matter of perspective. If you believe something is out of reach, then it will be. Take tennis, for example. You look at Serena Williams and say, 'I could never do that.' But at some point in her life, she told herself she could. I'm not saying that wishing makes it so, but if you put limiting ideas in your head, you will be limited. If you think positively, anything can happen." Luna patted Rita's hand. "Take five minutes. Set your watch, clock, phone. Pick a time of day. Even if it's the first thing you do when you get in your car at the end of the day. Before you turn on the ignition, sit back, close your eyes, and breathe in deeply. Exhale slowly. Do it ten times. Then start your car. It's amazing what you can shed from the day's work and stress just by tuning out for a couple of minutes." Luna was about to write down a few words on the sketch pad. That was when she realized she hadn't drawn anything when she was talking to Rita. She was drawing a blank. Maybe she was psychically fatigued. It was possible.

It takes a lot of one's personal energy to decipher someone else's. She blinked a few times and began to write: *Prosperity comes to me easily and effortlessly: physically, mentally, spiritually, emotionally, financially, and in all my relationships.*

She tore off the page and handed it to Rita. "Read this as soon as you get out of bed, when you leave work, and before you go to sleep. It will help you focus and put positive affirmations in your conscious mind and your subconscious."

"This is great. It will be enormously helpful. You are right. I need to do this. Thanks for the quick lesson."

"It's also called self-care. Too often people confuse self-care with selfish. 'Put your oxygen mask on first.' " Luna parroted a flight attendant's instructions.

They both laughed. "I wish I could tell you more about your friend. You said you have a photo?"

"Yes."

"OK. Next time we get together, bring it along. Maybe I can pick up some vibes from it. But meantime, the idea that she has been on your mind may mean she's thinking about you, too. Send out good thoughts. You never know where they will land."

Rita grabbed Luna's hand. "Thank you. I

231

feel much better now. What do I owe you?"

"What do you mean?" Luna furrowed her brow.

"For the reading."

"I didn't do anything." Luna made a frowny face.

"Not true. You reminded me that I need to give myself more oxygen." Rita smiled. "I've gotta run. My daughter has a cooking class and is insisting I be her guinea pig."

"I'm sure it will be delicious. It's in her DNA."

Luna walked Rita to the door.

"Thanks again, Luna. I owe you a caprese!"

"You've got a deal!" Luna waved, then dashed to where she had placed her earlier drawing and bolted into Cullen's showroom.

"Do you remember where I put that drawing I did about the trunk?" She was almost out of breath.

"It's on the worktable." Cullen's eyes followed his sister as she bounded toward the workshop in the back. Then he heard her squeal. He ran in to see if she was OK.

"What's wrong?" He looked concerned.

"Check this out." She flattened the two drawings on the table side by side. They stood in silence, comparing them.

"So, wait." Cullen raised an eyebrow. "The one on the right is the first one you drew. Where did the second one come from?"

"Today. A woman who I had never met came to me. She's having marital problems."

Cullen stared at the two charcoal drawings. "The one on the right is flames with a little boy. The one on the left is flames with two people slightly taller than the little boy who is also in the same drawing. That's strange, even for you."

"Right? They must be connected somehow." Luna's mind was spinning.

"Not necessarily. You had the diary with you. Maybe some of the energy jumped the psychic fence?" Cullen wasn't being facetious. Just his own way of dealing with the curiosity.

"I dunno, Cul. I have an odd feeling about this."

"Odd? You?" Cullen chuckled.

She gave him a slight smack on the arm with the back of her hand. "Hey, be nice. Odd as in some kind of complexity."

"Didn't you say it was marital stuff?"

"Yes. That was her reason for coming here, but I think there's more to it." Luna squinted her eyes as if it would help her think harder.

"Do you think she was the one who sent the trunk?" Cullen was intrigued.

"No. Not her. But there is a connection somehow."

"Well, I don't know when you've been wrong about something intuitive."

"That's the whole point of intuition, dummy." Luna shook her head and smirked. "But somehow there is a connection here."

"Oh boy." Cullen looked up at the ceiling. "What was her demeanor?"

"It was obvious she was nervous. She kept twisting her napkin in her lap. There was a sadness about her."

"Aren't most of your clients sad about something?" Cullen was being serious.

"True, but . . ." Luna got a wild look in her eyes. "The coffee cup."

"What coffee cup?" Cullen was now talking to the back of her head.

"Be right back." Luna ran to the sink where she left the coffee cups. She was relieved that for once she hadn't compulsively washed each of them out. It had been a little hectic between Tori, the delivery, and Rita. She pulled the cup with the pink lipstick. Now, who could she get to run a DNA sample? She sent Cullen a text to come to the café and bring the drawings.

"What the heck is going on?"

"Here is the cup from Tori."

"So?" Cullen was very confused at this point.

"So, what if we can match the DNA on the cup with fingerprints from the things that were in the box?"

"I'm not sure that's how it works." Cullen looked doubtful.

"Well, maybe the fine marshal can suggest something. He said he would help. Well, kinda. Sorta. But it wouldn't hurt to ask him." Her eyes lit up as she dug into her apron pocket. "And I have this."

"What is it?

"A note she wrote."

"So what of it?"

"More tools for my research." Luna winked.

The weeks that followed, Luna was busy cramming clients into her schedule and making sure she ordered enough supplies. Sabrina was thrilled to cover for her at the café. Luna gave her specific instructions in case anyone asked for a reading. Take their first name and phone number and give them one of her cards.

She finally had an afternoon when she was able to sit down and go through the diary. The handwriting looked familiar. On one of her hunches, she pulled out the note the woman had left for her. Luna's eyes almost popped out of her head. She would swear the handwriting was similar. She would have to show this to Gaines and get his take on it.

Luna went into Cullen's workshop and asked for the box that was also wrapped in the blanket. She brought it back to her café and carefully took out the contents and spread them on the table. There were several movie stubs, but none had any specific information as to what theater they were from, but when she turned over one of the stubs, the word *Others* was scrawled on the back. It didn't look like the same handwriting from the diary. *Huh. Another piece of the puzzle,* she thought.

There was something that resembled a dried daisy and a few coins that appeared to be used for game machines. Or rides, perhaps. There were two flyers from traveling carnivals. Both said Brinkley Entertainment, but neither had a year. Only the month. One was from July, the other August. She jotted down the name of the company. Maybe they could give her some information as to when the flyers were made. If she got lucky, maybe they could give her their usual locations for those two months. *But for how many years?*

She went over to the corner workstation, where she kept her laptop and printer. She carefully uploaded the images of the flyers and ticket stubs to her laptop and printed out copies.

When she finished, she looked up Brinkley Entertainment on the Internet. Up came a website with a phone number. She grabbed her cell phone and dialed.

A pleasant Southern drawl answered. "Brinkley Entertainment. Y'all bring the people, and we'll bring the fun. How can I help ya today?"

"Hello, my name is Luna Bodman. I'm doing some research on carnivals and I came across two flyers with your name on them."

"Are y'all looking to book something?" the gentleman asked.

"Well, no. As I said, I'm doing some research. The history of carnivals in the South." Luna was surprised that she was able to conjure that lie so quickly. It just spilled out of her mouth. Although that wasn't anything new, really.

"Do tell," the man insisted.

"Do you have a few minutes?" Luna asked politely.

"I do. What can I do fer ya?"

"First, if I send you a photo of the flyer, do you think you'd recognize what year it's from?"

"Can't say until I see it."

"Good point. Can I e-mail you a copy?"

"Sure thing." The man gave her the e-mail address associated with the company.

"I'm going to send it over now. Meanwhile, if you don't mind answering a few questions?"

"Go 'head."

"How long have you been doing this?"

"Goin' on forty years now."

"Do you travel all over the South?"

"Mostly the Carolinas and Georgia now. But we keep busy."

"How many people attend the carnivals?"

"That depends. Anywheres from a couple hun'red to over a thousand. Sometimes we're the only family entertainment available to a lot of folks. Getting yer family to Disney World ain't no free walk in the park, if you get my drift."

Luna chuckled, thinking about the rambunctious kids who descended upon the center. "Yes, family vacations can be very expensive."

"You ain't kiddin'."

Luna was getting the impression the man had much more free time on his hands than a few minutes.

"While we're on the phone, can you check to see if my e-mail came through?" Luna did not want to drag out the conversation any longer than necessary. She feared he was going to tell her much more than she was interested in.

"Sure can. Hang on."

Luna could hear footsteps in the background. Some clicks that sounded like someone was typing on a keyboard. Then footsteps getting closer to the phone.

"Yep. One says 'Special Appearance by Wild Bill Harper.' That had to be 2000, 2001, 2002, I reckon. He's no longer with us. Thems were the two years he traveled with our troupe."

Luna could barely contain her excitement. She had it narrowed down to two years.

"And do you recall where you had the carnivals?"

"Lots a places them years," the man answered.

"Can you narrow it down a bit?" Luna crossed her fingers, hoping she'd get something geographical from him.

"Like I said earlier, mostly the Carolinas and Georgia. Usually started in Georgia and worked our ways back north. So, if I was goin' to make a guess, I'd say Georgia was

June, South Carolina would be July, and North Carolina would be August."

"Do you have any records on file that could confirm those?" Luna tried not to sound too pushy, but she felt she was getting close to narrowing it down.

"Used to, but all the paperwork got flooded after Hurricane Matthew back in 2016."

"I'm so sorry to hear that."

"Yep. It was a big mess for sure."

Luna refused to be disheartened. "I imagine someone like you would have a memory like an elephant?" She giggled to try to spark his recollection.

"I have to tell ya, at my age, I'm lucky if I remember to put on my underwear."

That was a vision Luna didn't want to imagine.

She chuckled again. "Well, if you think about anything that might be interesting for my article, please let me know. My contact information is on the e-mail I sent. I really appreciate your time, Mr.?" She realized she had never gotten his name.

"They call me 'Chief.' Don't know exactly how that came about, but I've been Chief for a coupla decades now."

"Well, thank you, Chief, for all your help." Luna was genuinely grateful.

"You are most welcome, missy. Y'all have yourself a good day, and send me a copy of that article, will ya?"

Luna had a pang of guilt knowing there wasn't going to be an article. She thanked him profusely and promised to keep in touch. She couldn't remember the last time she felt so guilty. But she had accomplished something. Some things. Now she had to try to put the pieces together.

While she was musing over the carnival information, Ellie stopped in.

"Namaste, Luna!" She gave a short bow.

"Namaste," Luna responded in kind. "Can I fix you a coffee?"

"No, thanks. Just wanted to say hi and ask you to thank Chris for his idea about the security guard."

"Cool. Nathan seems like a really nice guy. Authoritative." Luna winked.

"Yes, the evil plan is working. The Mommy Club Winos were flying solo without their children this week. All it took was one afternoon with Nathan staring them down, and they were too scared to come back. As long as the mommies keep spending their money and there is peace in the center, all is good."

"I wonder what they did with the kids?"

"I honestly don't care, and I certainly

didn't ask. Heaven forbid they think that I miss the little monsters." Ellie chortled. She looked over at the table where Luna was working. "What do you have there?"

"This was the stuff that was in the box from the trunk. And guess what?" Luna was overjoyed to share her news. "I tracked down the carnival company and they were able to narrow down the time from 2000 to 2002."

Ellie moved to where Luna was standing. "Let me see. I vaguely remember now. Wild Bill Harper rings a bell. He brought a bit of rodeo with him. Richard and I went one year."

Luna's eyes lit up. "So that almost confirms that the diary was written around that time. And check this out." Luna showed her the note and the first page of the diary. "Do any of the letters resemble each other?"

Ellie squinted and pulled up the reading glasses she wore on a handmade crystal chain. She had a set for almost every outfit. "It's hard to tell. The diary is in long-hand, but the note is printed." Ellie knew Luna was hoping for some kind of confirmation. "Where did the note come from?"

Luna recounted the brief meeting she had with a woman named Tori.

"How about this?" Luna unrolled the two

drawings. "This one is from my first impression of the trunk." She pointed to the other one. "This is from when I was speaking with her."

Ellie gasped. "That's a little eerie, don't you think?"

"Creepy, too." Luna stared down at her primitive artwork. "You know what else is odd? There is very little in this diary. Even the author admits there isn't much in there except for the last entry. She sure sounded desperate. And young."

"Let me look at that note again." Ellie peered at the note, then at the diary entry. She frowned.

"What?" Luna asked.

"The diary is signed with a *V.* The note is from a woman named Tori."

"Dang." Luna twisted her mouth to the side. "I still think there is a connection here." Luna chewed on her lip. "I'm going to bring these with me when I see Christopher. Maybe he can recommend a handwriting expert."

"That's not a bad idea. If you really want to go through all that trouble," Ellie said.

Luna gave Ellie a look. "This is me, remember?"

"Right. Dog with a sock in his mouth refusing to let go." Ellie chuckled.

"Bowwow," Luna replied. Both women laughed.

"Are you getting excited about the weekend?" Ellie knew that was a rhetorical question, but she wanted to engage Luna in more conversation.

"I'm a wreck," Luna admitted. "On the one hand, I'm really looking forward to spending some alone time with Chris, but I don't know how much he is looking forward to it."

"Oh please, don't start that again," Ellie huffed. "Truth be told, if it were up to me I would lock both of you in a room and not let you out until you had at least a heavy make-out session."

"Ellie Stillwell! How crass." Luna laughed out loud, knowing Ellie would take it as a joke.

"My dear. Life is short. And swift. Before you know it, another twenty years have dissolved into the mist."

"Yeah. I get it. I've had that conversation more than once. I'm such a hypocrite." Luna shook her head.

"No, not really. You understand the concept of enjoying life while you can, but too often we get caught up in the daily grind."

"My gosh, you are starting to sound like me!" Luna smiled.

"We're a good influence on each other, and if I can influence you into getting up close and personal with Chris, I will." Ellie folded her arms.

"You are such a good friend." Luna gave her a warm smile. "I appreciate your confidence in me. I wish I had more."

"You know he is very fond of you, and you are of him. Don't put any pressure on yourself. Just be the kooky, loving, warm, caring Luna that we all love."

"Aw." Luna's eyes got a little misty. "I promise I will not pull the emergency brake if he makes a move. How's that?"

"And what about you? A little physical contact couldn't hurt."

"Like what?"

"Touch his arm, put your hand on his back. Oh jeez, Luna, do what you always do when you're around him. If I didn't know better, I would think you two were having a thing."

"It's a thing all right." Luna snorted. "Just what *kind* of thing is the question."

Ellie rolled her eyes. "Whatever 'thing' you want it to be."

"OK. Enough high-school chatter. Let me ask you something."

"Of course."

"Do you recall any fires during those two years?"

"In the summer, there are always fires. Irresponsible campers, or some idiot tossing a lit cigarette out a car window."

"Maybe I'll go to the library and check out the local newspaper editions from those summers."

"That's an excellent idea. If you want I'll go with you," Ellie offered.

"Really? That would be great."

"If I remember correctly, this was going to be a group project."

"You are correct." Luna smiled. "When I get back from my adventure."

"You have a deal, my friend." Ellie gave Luna a hug. "I've got to run. Nathan and I are grabbing a bite to eat."

Luna perked up. "Oh? You and Nathan?" she said accusingly.

"It's not what you think," Ellie protested.

"Ha! We shall revisit this conversation at a later date." Luna gave her a knowing look.

Just as Ellie was about to leave, she said, "By the way, brilliant move on the Cullen and Chi-Chi front."

Luna looked a bit confused.

"I know you had your hand in that rendezvous. Ciao!" Ellie smiled and left the café.

CHAPTER TWELVE

After Tori's trip to Stillwell

When Tori returned home from her first junket to the art center her husband was at work. She carefully unwrapped the beautiful hand-blown magic ball. She looked around but couldn't decide where to hang it. It really didn't go with any of her boring, Early American décor. She had to think about the last time they bought any new furniture. It had been years. Some of the furniture had come with the house and it still remained, probably because they could never agree on what style to purchase. He didn't seem to care unless it was her idea. Then he would decide he didn't like it. When she asked him what he wanted, he'd shrug. "Anything but that," referring to her idea. She managed to get slipcovers for the sofa without any negative repercussions. Come to think of it, he never even mentioned it. She thought about buying new living-room furniture without him, then dealing with his objections, but it wasn't worth it. He would just sulk for days, and things were tight enough. After thinking about their inability to agree on most things domestic, that's when she decided to wrap the ball in its original tissue and place it back in the pretty shopping bag. She was going to stash it in her closet until, well, until she decided where it should go. For the moment, it was going to be her little secret.

She set the origami crane on the buffet chest in the dining room. She wondered if he would even notice it.

Tori went into the kitchen to fix herself some dinner only to find dirty dishes in the sink and the casserole dish from the stew sitting on the counter. She tossed the remains onto another plate and planned to pop it in the microwave after she began the ritual of cleaning up after him. She knew he wasn't a bad guy. Just selfish and lazy. *Must be a genetic defect with the Y chromosome.* She chuckled. That seemed to be the main complaint she heard from other women as well.

She was surprised to see he had left a note, smudged of course, but it said *Thanks!* She couldn't remember the last time he wrote down anything for her.

Before she pressed the start button on the food-zapping machine, she decided to change her clothes. When she went into the bedroom, she found a second note:

I'll be staying at Jack's tonight after my shift so we can get an early start tomorrow.

That was it. No, "love ya, love, see ya." Typical. At least she knew she would get a good night's sleep. If she *could* sleep. The half-hour drive home did not allow for any decompression from the day. And it had been quite a full day. Between the sensory overload of all the artwork and crafts, and her meeting with that Luna person, there was a lot of stuff in her head that needed sorting. One thing was for certain — she would be going back for an origami workshop, and again to see Luna. She was elated that she had made a number of decisions on her own. It was refreshing and invigorating.

Tori slipped into a pair of jogging pants and a sweatshirt and returned to the kitchen to heat up her dinner. She sat in silence, reliving the day. She stopped in the office. Drove to the center. Watched anxiously to see if she could get into the psychic's café. Bought a magic ball and made origami. Saw the psychic for a few minutes. But those few minutes were very revealing. There was no way that woman could know anything about Tori or her situation. She was convinced it was through divine intervention that she had heard about that woman Luna, and because of her journey, she discovered more things about herself. For one, she could make a decision, even if it was a small one. Secondly, she could take control over her life, as much as anyone could take control. Then she thought about the odd shop with the metal sculptures. *How odd,* she thought. *The honor system.* But then again, the entire place had a vibe about it. Mysterious, yet obvious. Exhilarating, yet relaxing. It was hard to describe.

She fixed a cup of tea and ran a bath. *Full circle,* she thought. Once again, she poured Epsom salts under the running water and let the level rise until it almost overflowed. She dimmed the lights, lit a few candles, and lowered herself into the tub. She put her hand on her belly. She wasn't showing yet, but she could feel something.

Tori lingered in the bath until the water became tepid. Time to step out and wrap up in a towel and robe. She padded her way into the bedroom and flopped on the bed. Tonight she would be sleeping alone. She figured it might be good practice. Even though her mind had been racing, she finally fell into a deep sleep.

When she woke the next morning, she realized that she and her husband hadn't spoken to each other the entire day. She had left for the center, he to work, stayed at a friend's, but not one phone call. That was out of the ordinary. He usually wanted to know every move she made. Maybe the artsy thing had turned him off. She could add that to her list of things her husband didn't like about her.

Tori fixed her usual breakfast of toast and decaffeinated coffee and got ready for work. It dawned on her that she was unusually relaxed. *Maybe the bath,* she thought again. *They should put it in pill form.* Then she realized there were a lot of pills that could make you relax but she had never tried any of them. Maybe she should have before she got pregnant. Maybe it would have made her less numb to the loneliness.

Tori put herself together but with a little more effort that morning. A little more eye shadow and blush and a good blowout with her hair. She looked in the mirror and gave herself a thumbs-up.

Satisfied that the house was in good order, she made her way out the door, into her car and off to work, stopping at the coffee shop on the way. She figured Mr. Layton, George, might need a little pick-me-up donut after a frustrating day of golf. She could not remember a time when he had been happy about how he played. But from what she understood about the game, it was frustrating to a lot of people. She wouldn't know. She had never played.

Tori pulled into the parking lot and entered the shop. She realized it was Thursday and looked around for the woman who wanted her to go to Ringo's but didn't spot her. She had hoped to get more information from her. She shrugged and ordered the usual, paid the check, and headed to the office.

When she reached her desk, she pulled out the pad and paper of the notes she had made about divorce in North Carolina. Did she really want to go through with it? Should she try to have a conversation with her husband and air her issues? That would seem like the reasonable, adult thing to do, but she wasn't sure if he had ever reached adulthood in his emotional intelligence level. They had loved each other once. Or it had felt like love at the time. Then again, she had only been eighteen, with no idea what life was about and what was expected of a spouse, a job, a friend. Responsibility.

To each other first. The rest of the world came second. She thought about that for a good long time until George Layton stood in his doorway and asked her to come in.

"Have a seat."

"Am I in trouble?" Tori felt more nervous than usual.

"Not at all." He gave her a warm smile. "I see where you were going through some of the law books about divorce."

Tori was surprised that he knew she had been researching the subject.

"You left one of the books upside down," he said kindly.

"Oh, dear." Tori was embarrassed. "I hope you don't mind that I went into your office when you weren't here."

"That's not a problem, Tori. But if you have questions, you can always come to me with them."

"Thank you. I very much appreciate that. It's just that I didn't want to bother you with it. You have been so kind to me." Tears welled up in her eyes.

"Have you discussed any of your issues with your husband?" he asked.

"No. Not really. Actually, not ever." Tori dabbed her eye with the back of her hand.

"Don't you think that would be a better place to start?"

"I . . . I guess so, but he can be so stubborn I was worried it would blow up into a horrible fight."

"Has he ever been violent?"

"No. Not to me."

"So what is stopping you from trying to have a conversation with him?"

"I guess it's because he can be intimidating. He's forceful in his opinions."

"So you'd rather avoid any confrontations with him, is that correct?" Layton was starting to sound like a lawyer.

"I suppose." The tears were now streaming down her face. "I don't know why. Maybe it's because when I was growing up, there were always fights between my parents, and I never knew if they would blow up at me. Well, at least my dad was reasonable when he was around, but that was usually never."

George put his hands behind his head and leaned back in his chair. "May I offer you a bit of advice?"

Tori sniffled. "Yes, of course."

"Try having a talk with him before you pull the plug. He can't magically know what you're thinking. He deserves that much, at least." He sat upright to stress his point. "Unless you tell him what's on your mind, he will never know." He snickered a bit.

"Men don't have the same kind of instincts women have. We're a bit dense."

Tori smiled. "You are right about that, Mr. Layton. No offense. I mean George."

"I would suggest you do it in a neutral place. Not at home. It's too easy to go into another room and slam the door behind you. But someplace public, maybe a park?"

Tori had a blank look on her face. "But isn't it too public to have a private conversation?"

"I'm sure you could find a quiet bench somewhere. We have plenty of parks around here. Plus, if for any reason you felt you were in danger, you would be in earshot of a passerby."

Tori looked horrified. "I cannot imagine him getting violent, but you have a point. It would kind of force us to have a reasonable conversation if he knew people were in the background. Plus, he's a cop, and a lot of people know him. He wouldn't want to show a bad side of himself in public."

"See? You are getting my drift. Pack a lunch. People usually function better if they're not hungry."

"So I should invite him on a picnic?" She looked at him curiously.

"If that's the excuse you have to use. The other option is to go to a counselor and have a mediator."

"Oh, I don't think he'd ever go for that. He wouldn't want a stranger learning anything about him. Plus, that would be an admission that things aren't great in paradise."

"Well then, try to get him to spend a little time. Tell him you need to talk to him about something important."

"He'll just say 'go ahead.'"

"That's when you need to be firm. Not nasty. Not mean. Just firm. Don't waffle. And if he doesn't want to give you the opportunity to have a discussion, then you could threaten him with a separation."

Tori looked horrified. "Wow. All of my thoughts are coming to life. It's one thing if you're thinking about doing something. It's an entirely different matter when you actually have to do it." Tori sighed. "I know you're right. I'll muster up the courage to ask him to take a walk with me. I might leave out the 'talk' part until we're actually outside."

"You don't want to blindside him either." He leaned in her direction. "Give it some thought. Write down what you want to say and memorize it. I always find writing something down gives you more clarity."

"Thank you so much. This has been a big

help." Tori was no longer misty. "You're right. I can't expect him to know what's on my mind if I don't tell him."

"You said you had 'grown apart.' Maybe you can replant some seeds. Oh my, no pun intended. Sorry." Layton's face went red.

Tori chuckled. "That's OK. Kinda funny." She sighed. "I'll try to remember what it was about him that made me like him. The running-away part is kinda obvious. We were both running away from bad situations."

"You know what you were running away *from*. It's never too late to figure out where you want to run *to*."

Tori got up from her chair and returned to her desk. She answered the dozen-plus e-mails that had arrived the day before. They had lunch delivered and ate in the break room. Tori looked around and imagined how she would arrange it so it was comfortable for a baby. Maybe a new paint job, move a few things around, and create a comfortable space in the corner. She thought a nice folding screen would provide privacy but also add a little style to the room. She would also put something cheerful on the walls. Right now it was an outdated yellowed map of the state. She decided the lighting could be better instead of the old, ugly, buzzing fluorescent tubes. A couple of inexpensive floor lamps would create ample illumination. They could always turn on the ugly lights if necessary. Yes, a DIY remake of the break room wouldn't take much and it would be a nice distraction. The idea elevated her mood. Once again she was feeling more in control. Little by little, but it was progress.

After lunch, she did some research for a case of land encroachment, and before she knew it, the day was over. She cleared off her desk and said good night to everyone. She checked her phone. Nothing from her husband all day. It had been over twenty-four hours. Maybe his phone battery had conked out while he was fishing. That thought made her wonder about dinner. Would he be bringing home a freshly caught fish? She decided to call his cell. It went straight to voicemail. She sent a text.

> Hope you're having a good day.
> What do you want to do about dinner?

It took several minutes for him to respond.

> Didn't catch anything. Heading to Ringo's.
> Be home later.

That's when Tori decided to take that

strange woman's suggestion and go to Ringo's that evening.

When she got home, she changed her clothes and fixed a salad. Maybe she would grab a burger at Ringo's. She was feeling the need for red meat. She wasn't sure if she should let him know she was coming. Maybe showing up would be a nice surprise for him. Show him she was interested in what he did in his time off. It would also be a good opportunity to tell him she wanted to have a conversation with him. Maybe over the weekend.

Tori decided to wear a nice outfit and do her makeup as if she were going out somewhere special. She knew he would be puffed-up proud if she showed up looking her best. After all, she was a pretty woman, especially when she did her hair and dolled up her face a bit.

She pulled out a navy-blue jumpsuit from the closet. It had an empire waist, and she thought she might still be able to fit into it. She stepped through the pant legs, then the armholes, and then zipped it. Now she remembered why she rarely wore it. It was a production when you had to go to the bathroom. Why didn't designers make them with . . . ? With what? Velcro? Or maybe stretchy straps so you could pull it down instead of having to unzip it and practically disrobe. This would be the jumpsuit's farewell performance. She looked in the mirror. It looked great on her. No baby bump yet. She still had maybe two more months before she started to really show.

Her hair was now down to her chin, so she tucked one side behind her ear. She donned a nice pair of costume-jewelry earrings. Nothing flashy. Just enough to draw attention to her face and her pretty eyes. She added just a touch more makeup than usual. She took another look in the mirror. Maybe there was hope for her yet.

She'd grabbed her purse, keys, and phone and started on her way to Ringo's when a burst of panic hit her. What if he got mad that she had showed up at "his" place? Would it be embarrassing to his friends? She stopped and calmed herself. *Walk in with a smile and say hello to everyone as if you belonged there.* His coworkers liked her, so they would probably be glad to see her. Maybe not glad, but they wouldn't be annoyed. Men generally liked to look at pretty women. And vice versa. Women liked to look at handsome men. It's just that women rarely said it out loud.

Tori parked the car and walked toward the outer door. It was an enclosed porch entrance with an interior window that looked into the bar. As she swung open the screen door, she spotted her husband through the glass. She also spotted a rather sleazy-looking woman hanging on him like a Christmas ornament. Tori froze in place. She watched the woman playing with her husband's hair, and he wasn't doing anything to dissuade her. She moved to the side of the window where she could still watch in shock but not be seen by the people inside. She pulled out her phone and sent him a text to see what he would say.

Hey. Any idea when you'll be home?

His phone was sitting on the bar with what looked like cash and his keys. He glanced at the phone, then turned his attention back to the bleached-blond-bad-hair woman without answering Tori's text. Tori switched to the camera app and secretly started taking photos of her husband and whoever the floozy was. She also noticed the time stamp. It read 9:00, which was the precise time the woman from the coffee shop said she should show up. That gave her the willies. Who was that woman and how did she know? Instead of breaking up the two lovebirds, Tori decided to turn

261

around and head back home. Now she had a real reason to demand a conversation with him.

Her hands were shaking as she gripped the wheel. Her mind was racing as she came upon a tight bend in the road. An oncoming car horn blasted as it swerved to avoid clipping her. She could hear the driver screaming as he drove past. "Slow down!"

Tori immediately hit the brakes and regained control of her car. She pulled over to the side of the road to regroup. Seeing her husband with another woman in a place where he hangs out with his friends was truly not what she was expecting. What to do? What to do? She knew this time she couldn't do nothing. She had to do something. That was becoming an anthem with her. Then she decided that doing nothing for the time being was actually doing something. She was going to wait for the right opportunity. She wasn't going to react when she was in a state of shock.

As she returned to the road, she thought that maybe she would text him the picture she just took of them. Yes, but not now. At the moment, she was in charge. She had the power in her little art form. If he didn't agree to take a walk with her, then she might show him her slideshow of his infidelity. Or was it? Was he simply flirting with that floozy? Showing off for his friends? She was going to get to the bottom of it. When she was good and ready. She had a lot of thinking to do. Again.

As the water filled the tub, she looked at the photos again, making them larger to see if she could identify the woman. Tori flinched at the first enlargement. The woman was much older but trying to look younger. The fake-colored hair and the heavy black eyeliner with blue eye shadow was not doing the woman any favors. "If that's what he wants, then that's what he can have." Tori was baffled. Why on earth would he be with someone like that? She decided to go to the diner the next day and see if she could get more information from the woman who had told her to go to Ringo's in the first place.

After her bath, Tori got into bed and willed herself to fall asleep. She did not want to be awake when he got home.

The following morning, Tori got out of bed unnoticed. She hurriedly got dressed and bolted out the door. When she arrived at the diner, she checked her face in the visor mirror. She took in a deep breath and told herself she was in charge of this situation.

She walked up to the area where you placed your order and asked about the woman. "Good morning. I was wondering if the woman with curly gray hair is in today?"

The waitress gave her an odd look. "What woman?"

Tori began to describe her. "Late sixties. About this high." Tori held her hand to indicate the woman was about five feet tall. "Short, gray curly hair. Wore glasses on a chain around her neck."

The waitress still looked puzzled. "There is no one here that fits that description."

"Are you sure?" Tori was certain she had given the woman an accurate assessment.

"Absolutely. It's just me and my three sisters. My dad owns the place, so I would know if someone worked here who looked like that."

"So, no one who even remotely resembles her works here? Not even a couple of weeks ago?"

"No, hon. Sorry."

"But I spoke to her last week when I came in for donuts. You were at the cash register." Tori was becoming impatient.

"Yes, I remember you, but I never saw you speak to anyone else. Not to my recollection." The waitress was giving Tori an "are you all right?" kind of look.

"So you don't recall me talking to anybody? Ever?"

"Listen, sweetie, I don't keep track of who my customers talk to every time they come in here. But I know who works here, and that lady you described does not." The waitress was getting a little exasperated.

Tori knew she hadn't imagined it. How would she have known to go to Ringo's at that exact day and time?

"OK. Thanks. Sorry to have bothered you."

"No bother. Maybe it was a different diner or coffee shop?" The waitress could see the look of concern on Tori's face and offered an alternate explanation.

"Yeah. Maybe." Tori smiled but knew exactly where she had spoken to the mysterious woman. It was right there, only a few feet away from where she was standing.

In the weeks that followed, she maintained the status quo. He had been unusually quiet. Almost kind. She wondered if anyone had seen her that night and told him. He hadn't pressed her for sex, and if he had, she would have brought down the hammer. She surely wasn't going to have sex with someone who was doing God knows what with other women.

She sent a text message to the psychic woman, Luna. Now she had more questions that needed answers. Luna texted her back to meet with her the week following Tori's origami workshop. She had hoped it would be sooner, but she could wait. She had waited this long. What was another two weeks?

CHAPTER THIRTEEN

Marshal Gaines couldn't remember the last time he had been so nervous. He couldn't remember the last time he had a woman spend the night either. He realized that Luna would be staying in Carter's room. But still. He hired a professional cleaning service, which made sure everything was spotless. He wasn't a messy person, but he wanted his home to be pristine considering it needed a lot of work in the décor department. He wasn't sure what arrangements he should make for dinner. Dine out? Eat home? Takeout? Grill? He peered into the refrigerator. He had two rib-eyes, salad fixings, and asparagus. He then checked the pantry. A few Idaho potatoes. He would offer to cook, but if she wanted restaurant food, that would be fine with him as well. He would leave the decision to Luna. Although, he fancied the idea of cooking together. He knew they worked well in the field. Cooking would be a good opportunity to see how well they worked in the kitchen. Preparing a meal with someone was like choreography. You needed to move in sync with the other person.

He smiled as he thought about having that wild woman in his kitchen. They would share a bottle of wine, cook, then sit by the fire and have dessert. Dessert? He snapped his fingers. Then he remembered he had a pint of ice cream in the freezer. That should work. He knew Luna wasn't much of a dessert person, but she had ordered ice cream or gelato on more than one occasion. Satisfied he had the dinner part of the evening under control, his mind moved on to breakfast for the next morning. Eggs? Check. Bacon? Check. English muffins? Check. He was beginning to relax, knowing there was enough food for two meals for both of them.

His next challenge was what to wear. How casual? Jeans and a navy-blue long-sleeved cashmere button-down shirt? Why not? Unless they would go out to dinner, then he'd put on a blazer. But he really hoped they would stay in.

He checked Carter's room to make sure there weren't any adolescent remains such as dirty socks, laundry, stinky sneakers, and who knows what else. He knew he was being a bit obsessive, but he wanted Luna to be comfortable. The cleaning people did the laundry and put fresh linens on both beds. Clean towels were in place in the bathroom, and a clean set for Luna was on Carter's bed.

He took another long look around. The place was acceptable. He thought fresh flowers for the table would add a nice touch. Nothing too girlie. He phoned the local florist and spoke to Nancy. He explained he was having a guest for the weekend and he wanted to spruce up the dining-room table, but he didn't want it to be overdone. She said she knew exactly what do to. Two hours later, she arrived with a rectangular wooden box with an arrangement of greenery including eucalyptus and white dogwood branches. It made the long plank table that once served as a door look a little less like a flea-market find. It was just the right touch.

Then he thought about wine. He had a very nice bottle of Seamus Olde Sonoma Cabernet Reserve he could serve with the steaks. It was a sixty-five-dollar bottle someone had given him as a housewarming gift. Maybe it would help warm up the house that coming night, he thought to himself. He checked the balloon wineglasses and polished them. Dinnerware, flatware, and cloth napkins were in the pantry. Music? He went through his vinyl record collection and pulled out a Wes Montgomery album. It was classic California smooth jazz, a style Montgomery had made famous. Keeping in line with the genre, he also set aside albums by Earl Klugh and George Benson. That should cover a couple of hours. He checked the liquor cabinet. He also had a bottle of vermouth they could have after dinner in front of the fireplace. "Get a grip, Gaines," he said out loud. "Let's not get ahead of ourselves."

Then he remembered he should check that he had a decent pair of loungewear. Normally when he puttered around the house, he wore sweatpants and a T-shirt, or a U.S. Marshal sweatshirt. Did he have something he could put together so he didn't look like a gym rat or a slob? He sprinted into his bedroom and rifled through his drawers. He dug out a pair of gray flannel pants, sniffed them to see how fresh they were. Not enticing. They must have been sitting at the bottom of the drawer since he moved in. They would need to go into the wash. He looked at the digital clock on the footstool that served as a nightstand. He had at least four hours before Luna arrived. He dug through another drawer and found a new U.S. Marshal warm-up jacket he had been saving. *For what?* He couldn't remember. *Some special activity?* Luna coming for the weekend fit the bill. The warm-up jacket was gray and navy. It would look good with the pants, casual but put-together. Thankfully, his moccasins were in good shape. He scanned the room to see if there was anything else he or the cleaning people might have left behind. Nope. Just the two items he had in his hand. He bolted down the stairs to the basement and tossed the clothes in the washer. He spotted a few old trophies from when he played baseball. Should he put them on display? He quickly thought, *Don't be ridiculous. We don't need any "Glory Days" reminders. Such a guy thing.* He climbed back up the stairs, taking them two at a time. Then he thought about candles. Did he have any? Would that be over the top? Maybe a quick trip to the drugstore and get one for the kitchen and one for the bathroom. That wasn't too fussy. Or weird. Or was it? Who could he ask? Minnie. He pulled out his cell and punched speed dial.

"Hello, mate! To what do I owe this pleasure?" Minnie's Yorkshire accent always made Gaines smile.

"Hello, Minnie. How are you today?"

"I'm ducky, love. And you?"

"Fine, thank you."

"What are you doing on such a lovely morning?"

"Luna is coming this afternoon to help me decide what to do with my house."

"Brilliant! How is she doing now that she is working with her brother? Does she miss child services?"

"The art center is doing well. It's become a destination spot. Her brother has been quite busy with restoration projects. She's been consulting for him and running the adjacent café."

"She's a love. So, what can I do for you?"

"I want the place to be comfortable in spite of the condition it's in." Gaines wasn't sure how to broach what seemed like a ridiculous question. He looked around the room and frowned. "Candles. Yes or no?"

Minnie chuckled. "A few wouldn't be a terrible idea, but nothing too overwhelming. Stay away from lilac and coconut. You don't want your place to smell like old ladies or suntan lotion, now do you?"

Gaines smiled. "Correct. I certainly don't want this to turn out to be a damp squib." He chuckled, using one of Minnie's favorite terms for a total failure.

"Oh, I doubt that, but I understand. You

want to make a good impression and not look like you're desperate."

"Desperate?" Gaines balked.

"Oh, lovie, it's obvious you have a sweet spot for her. I am sure everything will be aces and do get vanilla candles. But not too many."

"Will do. And thanks, Minnie."

"You are quite welcome. Have a wonderful time. Give Luna my regards. We miss working with her."

"I will. Gotta dash and go buy some candles. Thanks again, Minnie."

"Cheerio."

Gaines hopped into his Jeep and drove to the local pharmacy. He wandered aimlessly through the aisles. Heaven forbid he ask someone where the candles are kept. As he walked down the third aisle, he realized he was probably being watched by security. What was a grown man doing meandering through the women's hygiene section of the store? He picked up his pace and moved as quickly as possible into the toothpaste section. Nope. Not here either. He finally succumbed to his ignorance of product placement and asked a woman who was taking inventory of the dental floss. "Excuse me. Can you point me in the direction of candles?" He didn't know why he felt embarrassed, but he did. Maybe because he couldn't remember the last time he had thought about candles.

"They're right over there." She nodded at an endcap.

He must have walked past them at least twice. Now he really felt ridiculous. "Duh. I should pay better attention. Thanks!"

The woman gave him a "most men don't pay attention" shrug.

He stared at the shelves. Some of the names were vague. *Summer Delight. Serene Sanctuary. Home Sweet Home.* He took a whiff of it and his eyes almost teared up. That was one home he didn't want his to smell like. He searched for vanilla but there were none. He gingerly pulled the Serene Sanctuary closer to his face, concerned it would make him sneeze. Much to his surprise, it had a clean scent. Once again, he was befuddled. He brought the candle over to the same woman who had directed him to the shelf. "May I ask you something?"

She shrugged again. "Sure."

"I'm having guests and I want to give my place a little more, I dunno, umph, I guess. Would this be all right?" He handed the candle to her.

"Divorced?" she asked.

Gaines laughed out loud. "Is it that obvious?"

She gave him a deadpan look.

"Understood." He nodded. "Due to my candle ignorance, could you please advise?"

She handed it back to him. "This is fine. Has a little sandalwood so it's a bit more masculine than the others. Go for it."

"Thanks. I appreciate your help."

"She's a lucky woman," the clerk replied, as he was walking away.

He stopped suddenly, turned, and grinned. "I think I'm the lucky one."

"Even better. Good luck." The woman finally smiled.

Gaines bought three large candles and a lighter and headed back to his place. He set one on the dining-room table, one on the fireplace mantel, and one on the bathroom vanity. He decided to light one just to be sure he wouldn't have another olfactory reaction. He checked his watch again. Three more hours. He didn't want to start any new projects. The house was in a state of suspended animation, and he didn't want to open any work files. He couldn't remember the last time he actually had time on his hands. He sat on the sofa and looked around for the umpteenth time. Not very homey. *It is what it is, and that's why she's coming. I should be thankful it looks the way it does.*

The weekend

Luna must have packed and unpacked her bags three times. Wiley watched her move back and forth from the closet to the week-ender suitcase propped on the chair in the corner. She held up a midi dress with long sleeves. "What do you think? Too caj? Too dressy?" Wiley didn't make a move. "OK. So that will go back on the rack." Her closet was squished. She dug through more clothes, shoving each garment into the next. "Wow. I never realized I had so much stuff." She looked at Wiley. He yawned. "And I can't figure out what to wear or pack." She threw herself backward on her bed and began to stare at the ceiling. She was nervous. She knew it. Talk about practicing what you preach. She stunk at it. Maybe this was a good time to put her own words to good use. She didn't have to be on the road for another couple of hours. She had time to decompress and hit the reset button. She got up and dimmed the lights, pulled down the shade, put on some New Age music, and set the timer. She would try to be still for forty minutes, regardless. No thinking allowed. She closed her eyes and began deep yoga breathing, inhaling and exhaling to the rhythms of the ocean waves in the background of the music. She drifted off to the guided meditation taking her to the tranquility of lush, beautiful gardens.

Before Cullen left for work that morning, he set out the clothes he planned on wearing to dinner with Chi-Chi. Of course, Luna had a major hand in it. A Hawes & Curtis green-and-blue Italian linen blazer, navy linen pants, a dark green shirt, and a blue-and-green-checkered tie with a pocket square to match. Cullen was always very buttoned up. Literally. During the week, he would spend most of his time in the workshop renovating something. But under his work apron was a button-down collared shirt. The only thing that gave a hint of his creative side were his socks. They were always something different than one would expect. Something interesting. Most people didn't realize it because he wore work boots in his studio and workshop. But under that Brooks Brothers appearance was a pair of Looney Tunes, Rocky & Bullwinkle, Oreos, SpongeBob, or some other wacky footwear. Even at a black-tie event, he would wear white socks with black bowties. Rarely did anyone say a word. It was such a dichotomy from what people generally recognized. Now the dilemma was which pair to wear to dinner. Then he remembered he had a pair of green paisleys. Perfect. Dark maroon loafers with tassels, of course. He then started second-guessing himself about the tie. It would depend on how nervous he was and if a tie would make him feel like he was choking. He'd tough it out. The ensemble Luna had picked was impeccable, and he wanted to impress Chi-Chi. Satisfied his evening wear was ready, he left for the showroom and workshop. It was Saturday. He wouldn't be working with paint, sawdust, old metal, or whatever would arrive in desperate need of refurbishing. He wanted to be sure he wouldn't find the need to bathe in turpentine before he showered for his dinner date.

He had started working on the trunk the previous week. It took several days to get it clean and down to the original wood. He was surprised it was in decent shape considering how it had smelled when it arrived. It still had a smoky odor, but he figured that would dissipate over the next week or so. Then there was the refinishing, which would add its own aroma to the mix.

Luna had some crazy ideas about the origin of the trunk and the measly contents, but she had been busier than usual, probably because she was taking a weekend off and had to cram in more time during the week. Plus, she had to shop for her trip. Cullen smiled, thinking about her and Marshal Gaines. Individually they were fun, funny, and interesting, but when they were together, it grew exponentially. And it was contagious. Even during serious conversations, the four of them would find a silver lining. He once joked "that silver lining is a bolt of silver lightning." That fueled a conversation about old adages with a twist. "Even at its lowest ebb, the tide will turn . . . and swallow you in the undertow." Then there was "Tomorrow's another day . . . hope it's not your last."

Cullen wondered what dinner alone with Chi-Chi would be like. He tried not to think too much about it. He didn't want to talk himself into sabotaging it and hoped Luna wasn't doing the same thing in her situation.

On the drive to the center, Cullen turned on the radio to get the local news and weather. He almost drove off the road when the song "Smooth Operator" by Sade came on. He had known Chi-Chi for about a year, and it finally hit him. That's who she reminded him of! Sade Adu, pronounced Shaday. She, too, was Nigerian. "I'm such an idiot. I can't believe I missed that," he muttered under his breath. "Maybe because I haven't heard it in a long time? That song came out around the time we were born," he said to no one. But it reinforced his opinion about music and reminded him of the conversation he had had with Chi-Chi and Luna about contemporary music. He smiled to himself, anticipating the coming evening. He wondered if it was going to be awkward without the crew. He also wondered if there were any subjects that were off-limits. They rarely discussed race. Culture? Yes. General politics? Yes. Religion? Often. Luna considered herself a "spiritual" person but not tied to any particular religion although Christianity had a lot of good points, she concluded. Chi-Chi also had a Christian background with a smattering of traditional Nigerian beliefs in higher beings. She once compared them to saints. Each one covered a particular subject, idea, or territory. Cullen considered himself a Christian and attended church on holidays and other occasions. At least he knew religion wouldn't be a problem. He was learning more about Chi-Chi's culture and upbringing, which seemed to be strict but loving. He smirked, thinking about the time he had driven Chi-Chi to her car and told her men needed an invitation to kiss a woman. He now realized it was a bit of an exaggeration, and perhaps she might have misinterpreted what he had said. He'd find out soon enough. He hoped. In a good way.

Luna bounced up when the timer went off. She had fallen into a deep state listening to the New Age music. She checked the clock. It was almost eleven, and she still hadn't finished picking out her clothes. She had the essentials packed. Toiletries, the new teal silk pajamas with navy piping and a matching robe. Luna shuddered when she thought about the $500 she had spent on sleepwear. It was the most she had spent on any type of clothing in her life. But the company was called Lunya and she rationalized that it was a "sign." Chi-Chi chortled at Luna's explanation for her extravagance. "But it does look lovely on you." Chi-Chi supported her the day they had gone shopping.

Trying not to waste more time, Luna pulled out a pair of jeans and a light, cream-colored sweater for the next day, a silk scarf, and a pair of slip-on canvas shoes with rubber soles. But what to wear now? She wanted to make a good impression, which was always the case, but this time it was special. Really special. Chi-Chi had suggested a baby-blue maxi dress with the tribal print split neckline, and a light denim jacket. She finished it off with her shooties — the booties with an open toe — bangle bracelets, and hoop earrings.

The night before, Chi-Chi had braided Luna's hair in the same fashion as during their emergency makeover a few weeks before. It fell beautifully over her left shoulder, and she could undo it if she wanted to go wild and wavy.

Luna turned and looked at her bed. It was covered in a pile of rejected outfits. "Wiley. Why did you let me do this?" He offered a disinterested woof. "Yeah, yeah. Enough of fashion week. I'm going with Chi-Chi's idea." Wiley's head perked up in agreement. "You should have said something earlier." She laughed and gave him a big smooch on the head.

She applied her makeup very carefully. She didn't want to look like she was overdoing it. "Casual. I'm casual," she kept repeating to herself. She also decided to wear her contact lenses instead of her granny glasses. She plopped them in a case and stuck it in her bag. She considered it might be time to trade them in for something a little more modern. Then she laughed at the thought. No one would recognize her!

She took a long look in the mirror and turned to Wiley. "What do you think, pal?" He gave her his particular woof of approval, his tail banging an affirmative on the floor. "Come on. You're staying with Uncle Cullen tonight."

Luna was worried that having to take care of Wiley would interfere with Cullen's evening, but Cullen insisted. "He's no trouble at all."

She took one last look before she locked up and set the alarm. Cullen knew the code if he needed to get in for any reason. Ellie was the backup. Confident she was ready for this new adventure, she harnessed Wiley in the back seat of her SUV and put her weekender bag in the back. She checked her tote bag for a sketch pad, tape measure, and fabric samples. Then it dawned on her that she didn't have a gift! You never go to anyone's house without bringing something! With all the excitement of shopping and preparing, she had forgotten a house gift. The thought of a candle crossed her mind, but she felt that would be too girlie. She hit the button on the console. "Call the Flakey Tart." The electronic voice repeated "Calling the Flakey Tart." After two rings, Heidi answered with her usual greeting. "What sweetness can we bring into your life today?"

"Hey, Heidi! It's Luna."

"Hey, Luna. I thought you were going out of town this weekend."

"I am, but I'm such a knucklehead I forgot to pick up something for the host."

Heidi laughed. "I have just the thing. I made a beautiful apple strudel that came out of the oven about an hour ago."

"Sounds scrumptious. I hope I don't eat it on the way!"

"I'll throw in a scone for your trip." Heidi chuckled.

"Thanks. Come to think of it, how about a couple of them. Do you have any brioche?"

"Yep, I do. Want me to put a box together? Three of each?"

"Fantastic! But make sure you put an extra scone in a bag for me!"

"No problem."

"I'm on my way over now. Uncle Cullen is doggie-sitting for Wiley."

"Great. See you in a few."

Luna was relieved. She would have brought something for the house but she didn't know what he needed. The first time he visited the center, she had given him a tour, and he bought dinnerware and glassware. If she had more time, she would have looked for something appropriate. But a good apple strudel wasn't terrible. Plus the breakfast goodies. She was satisfied with the pastry party she was going to offer.

Chi-Chi unlocked the safe and was beginning to put the jewelry on display when her phone rang. It was her brother. "Hello, sister. I am an hour away." His cheerful voice was loud and clear.

"Abeo! I thought you were coming day after tomorrow." Chi-Chi's voice was nervous.

"Do you not want to see your older brother?" he kidded. "I have those stones you asked Father to send from Nigeria."

"Of course I want to see you. And yes, I need the stones."

"What is the problem, then?"

"I wasn't expecting you until Monday, and I made plans for the weekend." Chi-Chi wasn't sure what might unfold and she didn't want her brother to interfere.

"Should I turn around and go home?" he asked with a hint of sarcasm.

"Don't be ridiculous." Chi-Chi knew he had driven fifteen hours. "I cannot change the plans, so you will have to be on your own for the evening."

"I think I can manage that. What are your plans for the evening?"

"I am having dinner with a friend."

Abeo's voice brightened. "And what kind of friend?"

"A friend. Must you be so nosy?"

"Oh, do not disrespect me." Abeo was half serious.

"You are being ridiculous again. I am not disrespecting you. But I am a grown woman and capable of making plans with friends without your permission." Chi-Chi knew she was being curt, but she couldn't help it. She wasn't prepared for this kind of monkey wrench being thrown into her evening.

"Oh my. Are you in a mood today?"

"Sorry. No. I am trying to get the shop ready, and now you surprised me with an early arrival. That's all."

"I see. So let me come to the shop and help you today," Abeo offered.

Chi-Chi wasn't sure that was a good idea either, but she knew she had no choice. "That would be very nice. See you soon." Chi-Chi thought she might throw up in the back of her mouth.

A little over an hour later, Abeo arrived at Silver & Stone. "I am very impressed." He scanned her shop from one end to the other.

"Thank you." Chi-Chi smiled demurely,

286

hiding her anxiety. She didn't know what to say if Cullen came into her shop. Of course, she would introduce him to her brother. He was a friend after all. But she knew her brother was a bit nosy and might press her for details about her dinner arrangements. Why did her brother have to come to town so soon? It was just like him to disturb her plans. Ever since they were teens, Abeo enjoyed getting under his little sister's skin. She loved him dearly, but there were times she wanted to smack him with a stick.

"Lebici, what have you done with your hair?" He peered closely at the pin-straight ponytail that ran the length of her back. "I don't remember your wearing it like this?"

"I thought I would try something new," Chi-Chi replied. The night before, after she had braided Luna's hair, Luna returned the favor by flat-ironing Chi-Chi's.

"Do you not like it?" She really didn't care if he did or not, but she had to be polite.

"It looks lovely." Abeo hugged her. "Tell me about your plans for the weekend."

Chi-Chi maintained her reticence. "I am having dinner with a friend. His sister is away for the weekend." She wasn't sure why she had thrown that into the conversation. Maybe because she didn't want her brother to think it was a date date. Just as she wasn't sure if it was a real date, but it felt like it might be. Even though her family accepted the idea that Chi-Chi might not marry a Nigerian, they were far more concerned that she might never marry at all. Single women over the age of twenty-six were considered "thornbacks," while women aged twenty-three to twenty-six were "spinsters." But nowadays, it's not unusual for a woman to marry well into her thirties. Chi-Chi must have explained that to her parents ad nauseam.

"But you are almost halfway to forty," her mother reminded her at every opportunity.

"Is it that Cullen fellow? His sister is Luna?" Abeo hadn't met them before, but Chi-Chi had spoken about them numerous times. Her parents had met them at the grand opening almost a year ago while Abeo was in Nigeria doing business for his father.

Chi-Chi was taken aback. "Yes, if you must know."

"I didn't mean anything by that, dear sister, but you speak of them often. I am sorry I will not be able to meet your friend."

Chi-Chi was hoping he wouldn't meet either of them, at least not anytime soon.

"It is nice you can keep someone's brother company but will not keep your own brother company?"

Chi-Chi wasn't sure how to answer that. "Abeo, I made these plans weeks ago. You were not supposed to arrive until Monday. You cannot expect me to be rude and cancel my plans simply because you changed yours."

Abeo was surprised at his sister's straightforwardness and logic. "You are right. I apologize for making things inconvenient."

"Do not be cynical with me." Chi-Chi was hoping the conversation wouldn't take a bad turn. She didn't want to ruin her attitude about her dinner plans.

Abeo looked crestfallen. "I am not being sarcastic. Most sincerely. I forget that you have a life and a business. I keep thinking you are still my baby sister."

Chi-Chi wrapped her arms around him, then looked him straight in the eye. "I love you. I love Mommy and Daddy. And I also love my life here."

Abeo's eyes got misty. "I am very proud of you. Again, I apologize for being an interloper."

"You are not an interloper, but you are also not getting an invitation for dinner tonight." She gave him another hug.

He grinned at her. "I suppose my usual guilt trips will not work on you any longer?"

"That is correct." She patted him on the

shoulder. "Come. Make yourself useful." They retreated into the back office, where Abeo opened the stainless-steel case he carried. Chi-Chi gasped and put her hand to her chest. "These are beautiful!" She picked up the watermelon tourmaline. "You know this stone supports inspiration and happiness." She turned it over in her hand several times.

"A similar meaning as my name. 'Bringer of Joy.'" He gave her a broad smile.

"Yes, I think they made a mistake on your birth certificate. False advertising." Chi-Chi bit her lip, trying to keep a straight face.

Abeo shook his finger at her. "Tsk. Tsk. Do not be disrespectful."

"I am not. I blame it on the hospital." Chi-Chi couldn't contain her laughter any longer.

"Oh, Lebici, I do miss you very much." Abeo beamed at his sister.

"You should visit more often," she said absently, as she reached for the aquamarine stones. "These will make beautiful earrings." She was already envisioning them dangling from wavy fluid silver. "I think the white fire opal should be a necklace. They are fragile stones."

Abeo watched his sister delicately examine the pieces. "You are pleased?"

She looked up and kissed him on the cheek. "I am very pleased."

Chi-Chi noticed that it was getting close to lunchtime. "Do you want to get some sandwiches and sit outside? I can call one of the pages to watch the store for a half hour."

"That sounds like a splendid idea. And then you can show me around."

"Abeo, I have to run my shop today. We will do the tour on Monday as we originally planned."

Abeo feigned a pout. "If you say so."

"Yes, I do." Chi-Chi picked up the walkie-talkie and reached out to Lucy, another page from the local college. The crackling sound was followed by a woman's voice. "Lucy here."

"Hi, Lucy. This is Chi-Chi. Could you watch the shop for about a half hour? My brother surprised me, and I want to get him a sandwich and show him the park."

"No problem. How soon?" Lucy answered.

Abeo bobbed his head in anticipation.

"Can you come now?"

"Sure. On my way."

"That is very impressive," Abeo noted.

"Yes. Ellie Stillwell, the woman who built this center, put a great deal of thought into it. Not just a place for artists but also how to operate efficiently."

"I would like to meet this Ellie Stillwell."

"You most likely will. She is in and out during the day. If you see two German shepherd dogs, then you will know she is in the building."

"Dogs?" Abeo looked perplexed.

"Yes. Dogs. We have a dog park outside as well. And there is a young man on doggie patrol. He supervises when people drop off their pets. He is responsible for keeping it clean and making sure that the dogs behave themselves. He was a veterinary student but decided he enjoyed doing this much more."

"Is this a day-care center for dogs?" Abeo's eyes widened.

"Not exactly." Chi-Chi explained about the service the center provided for tenants and guests with dogs.

"And no cats?" Abeo joked.

"No, dear brother."

A few minutes later, Lucy strolled into the shop. "Hello, Lucy. This is my brother, Abeo."

Lucy held out her hand. "Nice to meet you."

"Likewise."

"We'll be getting some sandwiches and taking them to the patio if you need me."

"No problem," Lucy chimed.

Chi-Chi and Luna often joked that "No problem" was a standard answer from the pages. Chi-Chi and Abeo walked across the atrium and into the Blonde Shallot. Chi-Chi introduced her brother to Rita and picked two of the day's specials, then signed the check. As they were heading toward the patio, they bumped into Luna rushing past them with pastry boxes.

"Hey!" Luna said with a surprised look on her face.

"Luna, this is my brother, Abeo. He arrived two days early." Chi-Chi rolled her eyes.

"Nice to meet you, Abeo. Chi-Chi has told me so much about you!" Luna was trying to do a Jedi mind trick to see if Chi-Chi and Cullen's plans were still on track.

"I told Abeo he would be on his own tonight. He wasn't very happy."

Voila. It worked. Luna chuckled. "I am sure you will find something interesting to do. The center is open tonight for a music ensemble. A string quartet. Sorry I am going to miss it. Listen, I have to dash. I am already running behind. Enjoy your dinner. See you Sunday. Bye!" Luna raised her one free finger, waved, and scooted away.

"She seems interesting." Abeo watched

the whirling dervish exit the atrium.

"Yes, she is. Very. Come, we don't have a lot of time, and I want to enjoy my lunch."

They walked through the beautifully landscaped atrium. Abeo looked around in awe. "I can understand why you like it here. The creativity, the openness, the landscaping inside and out. It is a haven for artists."

"And visitors alike." Chi-Chi unwrapped her roast beef, cheddar, bacon, and horseradish sandwich. "Ellie wanted it to be a destination point for people to see artists work but also for people to congregate. We have monthly events. Some artists hold workshops. It is truly a work of art in itself."

"And so is this sandwich." Abeo grinned with delight.

During the next half hour, they chatted about Abeo's trip and their parents. Neither of them were married and they commiserated about the underlying pressure they would get from their mother and father. Abeo mentioned that their mother had tried to match him up with the daughter of one of her friends, but Abeo said the woman was spoiled and demanding. "More than usual," he joked.

Chi-Chi looked up and saw Cullen walking in their direction. He hesitated for a minute, then Chi-Chi waved him over.

"This is my brother, Abeo. He was supposed to arrive on Monday, but here he is."

Cullen was just about to say something when Chi-Chi continued, "But I told him that I had plans for this evening, and he would have to entertain himself." Now it was her turn to try to flash a message to Cullen: *Do not ask him to join us.*

Cullen got the message loud and clear. "There is a wonderful string quartet playing here tonight. There will be wine and cheese, and the Blonde Shallot will be serving petit fours."

"Ah. Those little sandwiches?" Abeo asked.

"Yes. From the same place where you got the big sandwich you are eating." Cullen smiled.

"Oh, then I most definitely must come back!" Abeo was grinning again.

"I will introduce you to several other artists before I leave. This way you will have people to talk to."

"Excellent idea. I bet Jennine would love to meet your brother." Cullen was referring to the pottery artist who was the epitome of Blanche from *The Golden Girls.*

Chi-Chi laughed out loud.

"What is so funny?" Abeo gave her a look.

"Jennine is what they call a handful,"

Cullen added. "She's *very* friendly."

"Yes. *Very,*" Chi-Chi noted.

"Then I would be very happy to meet her," Abeo said innocently. He had never seen the television show and wouldn't understand even if they tried to explain.

Chi-Chi bit her lip. One thing was for certain — Abeo would be very busy fending off the overtures that would certainly be coming from Jennine.

"Then I shall introduce you to her now." Chi-Chi began to gather the paper wrappers from the sandwiches and the empty bottles of water. "Come." She gave Cullen a look and shook her head.

Cullen also tried to restrain his amusement at what was in store for Chi-Chi's brother. "Nice meeting you, Abeo. Enjoy your day."

Chi-Chi was relieved the subject of dinner did not come up. However, she also realized that Abeo would see Cullen when he came to pick her up, unless she could get Abeo to stay at the center for the duration of the afternoon into the evening. The two walked toward Clay-More, the pottery stall. Jennine was wearing a wild-looking chiffon outfit. Chi-Chi wasn't sure if it was supposed to be lingerie or not.

"Jennine, this is my brother, Abeo. He

brought me wonderful stones from Nigeria."

"Well, hello there, big guy." Jennine did not disappoint. She immediately looped her arm through his. The woman had no shame and the twenty-plus-year discrepancy in their ages made not one lick of difference to her.

Abeo became immobilized. His usual outgoing demeanor deserted him. "How do you do," he replied politely. He gave his sister a frightened look, as Chi-Chi suppressed a grin.

"I do *very* well. And you?" Jennine was clinging to his arm as if it were a life raft from *Titanic*.

For the first time Chi-Chi could recall, Abeo had a look of abject fear in his eyes, while Chi-Chi's were filling up with tears of laughter.

"I . . . I am doing well, too." Abeo tried to disengage the death grip Jennine had on his arm, but she wasn't letting go.

"How long will you be in town?" Jennine asked demurely.

Abeo's first instinct was to say, "Not very long," and try to escape, but he smiled calmly, and said, "I will be here until Monday."

Chi-Chi could not help adding fuel to this little campfire. "Abeo is interested in attending the music ensemble this evening, but I am not available. Would you mind showing him around and keeping him company?"

She thought Abeo was going to faint.

"I would be delighted." She patted his arm. "I will take good care of him. Who will be minding your shop?"

"Alex. He finishes his doggie work at five. Ellie decided to close the dog park for the evening, and he was happy to oblige."

"Ah. Alex. He's a cutie-pie," Jennine said, her voice indicating just how man-crazy she was.

Abeo's eyes grew wider. He was beginning to think he had made a big mistake trying to surprise his sister. Now she was surprising him by letting this desperate woman take charge.

"So, Abeo, I will come fetch you around five. We can have some wine and get to know each other. The music starts at six."

Chi-Chi was tickled pink. Problem solved. Abeo would not be at her house when Cullen came to pick her up. She would deal with his ire later. After all, Abeo was a grown man approaching his fortieth birthday. Who knows? He might actually enjoy himself.

"Come. We need to get back to the shop." Chi-Chi pried her brother's arm from Jennine's and put it through hers.

"See you later, handsome," Jennine said, batting her very long, very fake eyelashes.

Chi-Chi hurried them out of Jennine's grasp. Chi-Chi was having second thoughts about that introduction. Then she reminded herself again, *He's a grown man.*

Abeo finally let out a long breath of air. He didn't realize he had been holding it for what seemed like half a lifetime. He muttered under his breath, "What are you trying to do to me?"

Chi-Chi slowed her step. "Oh, *buroda,*" she said, addressing him in Yoruba, "she is a very nice woman. Perhaps a little too friendly at times, but you will certainly be entertained."

"And who knows what else?" Abeo was still trying to comprehend what he had just witnessed. "That woman is a cheetah!"

"You mean cougar?" Chi-Chi snickered.

"I know the difference, dear sister. The jaguar may have the strongest bite, but the cheetah is the fastest animal on land."

Chi-Chi burst out laughing. "You know they refer to women of a certain age who hunt younger men as cougars?"

"She is still too fast for me." Abeo shook his head.

Chi-Chi chuckled. "You can take care of

yourself."

"Maybe I need a chaperone?" Abeo's mood lightened.

"I will introduce you to a few more people so if you need to escape the claws of Jennine, there will be someone you can hide behind." Chi-Chi was very amused at the situation she had created.

"I hope so." Abeo fanned himself with his hand. "She is a few degrees warmer than most other women."

Chi-Chi started to cackle. "And you thought you would have to entertain yourself tonight."

Abeo gave her a sideways look. "I should have kept my original plan and waited until Monday."

Chi-Chi elbowed him in the side, then kept her word and made sure Abeo met several other artists and vendors, subtly dropping the news that he had been introduced to Jennine. Vic from the Wine Cellar gave Abeo a knowing look, as did Brian Tucker from the Cheese Cave. The women simply smirked. Jennine was truly a nice person. She would go out of her way to be helpful. But when it came to men, her hormones were like a nuclear missile aimed right at them.

It was nearly five, and Chi-Chi was scrambling to put away the high-end jewelry. Most people who attended the open-house events weren't interested in spending oodles of cash. Her more moderately priced items, those under $100, were popular. During a fund-raiser, she had a broad assortment because a portion of the proceeds went to the charity. Rather than keep the items that fetched $1000 or more on display, she had large, silver-framed photos of her work throughout the shop. This way she had both ends covered.

Abeo was standing in the doorway, taking in the activities in the atrium. Chi-Chi called out, "Abeo, I am leaving now. You stay out of trouble. I am leaving a key to my house on my desk in the office. Do not wait up for me."

"Ah, and sister, do not wait up for me either!" He had the widest grin of the day on his face.

Tori was proud that she had remained calm and cool since the unexpected result of her evening outside Ringo's. Her husband had been reasonable and more attentive than usual. He had even brought dinner home one night. Tori figured it was guilt, which was fine with her. She was much more relaxed knowing she had something on him.

But it didn't make her any happier. Power-ful? Yes. That was better than where she had been a few short weeks ago.

She climbed out of bed and got ready to head back to Stillwell. It was her day to attend the origami workshop. It dawned on her that he hadn't noticed the crane until she mentioned it to him a few days before.

"I'm going to take a workshop this week-end," Tori announced.

His head jerked back when she told him. It was the first time she made a decision without consulting him first. "Oh?" He sounded much more surprised than an-noyed.

"Yes." She brought the crane into the kitchen where he was sitting. "Origami."

"That Chinese or something?" he asked.

"No." She stopped herself from saying, "You idiot." "It's a Japanese paper-folding art form. Thousands of years old."

"What? That thing is a thousand years old?"

Cripes, could you be any stupider today? she thought.

"Yes. I got it from an archeological dig." She sneered.

"Ha. Oh, I get it. A little snarky, are we?"

"Sorry. I made this when I went to the art center. Doing origami is very interesting and relaxing. The woman who owns the shop is having a workshop today, and I signed up for it." Tory was standing her ground, and she wasn't about to divulge either of her secrets.

"Well, good for you, I guess. What are you going to do with your newfound talent?"

"Who's being snarky now?" She put her hands on her hips.

He put up his hands. "I give up. You go and fold your papers. I'm going to shoot pool."

"Ringo's?" Tori waited for his reaction.

"No. A new place. It's an arcade in Chester."

Chester was a town about eight miles north of where they lived.

"Who are you going with?" Tori again waited for a reaction.

"Jack and a few other guys."

"Well, OK. Have fun." The chill was gone from her voice, and she headed out the door.

"You too!" he called after her.

Tori knew she was going to have to confront him soon. She was starting to feel a bit puffy, the way pregnant women look before their bellies start to bulge.

Two major things to discuss was going to take a lot of strength. *I'm pregnant, and you're cheating.* How does one start that conversation?

Tori plugged the address to the art center into her GPS. She knew the way but she liked to know if there were any detours and how long it would take to arrive. According to the calculation, she should be pulling into the Stillwell parking lot in forty minutes. There was very little traffic, and she cruised along to the sounds of country music singer Miranda Lambert. Not only was she beautiful but she had a lovely, lilting voice. Tori remembered the humiliation Miranda had suffered when the tabloids were all over the Blake Shelton and Gwen Stefani affair. Who knows when it had started, but it was clear Miranda was devastated. Speculation was that he chose being a judge on the show *The Voice* over his marriage.

Tori took comfort knowing that if someone like Miranda Lambert had marriage problems, anyone could. Plus, if Tori's personal issues became public, at least they wouldn't make it to national television.

The drive to the center took less time than she'd thought. She had over an hour to spare before the workshop began. Tori decided to get another one of those excellent sandwiches and do a little more window-shopping.

As she passed the Jimmy Can-Do Shop,

she stopped abruptly. Out of the corner of her eye she thought she spotted something that resembled a double-wide trailer. Chills went up her spine. She was drawn to it and repulsed at the same time. She cautiously moved past large metal palm trees, an assortment of animals, both wild and domestic, vases, sundials, and weather vanes.

She moved closer to the three-foot replica of the trailer-style house. It gave her the spookiest feeling. A major flash from her past. She peered at it intently. Even the details looked familiar. More goose bumps went up her spine and down her arms. She couldn't get out of there fast enough. If she weren't pregnant, she would have run to the wine shop and bought a bottle. Instead, she bolted to the Namaste Café for a cup of chamomile tea. A young woman greeted her at the door. "Welcome to the Namaste Café. How can I make your day better?"

Tori was caught off guard. Her first thought was *Get that thing out of there!* But she knew that her guilt was getting the better of her.

CHAPTER FOURTEEN

The weekend

Luna mapped out her route to Charlotte and entered Gaines's address into her GPS. She broke up the scone in several pieces so she wouldn't be messing with it when she was on the highway. The GPS gave her two choices, and she decided she would take Interstate 40 to 321 South. Route 74 was more scenic, but she wanted to get there by the most direct route. Today she wasn't interested in the flora and fauna of the countryside. She was nervous enough. The sooner she got there, the better. If all went well, the trip would take two hours. She picked a playlist of music to listen to on the way. It occurred to her that she didn't know much about Gaines's taste in music. She knew he wasn't into heavy metal or rap, but she wondered what he listened to when he was home. She guessed she would find out soon.

Between verses of "Love Shack" she

chewed happily on the sweet dough.

The ride went without a hitch and she was soon pulling into Gaines's driveway. It was exactly how she pictured it, with large shade trees and a meticulous lawn. The driveway was wide enough for two vehicles, so she parked next to his. As she unlocked the cargo door, Gaines appeared in his doorway. He hurried to the car to help her with her bag. This time there was no debate about a welcome hug. And it was a good one. Luna thought he just might swing her around.

He still held her close. "Good to see you." His smile and eyes were like neon welcome signs. He could not contain his delight. "Wow. You're really here!" He finally let her loose and took a step back.

"I am indeed." Luna could hardly believe it herself. Luna popped the tailgate as Gaines moved to the back of her car.

"Let me help you with your things." He grabbed her weekend bag. "You pack light." He chuckled.

"Oh, you should have seen what I started with!" Luna was surprisingly relaxed now. When she first got in her car, she was gripping the wheel for almost an hour. Now that she was finally at his place, she felt she could breathe normally. *Just be yourself,* she kept telling herself. "Your trees are magnificent." She gestured toward the red maples and the willow oaks.

"Wish I could take credit, but they were here long before I bought the place." Gaines smiled. "Come on."

He led the way to the front door.

It was exactly how she pictured it. A small step down into a living room that ran from the front to the back, with a large picture window that looked out onto the yard. A fireplace was on the left and a wall on the right separated it from the kitchen. The dining area was to the right of the living room, in front of the kitchen area. To the left was a hallway that led to the bathroom and two bedrooms. For its modest size, it had an open feel to it.

"Welcome to my humble abode." Gaines set down her bag.

"It's great. The way you made it sound, I was expecting a tumbled-down shack!" Luna replied. "But I see what you mean about brown." The old walnut-colored paneling was a throwback to the 1950s.

"Wait until you see the kitchen." Gaines chuckled.

"What's left of it, that is." He walked through the living room, skirting the big ugly brown sofa, and turned the corner into the dining area.

Luna set the pastry boxes on the makeshift table. "What a beautiful setting." Luna noticed the flowers immediately. "Don't tell me you arranged them yourself," she taunted him.

"I arranged for them to be delivered. Does that count?"

"Most definitely." Luna peered through the skeleton walls where he had ripped down the Sheetrock.

"A little renovating?"

"Yes. This is where I'm stuck. I have to remodel this kitchen, but I'm not sure how to approach it."

"My first suggestion is to eliminate this wall if you can and put an island with a snack bar on this side."

"That's exactly what I was thinking, but it's a load bearing wall, so it would need to be supported."

"Put decorative columns on each side of the island." Luna pointed to the two-by-fours. "Then you can put a cabinet with glass doors if you wanted over the island. Or some cool lighting." Luna was still holding her tote bag and pulled out her sketch pad.

"Hold on there, missy. Let's get you settled first. Follow me." Gaines led her to the other side of the house and into Carter's room. That, too, was just as she had pictured it. Single bed with pennants and posters; a bookcase with trophies; and an assortment of Power Ranger figures; a small desk and a bean bag chair.

Luna laughed lightly. "No mistaking this for anything other than a teenager's room."

"I scoured the room for anything, uh, adolescent."

Gaines was referring to the possibility of girlie magazines.

"They don't need magazines for that." Luna laughed out loud. "Remember when water was free and you had to pay for porn?"

Gaines let out a guffaw. "Now *that's* funny."

"Not that I would know about that." Luna looked quite sincere.

"I don't doubt you." Gaines smiled. "Do you need to hang anything in the closet? That's one area I didn't check, but there are hooks on the back of the door. I'll grab a couple of hangers."

"Not necessary. I can keep everything in my bag."

Gaines cleared a small bench. "You can put it here."

"Thanks. You are a gracious host." Luna wanted to kiss him right then and there.

"Are you hungry?" Gaines asked. "I have

some cheese and fruit if you'd like."

"That would be great. Thanks! I had a scone on my way." She looked down and noticed a few crumbs on her jacket. "Leftovers." She picked off the scraps and handed them to Gaines.

"You are too kind."

"But seriously, I have something for you." Luna went back into the dining room and handed him the two boxes from the Flakey Tart.

He took a whiff before he opened them. "You shouldn't have."

"I know. But I did."

"Please sit." He pulled one of the mismatched chairs out for her while he fixed a plate of brie, Manchego cheese, and grapes. "What would you like to drink?"

"What time is it?" Luna giggled.

"A little before three."

"OK. I'll wait until five, then have a glass of wine. If that's OK with you?" Luna knew one glass would help her relax a little more.

"Speaking of dinner," Gaines threw in.

"Was I?" Luna gave him her sideways glance.

"No, but I am. Would you like to go out to dinner? There are a number of fine restaurants in town. Or." He paused. "I have two very nice prime steaks, Idaho potatoes, and salad fixings if you want to hang around here."

"You know what? I think hanging around here would be swell. We eat out so often that a nice relaxing home-cooked dinner would be super."

"Not exactly a home-cooked meal, but steaks on the grill can be delicious."

"If you're cooking, then it's home-cooked as far as I'm concerned."

Gaines brought the plate of cheese and fruit to the table, plus two glasses and a bottle of water.

Luna noticed the bottle was similar to those they have in restaurants. They were often referred to as French water bottles. Why? Who knew?

"Did this come with the house?" Luna asked, tapping the side of the bottle with her pen.

"No. I got it at a big-box store actually."

"I like it. Makes me aware of how much water I'm drinking. Or should be drinking."

"That's exactly why I bought it. I know I have to finish one of these a day."

"Great minds . . ." Luna added.

She pulled out her sketch pad, a ruler, and a tape measure and began to draw her concept of what the island cabinet would look like.

"I don't know about you, but I prefer an open floor plan. It makes the chi-chi flow better."

"Chi-Chi?" Gaines was a little confused.

"Oh, not *our* Chi-Chi!" Luna cackled. "Chi-chi as in energy."

"I knew that." Gaines faked a response.

"I know you know about chi-chi energy, but it can be a little confusing at times."

Within a couple of minutes, she presented a rough sketch of an island cabinet with a countertop, two pillars, and three hanging lights.

Gaines stood behind her and placed his arms on either side of her, leaning over her shoulder. She could feel the heat from his breath on her neck.

"Where did you learn how to draw like this?"

She tried not to stutter. "It's innate. Maybe I was an architect in a previous life," she joked. Sorta. "When I was in sixth grade, we had an assignment to draw a floor plan of our bedroom. It had to do with windows and air flow. I had graph paper and did an impeccable job. It was so good the teacher called my parents to see if I had cheated!" She tapped her pencil. "They didn't even know about it. To me it was just another homework assignment, except it was the kind of homework I enjoyed."

"So why didn't you pursue architecture?"

"Because the mechanical drawing teacher wouldn't let me in the class. He said he didn't want a girl distracting the boys. Imagine that!"

"He'd never get away with that today, that's for sure," Gaines said.

"You ain't kiddin'. I was on the cusp of the sexual revolution. And it's still revolting. Women have to work much harder than men and get paid eighty percent of what they are for doing the same job, only better. But don't get me started." She laughed.

"I totally get it. I am glad I don't have to raise a daughter. Although I'm sure she would be a daddy's girl, but a son just seems much easier."

"Tell that to a mother chasing after a three-year-old boy!"

"Good point. I think that was one of the many arguments my ex and I had. She would be exhausted by the end of the day. And not in a terrific mood either."

Luna realized that was one of the very few times he had mentioned his ex-wife. "So now you're dealing with an adolescent."

Gaines chuckled. "Yeah. Lucky me. But he's really a good kid. As far as I know anyway." He slowly disengaged himself from his position and stood up. Luna thought she was going to faint. There was an obvious level of intimacy between the two of them. The question was who was going to make the first move? Or had they already? Maybe it was time for the second move. But who was going to be the one to do it?

She made a rough sketch of the existing kitchen floor plan. "Gas or electric?" She nodded at the old avocado-colored stove.

"Gas."

"OK. Basement?"

"Full size."

"Great. We'll remove the broom closet and move the fridge there. That will give you more counter space between the stove and refrigerator. You won't lose any cabinet space once you install the island. And we can put a pantry cabinet at the end of this wall." She pointed to the wall that separated the kitchen from the living room. "It will be a functional L-shape work space with the island in the middle." She scribbled her idea on the pad. "You'll have more counter space and room for a dishwasher." She showed him her idea.

"I hear the sound of a cash register." Gaines moaned.

"Look. You already took down the Sheet-rock. Yes, appliances are expensive, but you don't have to go all Viking or Sub-Zero. There are very good moderately priced appliances that are available, unless you're planning on doing a Martha Stewart cooking demo in here." She looked up at him and smiled.

"So, what do you think this production is going to cost?"

She took out her tape measure and nodded to him.

"Let's take some measurements."

When they were done, she did a few calculations. The area was twelve-by-twelve. She was talking out loud. "Allowing thirty-six inches for the refrigerator, thirty inches for the stove, twenty-four inches for the return cabinets, you can put a thirty-inch base between the stove and fridge, and either a twenty-four-inch drawer cabinet or doors. On the sink side, you'll have a pantry cabinet at the end, and there should be enough counter space if you want to make it a dry bar or wet bar. The island would be one solid piece. I think the biggest job will be the load bearing wall."

Gaines took a big deep breath. "I'm planning on doing a lot of the work myself, with the exception of plumbing and electrical work."

"Did you have a budget in mind?"

"Yes, but I think I was being delusional."

"For example?"

"I was thinking twenty grand?"

"If you don't use slate or granite, you might be able to bring it in under thirty."

"But isn't granite the big thing now?"

"There are a lot of options that are half the price. Trust me. You get light-colored cabinets, stainless appliances, good lighting, the countertop will not be the focal point. The island will be. You can use granite there if you want. But honestly, with a kid and his friends, granite can chip, and it's way expensive to fix. I'll go with you to pick stuff out when you're ready. And I bet Cullen can find you a really cool light fixture for the island. A few high-hat floods on dimmers. It will look great."

"You sure you want to take it on?"

Luna was imagining herself in the finished product. "Yes. It will be fun. Especially since I won't be paying for it!" She hooted. "Now, about all this brown." She stood and twirled her finger around the room.

"I get a headache thinking about removing it. Lord knows what's underneath. If anything." Gaines sighed again.

"What I suggest is a chair railing. You can cover the bottom section with a light-colored fabric and paint the top section white or light gray. Do it all the way around. It will make the place feel bigger, too." Luna looked down. "At least the floors look good."

"Before I moved in, I sanded them and put a few coats of polyurethane on them."

She glanced at the fireplace. "And . . . that could use a coat of paint, or something. But I'd wait until you get the walls done." Luna folded her arms, waiting for his reaction.

Gaines put his hands on each of her shoulders and kissed her on the forehead. "You are a genius, Luna Bodhi Bodman!"

It wasn't exactly the reaction she was hoping for, but the evening was still young.

Cullen must have tied his tie three times before he got it right and comfortable. He combed his hair back with a little gel. Then he wondered if it was too much. Over the top. Luna had told him to do it, and she had a very good eye for aesthetics. Plus, she would never steer him wrong. He was still a bit reticent about the cologne. Luna showed him how to apply it. Instead of spraying it directly on himself, he was to spray it up in the air, over his head. "You want to get the scent but you don't want to knock her out," Luna told him. "Women spray the space in front of them and walk through it so the mist settles on their body and clothes. For guys, you don't need the whole shebang. But, if your hair smells good, you'll smell good."

He felt ridiculous spraying expensive cologne in the air, but as Luna would say, "Go for it." He gave it a test run by spraying it a few feet in front of him. He got the drift. He chuckled to himself, *No pun intended.* Then he tried it for real, spritzing his Hugo Boss arm's length above his head.

He checked his tie for the zillionth time and decided he should get moving even if he was early. He was getting jittery and didn't want to second-guess his attire. Even if he had to drive around the block a few times, it would be better than standing in front of a mirror.

He grabbed his keys and gave Wiley a rub. "Anything in particular you want to watch on TV?" The dog looked up at him as if to say, *"Et tu, Brute?"*

Cullen responded with, "I know. I know. Everyone is abandoning you tonight. I should have planned a playdate with Ziggy and Marley." Wiley began to wag his tail. "Oh no, that's not what I meant." Wiley moved into a prone position and pulled his paws over his eyes.

"Jeez. OK. How about I put on Cartoon

Network for you?"

Wiley picked up his head.

"I think *Looney Tunes* are on. Maybe *SpongeBob*?" Wiley's tail began to bounce, and he lifted his head.

"You got it!" Cullen could not believe he was having a conversation with his sister's dog. But it wasn't the first time either. Cullen picked up the remote and set the TV to the channel as Wiley made himself comfortable on the sofa. Cullen chuckled. "You are one smart pooch!" Wiley woofed in agreement.

Chi-Chi didn't know if she should dress full-on Nigerian with one of her fabulous caftans or go urban with a black halter jumpsuit and one of her stunning necklaces and matching bracelet. She decided to show off her art and plucked the black jumpsuit from her wardrobe closet. She picked the silver plastron collier necklace with the large polished amethyst stones, with matching earrings and cuff bracelet. She wore amethyst eye shadow with a very thin silver eyeliner. Highlighter on her cheekbones and peach matte lipstick finished the look. And she looked good. Even if she said so herself. She pulled on a pair of two-inch block sandals so she would be slightly shorter than

Cullen. Chi-Chi stood five-seven in flats, so the spike heels were out of the question unless she wanted to look Cullen square in the eye. She opted to be slightly demure. Besides, the sandals were much more comfortable.

She kept checking her watch and thought about Luna. Chi-Chi resisted the temptation to call her while her sister by another mother was at Gaines's house. Maybe a text? Why not? Luna could choose not to answer. Chi-Chi picked up her phone and tapped.

How's it going?

Within a few minutes she got a ping.

Great. He's outside grilling steaks! I'm a bit nervous.

Chi-Chi tapped back.

Ha! Me too!

Luna responded.

OMG. He's here!

Chi-Chi typed back.

Have fun! Ciao for now!

Luna signed off.

Chi-Chi heard a car door open and close. She took a long inhale and an equal exhale, then opened the door.

Cullen had to catch his breath. She looked spectacular. He could barely speak. "Chi-Chi, you are radiant. Beautiful. Not that you aren't always beautiful, but . . ." He was sputtering.

Chi-Chi helped him out. "Thank you. You look quite handsome. The color of the shirt brings out the green in your eyes."

Cullen attempted to stifle a blush and took a slight bow.

"I am very excited to have dinner tonight." Chi-Chi was nervous *and* excited.

"Me too. Thank you for agreeing to join me," Cullen said.

"I do not think your sister would have it any other way." Chi-Chi smiled.

Cullen chuckled. "She is quite the Lunatic. Shall we?" He gestured toward his waiting vehicle. It was a town car.

"This is not yours," Chi-Chi stated.

"No. I didn't want you to have to climb into my SUV."

"Thank you, but . . ." She stopped herself and remembered one of Luna's teachings, *Accept the compliment or the act of kindness with grace. Do not stipulate.* "That was very thoughtful." She grabbed her clutch and a deep purple wrap with silver threads.

Definitely a knockout. He didn't want to sound too smarmy, so he only let that thought form a balloon in his mind.

The driver got out and opened the rear passenger door for them.

"This is quite a treat." Chi-Chi got comfortable in the soft leather seat. Cullen followed. The ride to the restaurant took just under twenty minutes. Chi-Chi was very chatty, recounting her afternoon with her brother and introducing him to some of the artists. When she got to the part about Jennine, she and Cullen were laughing so hard they were on the verge of tears.

When they arrived at the restaurant, the driver repeated the action. He put out his hand to assist Chi-Chi getting out of the car. She turned and smiled at Cullen, who got out on his side without the help of the driver. He quickly moved to her side as they entered the building and opened the door. He wanted anyone who was watching to know he was with this gorgeous creature. He thought she looked like a goddess.

The maître d' showed them to their table as a small jazz combo played in the background.

"This is lovely," Chi-Chi commented, as

the gentleman pulled out her chair. "Thank you."

"My pleasure, madam." He handed her a menu and turned to Cullen. "Monsieur. Your server will be with you shortly." He gave a short, quick nod, tossing his hair aside.

Chi-Chi repressed a giggle as he walked away. "He has watched many movies."

"A bit dramatic, yes." Cullen perused the menu as they waited for their server. "I haven't had escargot in a long time. I am sure it's one of their specialties."

Chi-Chi let out a soft grunt. "They are too slimy for me. But please, do not think you should not order them. I do not mind if other people eat them but I cannot open my lips to one of them."

The waiter approached their table. "*Bonsoir, madam et monsieur.* Would you care for a cocktail?"

Cullen was keen to reply with *"Oui,"* but Chi-Chi caught his eye and gave him a raised eyebrow. Instead, he responded by asking Chi-Chi if she wanted a cocktail or wine.

"I would like a Hendrick's martini with a crush of cucumber, please."

"Very well. And you, sir?"

"I'll have the same, but also please bring

the wine list."

The waiter rattled off the specials and they settled on the seven-course tasting menu. They would start with canapes, then on to hors d'oeuvres, fish, poultry, salad, cheese, and dessert. Cullen ordered a bottle of Alphonse Mellot Sancerre "Edmond." It had a 93 rating but wasn't going to break the bank. "This should go with all of our courses."

Chi-Chi started to giggle. "Remember the stories you and Chris told about ordering wine and champagne and didn't know the cost?"

Cullen chuckled. "At least here the prices are listed. I'm not going to make that mistake again."

The food was scrumptious and the presentations works of art. Both Chi-Chi and Cullen appreciated the aesthetic of the plating. And every course tasted better than the one before.

Just before the dessert course, Chi-Chi excused herself to go to the ladies' room. After a while, Cullen checked his watch. She had been gone for almost fifteen minutes. He wondered what was taking her so long. It could have been the jumpsuit. Even though he was a man, he knew it took a bit of gymnastics to get in and out of those things. He kept looking in the direction of the ladies' lounge. Still no Chi-Chi.

Luna set her phone down on the console table behind the big ugly brown leather couch. She went to the door on the far wall of the dining room. It led to a small mudroom, where Gaines had positioned the refurbished armoire Cullen rescued from a storage sale. Another door led to basement stairs, and an exterior door opened out to the carport. It was neat as a pin. The whole house was neat as a pin. You'd never guess a man with a teenage son lived in it. Granted, Carter was only there every other weekend and a few nights a week, but that was enough time for an adolescent to cause havoc.

She went back to the dining-room area, where a large sliding patio door opened to the deck. "How's it going?"

"Grill is almost ready. How are the potatoes doing?"

"Ten more minutes." She leaned on the railing. "This is really lovely."

"Thanks. I built the deck in the spring. I wanted to have some outdoor living space. I never understood why the previous owners hadn't done it. It's a great yard, with a lot of shade trees."

"Do you garden?" Luna queried.

"If you mean do I grow tomatoes? Yes. But that's it. Don't have much of a green thumb."

"Then who takes care of the bushes and perennials?"

"Believe it or not, Carter does. Last summer, it was a project for the Scouts." Gaines laughed. "Keeps me from getting down in the weeds."

"He sounds like a well-rounded kid."

"I like to think so." Gaines opened the grill, salted the steaks, and popped them on the grate.

"I'll go make a salad and set the table," Luna offered.

"I didn't plan on making dinner and putting you to work." Gaines gave her one of his "be still my heart" smiles.

Luna could swear he had a twinkle in his eye. "It's not work. I love to cook, but I don't do it enough."

"Tell you what. Before you dive into the greens, bring out the bottle of wine that's sitting on the counter. I'll uncork it and put in the carafe. It's a really nice cab. Needs a few minutes to open."

"I can do that." Then she thought twice. *Men like to do that sort of thing. Don't be so . . . Luna-ish trying to orchestrate every-*

327

thing. "On second thought, I'll let you do it. I would probably break the cork." She went back inside and returned with the bottle and corkscrew. Gaines skillfully uncorked the bottle and handed it back to her. "The carafe should be on the counter where the wine was."

"Capisce!" Luna snickered and went back inside. She poured the wine and put the carafe on the table. She was about to look for the plates and glasses.

It was as if Gaines was reading her mind because he called out, "Cabinet left of the sink."

She stopped suddenly. *How did he know what I was going to ask?* "Hey. How did you know I was just about to ask you?"

"Deductive reasoning. The salad fixings are obviously in the refrigerator."

"But what if I was about to ask where the salad bowl is?"

"Yeah. But you didn't." He chuckled. Two could play the woo-woo game.

"Huh." Luna shook her head. Yep. There was definitely a *thing* going on with them.

Before they sat down for dinner, Gaines lit a fire and placed the first album on his turntable. As he was dropping the needle on to the vinyl record, he smirked. "And they mocked me when I refused to let go of my record collection. Now it's one of the hottest medias for music. You just can't get the same sound when it's mixed for streaming."

Luna had to agree. And she liked his taste in his collection.

The steaks were grilled to perfection, the potato skins were crisp, the salad a medley of lettuces, and the luscious wine was a perfect pairing. Their conversation flowed easily. Gaines talked a lot about his son, Luna about her dog. They continued to gab as they cleaned up the plates. Gaines grabbed the carafe and their two wineglasses and brought them over to the makeshift cocktail table. It was two wooden crates with a piece of shelving on top. "I see another project for Cullen." Luna eyed the configuration.

Gaines poured a little more into her glass and sat next to her on the couch, their arms nestled next to each other. Chris put down his glass and took Luna's from her and placed it next to his on the table. He turned and leaned in to kiss her when her phone rudely rang. She huffed and glanced over. When she saw that it was Cullen, she panicked. She knew he wouldn't call unless it was an emergency. "I have to take this."

She grabbed the phone and barked. "You'd better be dying."

Cullen's voice was gasping. "It's Chi-Chi!"

"Chi-Chi? What happened is she all right?"

"Yes. Listen." Cullen stopped talking.

"Listen to what?"

"Chi-Chi. It's Chi-Chi," he repeated in a whisper.

"Cullen, get a grip. What are you talking about?" She put the phone on speaker.

"Just listen."

Luna looked up at Gaines and shrugged her shoulders. All she could hear was music in the background. A woman was singing.

"Cullen? Are you still there?"

"Sshhhhh," he whispered again.

"I think he's had too much to drink or he's having a stroke." Luna looked pleadingly at Gaines. Then it hit her. It was Chi-Chi singing "Sweet Love." "Holy smoke. I thought it was Anita Baker," Luna whispered.

When the song ended, Luna could hear the applause in the background and someone saying, "Ladies and gentlemen, that was Lebici Stone."

"Gotta go." Cullen clicked off the call.

"Well I'll be a monkey's uncle," Gaines

said with relief and surprise.

"Wow. I wonder how he got her to do that," Luna mused. She couldn't help but send him a text.

How?

He typed back.

Dunno. Big surprise. Gotta go.

"You can be the monkey's uncle, and I'll be his aunt," Luna said.

"That woman has some set of chops." Gaines was truly impressed.

"For real. But I could kill Cullen. He had me frightened half to death." Luna pouted.

Gaines thought that was a good opportunity to put his arm around her. Pretend he was offering comfort in her time of distress.

She snugged into his chest as if it were something they had done together many times before. The lights began to flicker. The flickering became more constant until the lights went completely dark.

"Oh, here we go," Gaines said, but didn't move. "Whenever we get a few gusts of wind, we lose power."

"Does that happen often?" Luna asked. But she didn't seem to mind.

"Often enough that there's an investigation going on. Someone is asleep at the switch, and no one is writing checks for maintenance."

"How long does it usually last?" Luna thought it rather romantic. "At least we have a fire."

"And a couple of candles." With all the activity, he had forgotten to light them. "Don't go anywhere." He got up and put one on the fake cocktail table and lit the one on the mantel.

He sat back down. "Now, where were we?"

Luna was happy to recall exactly where he was sitting, took his arm, and put it around her shoulder and nestled in closer. She rested her head on his chest, and he brushed the few wisps of hair from her cheek.

"I'm really happy you came out here," he said in a soft voice.

"Mmmm . . . me too," Luna cooed. With the power out, the only sound was the crackling of the fire and their breaths in rhythm with each other.

She looked up at him. "Did anyone ever tell you that you look a little like Jay Hernandez? The new guy on *Magnum P.I.*?"

"Wait until the lights come back on." Gaines laughed and disengaged himself from the sofa. "Don't go anywhere."

Luna let out a slight "nuh-huh."

Gaines grabbed the flashlight he normally kept in the living room for the many times the power went out.

He went into his bedroom and pulled two pillows against his nose. They were fresh and clean. Then he grabbed the coverlet that sat at the foot of his bed. Another sniff test. "Those cleaning people did a spectacular job," he muttered to himself. When he got back to the sofa, Luna was stretched out. He couldn't tell if she had fallen asleep. He moved carefully in her direction and squatted on the floor next to her. He gently lifted her head and put one of the pillows under it. Her eyes fluttered, and she made a soft murmur of contentment.

He whispered, "Do you want to stay here or go to bed?"

Luna reached up and touched his face. "Both."

As Chi-Chi made her way back to the table, Cullen shot up from his chair, took her hand, and gently kissed the back of it. "You are not only the most beautiful woman in the room. You are the most talented."

Chi-Chi fanned her face with her free hand. "I cannot believe I did that." Cullen pulled out her chair for her to sit.

"Honestly, I can't either, and it was wonderful. You had been gone so long, I thought you might have left," Cullen said.

"First of all, I would not do such a thing, especially to you. And second, I had to speak with the group's leader to see if they could play that song in my key. I am sorry if I caused you any discomfort."

"It was well worth it." Cullen couldn't stop staring at her.

A few minutes later, the maître d' came to the table with a split of Veuve Clicquot champagne. "Compliments of the house. That was an impressive performance." This time he wasn't as affected as when he had seated them.

"You are very kind. Thank you." Chi-Chi was on the verge of blushing. She was thankful her honey-toned complexion masked any embarrassing color that might have appeared on her face.

"Yes. Impressive." Cullen lifted his glass and made a toast. "To a most delightful and memorable evening."

"Thank you. I do not remember the last time I had such an enjoyable night." Chi-Chi smiled at Cullen. "I supposed we should thank your sister for suggesting this."

"Don't worry. She'll take all the credit." Cullen laughed.

They took their time with dessert and sipped the champagne. Cullen took care of the check, and they began to leave the restaurant. Everyone they passed said something kind to Chi-Chi about her singing.

"You're a bit of a celebrity." Cullen could not have been prouder.

The town car was waiting for them at the valet station. Again, the driver opened the door and ushered Chi-Chi in. Cullen followed.

Chi-Chi intuitively took Cullen's hand and held it the entire drive to her house. Both had few words to say. The energy and mood between them spoke volumes.

When they arrived at her house, the driver opened her side of the car. Cullen jumped out. "I've got it from here." He walked her to the door.

"I would invite you in, but as you know, my nosy brother is in town, and I do not know when he will be coming back. I could hope not until tomorrow, but Abeo can be unpredictable, as you discovered with his early arrival."

"I'll take a rain check." Cullen didn't mind. It would give him something to look forward to.

Chi-Chi took both of his hands. "But I would like to invite you to kiss me good night. Or allow *me* to kiss *you* good night."

"Permission granted." Cullen pulled her close and accommodated both requests. The fireworks between them was like the Fourth of July. They had been standing in an embrace for several minutes when they were startled by her brother opening the door.

"Ka a ale!" Abeo blurted with his big baritone voice.

"Abeo! Where is your car?"

A chipper voice from inside the house rang out. "Hellooo . . ." It was the familiar greeting from none other than Jennine, the pottery queen.

Tori arrived home around dinnertime. She felt light and invigorated. The creative spirit of the origami workshop was stimulating. Chatting with other people came much easier than she had thought it would. They had something in common, whether it was wanting to learn the art of paper folding or finding a respite from the busy world. She hadn't finished the mobile yet. She still had a few more animals to work on, so she decided to go again the following month. She realized she would probably be showing a baby bump at that point. Meanwhile, she had to figure out a way to tell her husband all the things that had been festering for the past twenty years. *Twenty years is a long time,* she thought to herself, but then again, it goes by lickety-split. She knew she should have spoken up years ago, but she hated confrontation. She also knew that was no excuse. *Put on your big-girl pants.* She giggled, thinking she would need them soon enough.

Her husband wasn't home yet from wherever he had been, so she sent him a text.

Hi. Just got home. Dinner?

She was surprised at his rapid response.

Be there soon. Need anything?

Tori looked twice at the number. It was his. *How odd.* He rarely, if ever, asked.

Dessert?
Anything in particular?
Surprise me.

As if she wasn't already surprised by his interaction. She supposed it was guilt.

She took a package of chicken from the refrigerator and soaked it in salted water for ten minutes. She was a firm believer in brining the chicken before cooking. It made it more tender.

She stirred together a marinade and let the chicken steep in it for a half hour. She sliced the potatoes and placed them in a single layer in a baking dish, then placed the chicken on top. It was a new recipe she had picked up from a magazine. The juice from the chicken and marinade soaked into the potatoes as they roasted in the oven. String beans almondine would be a side dish. She never realized how easy it was to make fancy vegetables. Sliced almonds browned in butter and then tossed through the steamed beans. She felt like a gourmet chef.

Twenty minutes later, her husband arrived with an apple pie and vanilla ice cream.

"Oh my goodness. Where did you get a fresh apple pie at this hour?"

He didn't want to tell her that he had made his own journey to Stillwell Art Center. He waited until she was on her way so she wouldn't know he was following her. She had been acting out of character, and he thought something was amiss. It was a good half hour before he went into the center. He had checked the floor plan of the center on the Internet and confirmed the existence of an origami studio and the workshop. He waited until a half hour passed before he went into the center and kept close to the foliage. He had been on surveillance several times so he was sure he could avoid her line of sight, especially with the studio being tucked away on the side wing. Relieved she was really where she said she going to be, he spotted a pastry shop where the aroma of fresh-baked pies wafted through the air. Even though they didn't bake on the premises, the smell of fresh pastry was undeniable. He knew he would have to come clean once they both got back to the house, but it would be a good opportunity for him to find out what was going on in his wife's head.

"I have a confession to make." He set the pie on the table and pulled out two chairs.

This was when Tori knew he was going to tell her about his affair. She remained calm and collected.

"OK. Go ahead."

"You are probably going to have a conniption fit," he said plainly.

She thought, *You have no idea. I have been waiting for this moment.*

She pulled her phone from her purse, set it on the table, and primly folded her hands. "OK. Go ahead."

"I followed you today." He looked up at her.

Tori was stunned. "You did what?" she said with some skepticism.

"I followed you to the Stillwell Center."

Tori was totally confused. "But why?"

"Tori, honey, you have been acting differently these past couple of weeks."

"Yes, I know I have." She still couldn't grasp what he was saying. "But why did you follow me?"

"I was trying to figure out what was going on with you. The way you've been acting lately, well, I —"

"Now, isn't that rich?" she said, with a huge amount of sarcasm. "Why don't we start with what is going on with *you*?" She flipped through the photos on her phone and pulled one up with him and the trampy-looking woman.

"Wait. What?" He grabbed the phone and increased the picture. "How the hell . . ."

"You tell me." Tori peered at him suspiciously.

"That's Jack's sister, Dana. She's a piece of work."

"Oh, she was working it all right. Obviously. I saw you with her at Ringo's."

"What were you doing at Ringo's?" Now he was the confused one.

"I wanted to try to be more involved with your life. I was going to surprise you.

Instead, you surprised me." She flipped through a few more photos. "I was standing in the entryway. You didn't answer my text that night, either." She gave him a cold stare. "I saw you ignore it."

"I just didn't want to get into anything. Dana was being a pest, and I was trying to dissuade her from mauling me."

"How good of a job did you do?" She kept her stare.

"She backed off and moved on to Joe. Why didn't you ask me about this? Is this why you've been acting, I dunno, distant?"

"I have to tell you something." Tori gulped a good amount of air.

"Are you having an affair?" he asked.

"What?" Tori blurted. "You can't be serious."

"Then what is it?" He had a pleading look in his eye.

For the first time, Tori felt that she could drive this bus. She was matter-of-fact. "Look, I haven't been happy for a very long time. Over the years, we've drifted apart. It's as if we're two strangers living under the same roof."

He buried his head in his hands. "I feel like I've failed you."

Tori was shocked to hear his words. "What do you mean?"

"When I talked you into running away, I had big dreams for us. I wanted to give you everything you never had. A big house. A nice car."

"We have a nice house and a big car," Tori said, with a slight bit of humor.

He snickered. "That wasn't exactly my plan."

"I think that's where we zigged when we should have zagged. We never had a plan. We were flying by the seat of our pants for years. Then when we got comfortable, we became complacent."

"I still love you with all my heart. I honestly do." His eyes were welling up with tears. Tori couldn't remember the last time she had seen him express himself this way. "I know I've been a prig at times, but I'm just mad at myself. I should have done a better job providing for you."

"That's not what I wanted. I can provide for myself just fine."

"Exactly," he muttered.

"What I wanted was a partner. Someone to share my life with, not just a roof over my head. We never talk. We never do anything together." She sighed. And then she realized that they were having the conversation her boss encouraged her to have. "We've made love maybe once or twice in the past eight months." She was sure it was at least once.

"I thought you didn't want me, and you were disappointed in me."

"It's the opposite. I want to share time with you. I want us to be together more. Look, I know you like hanging out with your friends, but that doesn't mean we can't have some quality time together."

He looked up at her, wiping the tears with his sleeve. "Wow. We should have had this talk a long time ago."

"I know, and I blame myself. I've always avoided confrontation. I thought if I brought up anything that you didn't like, we would get into an argument. I guess I was hoping for magic thinking." She used the term George Layton introduced to her during the conversation she had had with him.

"Huh. 'Magic thinking.' Yeah, that probably doesn't work very much, eh?" He finally smiled. "So." He paused. "Do you think there is a chance for us now?" He took her hand and looked into her eyes, pleading for her acceptance.

Tori almost fell off her chair. "Honestly? I would like to think there is, but I don't really know."

"Do you still love me?" His eyes were pleading.

343

"I've always loved you. The *you* I ran away with. This guy" — she pointed at him — "I'm not sure I know him very well."

"I guess I got a little too macho from the job." He nodded. "Then, when you got the job at the law firm and were making the same money as me, I really felt intimidated. I guess I've been acting out. And not in a good way."

She held her breath, and asked, "Would you consider us going to couples counseling?"

"Really?" He blinked several times but seemed genuinely interested.

"Really. And we can keep it to ourselves. No reason to broadcast it to any of our colleagues or friends. Not that I have many."

"I kinda blame myself for that, too." He truly looked forlorn. "I expected you to be the dutiful wife while I was being a half-assed husband. It's as if I had you in a cage."

"Something like that." Tori was happy the conversation was going in an unexpected direction. "I met some nice people today at the workshop. I discovered I like creative and artsy people."

"Wow. You deserve so much more than I've given you."

"Listen, I can only blame myself for keeping my thoughts and wishes from you."

"Honey, I really mean it. I want to have a life with you. A life where we both feel secure."

"OK. Who are you?" Tori grinned. "What have you done with my husband?"

"He's in here somewhere." He pointed to his chest. "Can we start over? Please? I really don't know what I'd do without you in my life."

"I'm willing to try if you are." She lifted his chin and looked him straight in the eye. "Besides, we are having a baby. The child will need a father figure in its life."

His head jerked back. "We are what?"

"Yes, you heard me. I'm pregnant. Imagine. At my age."

"You're still young. A lot of women have babies at thirty-eight now."

"So I've been told." She pulled her chair closer. "This is a big deal."

"You ain't kidding." He put his arms around her. "I am so sorry you've been unhappy. I promise I'll do better, and we will keep our family together."

Family. Tori thought about her abandoned family and was overjoyed she wouldn't be abandoning another one.

He rested his head on her chest. Tori stroked his hair, and said, "We'll both do better. I promise I will never keep any

345

secrets from you ever again," except for the psychic she was still planning on seeing. Tori wanted to get her take on it before she succumbed to a false sense of security. That had happened once. Not again.

The next morning, Luna woke up in the afterglow from the night before. She quickly replayed the night in her head. Had it really happened? Could it have been a dream? No, it was real. She pinched herself just to make sure. She and Gaines had made love for the first time. The passion they unleashed could have brought the power grid back to life, yet it was warm, sweet, and tender at the same time. They were enveloped in the sweet desire that had been kindling for a long time.

It started as a slow dance building to a crescendo in a well-choreographed tango. It was the stuff movies were made of. She smiled, thinking about the scene in an old film with Cary Grant and Grace Kelly. It was *To Catch a Thief,* directed by Alfred Hitchcock. In typical Hitchcock form, he left a lot to one's imagination. As Cary Grant kissed Grace Kelly, the camera zoomed in on fireworks against the Parisian sky.

She rubbed her neck. Two people sleeping

on the sofa was romantic, but not necessarily good for the posture. She stretched and looked around. She could smell the aroma of good coffee. She pulled on Gaines's soft comfortable shirt and walked into the kitchen. He was wearing a T-shirt and jogging pants. "Good morning, sunshine," he said over his shoulder.

"Good morning." She resisted the temptation of rubbing her eyes. Sleeping with contact lenses is never a good idea. She blinked several times, urging her tear ducts to snap to it. "Coffee smells good."

"Someone who owns a café encouraged me to buy one of these newfangled machines." He nodded to the Nespresso coffeemaker.

"She must be a genius," Luna cracked wise.

"I would have to agree." He leaned over to give her a kiss, which she was more than happy to accept.

"How did you sleep?"

"I'm not sure if I did." She stood behind him, wrapped her arms around his waist, and rested her head on his back. "When did the power come back on?"

"About an hour ago."

"I must have been sleeping because I don't remember hearing anything."

"You were out like a light. Ha. No pun intended."

"We seem to do that a lot, don't we?" Luna observed, and let go of her affectionate death grip.

"We do. So, what would you like for breakfast? Bacon and eggs? Scones? Croissants?"

"I'll start with coffee for now." She took the cup from him and sat at the dining-room table. She looked at what she was wearing. His shirt. So much for the $500 she had spent on silk pajamas. She peered through the two-by-fours. "What's on your agenda today?"

"Whatever you want." Gaines brought his coffee into the dining area.

"I didn't want to monopolize your day." Luna was testing him.

"You are here. You are my guest. You have my undivided attention."

"I appreciate that muchly." And she did.

"Do you think we could spend a little time talking over my project?"

"You mean the mystery trunk?"

"I do."

"Absolutely. By the way, you can stay as long as you want. If you want to go back tomorrow, that's OK with me. I don't have to be in until ten."

Luna thought about it for a quick minute. "I need to get back." She really didn't, but she also didn't want to overstay her welcome. They had finally reached a new level of intimacy, and she wanted to keep him wanting more. She remembered her mother's favorite expression, "Don't make yourself too available. Keep them chasing you until you're ready to catch them." As much as she wanted to spend more time with him, she didn't want to come off as clingy. So many women do that after they cross the line of a sexual encounter. Especially if it was mind-blowing sex. Which it had been.

"Like I said, whatever you need to do." He kissed the top of her head and took a seat across from her. It was as if this was something they did often.

Her tote bag was on the mismatched chair next to her. She immediately went into recounting her meeting with the woman named Tori. She described the rough sketches, too. "Wish I had brought them with me, but I do have this." She put on the pair of latex gloves she carried and took the diary out of the plastic bag, followed by the note.

"How was her body language?" Gaines asked.

"She was nervous. Kept twisting her

napkin. But she seemed sweet. Kinda innocent but troubled. There was a sadness
about her. Something in her past is haunt-
ing her, and she has a lot to think about for
her future."

"About how old?"

"Late thirties I'd say."

"When are you going to see her next?"

"Within the next two weeks."

"I can hear your wheels turning," Gaines
teased her.

"Yeah. Yeah." Luna smiled up at him. "But
I would bet there is a link here. Somewhere." She opened the diary, got up, and
walked behind him. Leaning over his shoulder, she continued, "There are very few
entries, but there's a similarity in the
scrawl." Luna then went on to explain how
she had tracked down the carnival company
and narrowed down the time frame. "Ellie
and I are going to go to the library this week
and check the newspaper archives for fires
that took place back then."

"You are becoming quite the detective."
Gaines squinted at the note and the diary.
"It's really hard to tell. The *R* and the *T*
look similar, but the diary is signed with a
V. And the note is signed by someone
named Tori."

"Yeah, that's one thing that is throwing

me off."

Gaines was reading her mind again. "Do you want me to recommend a handwriting analyst?"

"How did you know?" she asked coyly.

"I wouldn't expect any less from you." He grinned. "I have a guy in the office who does this for us. I'll make a copy of both the page and the note."

"Really?"

"For you? Absolutely. Besides, I know you won't stop until you put it all together. I'm just trying to save you some time." He gave her a wide grin. "And me as well." He chuckled.

"You are the best!" Luna threw her arms around his shoulders and kissed him on the cheek.

"So, what are we having for breakfast?" he asked.

"Something easy. Scones?"

"You got it. We'll grab some lunch later and take it to Freedom Park. How does that sound?"

"Sounds perfect, but it will have to do." Luna was over the moon, and Gaines seemed to be traveling at the same speed of light.

CHAPTER FIFTEEN

The weekend wrap-up

On her drive back to Asheville, Luna called Chi-Chi, using her Bluetooth. In unison, they asked, "So? How did it go?" Both laughed out loud

"You go first," Luna encouraged Chi-Chi. "You created quite a stir."

"I can't really say." Chi-Chi was hoping Luna would understand that she couldn't discuss anything at the moment.

"Nosy brother?" Luna chirped.

"Oh. That is not all."

"Now you have to tell me. What?" Luna was hoping it would be about her brother.

"I will have to call you back."

"Wait! You can't leave me hanging."

"I have to make coffee for my guests."

"Cullen? Abeo? Speak, woman, speak!" Luna was practically shouting.

"I cannot say." Chi-Chi was being cryptic, but she knew Luna would get it eventually.

"Is Cullen there?" Luna thought she was in a taffy pull.

"No," Chi-Chi answered.

"So Cullen isn't there but Abeo is and there is someone else?"

"That is correct," Chi-Chi replied. "By the way, do you remember that show we always talk about?"

"Show?" Luna was scouring her brain.

"Yes, the friends that live together?"

"Friends?" Luna knew that wasn't the correct answer. Then it came to her. "You mean *The Golden Girls*?"

"Yes, I believe that is the one."

Luna let out a yelp. "Whoa!"

Chi-Chi had to pull the phone away from her ear.

"Yes, dear. I must get off the phone now."

"No! Wait!" Luna protested.

"But I must," Chi-Chi said.

"OK, but you will meet me at my house at six tonight. Understood?"

"Yes. I will see you later." Chi-Chi clicked off the phone and returned to her houseguests. She was in a state of disbelief. Jennine had nailed her brother. *Literally,* as the saying goes.

Chi-Chi fought fervently to keep her cool. How could her brother, a guest of hers, bring a strange woman into her house?

Strange. Yes, in two too many ways. Regardless of the culture, most men are the same. *They cannot help themselves. It has to do with hormones.* Chi-Chi tried to reconcile her brother's behavior. She maintained a modicum of civility and offered Jennine coffee. Chi-Chi didn't know how to move this situation along and out the door. She was dealing with Jennine. Jennine had no external radar. She was swirling in her own man-crazy tornado, displacing everything that came into her path. Again, Chi-Chi reminded herself that Jennine was not a bad person. She just had this over-the-top thing about men. Any man. Any age. Any height, weight, history, culture. She was her own stereotype. But as Luna would say, "As long as she is happy and not hurting anyone, better to have a happy crazy person than an angry crazy one." Some consolation.

Finally, Chi-Chi had to step in. First deal with Jennine. Chi-Chi approached her in the kitchen. "Excuse me, Jennine. My brother and I must leave for church in thirty minutes. If you don't mind, we need some time to get ready."

Jennine might be a nymphomaniac, but she wasn't dense. "Of course, sugar. I'll get out of your way. Abeo? Thank you for a dazzling evening." She blew him a kiss and ad-

354

dressed Chi-Chi. "See you 'round campus! Ta-ta." She twirled her silk caftan and slithered out the door.

Abeo looked like he had just come out of a drug-induced coma and flopped on the sofa. Chi-Chi decided to accept it as something her brother engaged in. It wasn't her problem, as long as Jennine didn't become a fixture in her house. That's when she decided to ask, "Abeo. How long will you be in town?"

"Sister, why do you ask?" he answered in a zombielike tone.

"Because you keep surprising me, and I would like to know how much longer I can anticipate disturbing behavior from my brother?" Chi-Chi folded her arms, waiting for an answer.

"I will be here two more days. Unless that is an issue for you?" he replied sheepishly.

"So you will be leaving on Tuesday?" Chi-Chi wanted it to be abundantly clear.

"That is correct, dear sister. Please accept my most sincere apologies for the discomfort I have brought upon you."

"You have no idea." Chi-Chi blew out a big burst of air. "That woman will never leave me alone now. Every day it will be, 'How is your brother? Will he be coming back soon? Has he asked about me?' It will be painful."

"Oh, dear sister. Again, my most heartfelt apologies."

"Tell me. How did you manage all of this? Or should I say, how did *she* manage all of this?" Chi-Chi folded her arms again, waiting for an answer.

"She plied me with alcohol." Abeo shook his head.

"You hardly drink."

"That is the problem." He kept shaking his head. "The champagne was delicious and she kept refilling my glass. Before I knew it, I was getting tipsy. I did not want to drive. She offered."

"And then she didn't leave!" Chi-Chi was beside herself.

"Do not worry. Nothing happened."

"I find that hard to believe." Chi-Chi was standing over him now.

"It is the truth, dear sister. I passed out."

"Thank goodness for small favors. Although that might mean she will want to take another shot at you."

Now it was Chi-Chi's turn to shake her head.

"Do you really think so?" Abeo tried to play innocent.

"I know so." Chi-Chi sighed.

"I do not plan to come back for several

months. Maybe she will forget." Abeo attempted a smile.

"I doubt it," Chi-Chi replied. "Come on. You need to go to church." Chi-Chi hauled Abeo off the sofa and shoved him toward her guest room. "And please replace the sheets before you leave on Tuesday."

"But I told you nothing happened." Abeo was insistent.

"All the same. You will be doing laundry before you go." She tapped his foot with her shoe. "Now clean yourself up and get ready for church," Chi-Chi barked at him.

"Church?" Abeo's eyes went wide.

"Church. If anyone needs it today, it is you."

Luna pulled into Cullen's driveway around five. She could hear Wiley yapping. "Mommy's home!" Luna called out.

Cullen greeted her at the door. He looked like the cat who ate the canary. Or was that her own expression on her face?

"Well? So?" Both were sputtering.

"You go first." Luna squatted to give Wiley a big hug.

"Well, you know part of it."

"Yeah. And thanks a pantload for scaring the hell out of me!" She gave him an affectionate punch in the arm.

"Sorry. I hope I wasn't interrupting anything."

"Well, you were."

"Do tell?"

"Oh no, mister. You have to recap first since you did interrupt me."

"First I have to say, she looked absolutely exquisite."

"I would not have expected any less." Luna nodded.

"We ordered a seven-course tasting menu, then she disappeared just before dessert. She said she was going to the ladies' room but she was gone for almost fifteen minutes. I thought she had left."

"Chi-Chi would never do such a thing."

"Of course not, but I was a little worried. I know she was wearing a jumpsuit, and from what I've been told, it's a circus act getting in and out of them, but . . ." Cullen took a breath. "Without any introduction or notice, she appeared in front of the jazz combo and started to sing. I almost fell off my chair. That's when I called you." Cullen was almost out of breath.

"Yes. Duly noted." Luna started to giggle. "I thought it was Anita Baker singing and couldn't figure out why you were calling me to play a song over the phone."

"Well, I thought you would appreciate her

live performance other than inside my car." Cullen smiled.

"Yes. I put you on speakerphone so Chris could hear it, too. He was quite impressed."

"Speaking of Chris, how did it go?" Cullen was anxious to hear about Luna's special weekend.

"Oh, wait a minute. You haven't finished your story. Continue," she directed.

"After she sang, the place went crazy, and the maître d' sent over a split of champagne."

"Only a split?" Luna was referring to the half-size bottle.

"It was Veuve Clicquot." He grinned.

"Well, in that case, I suppose it was appropriate."

She smirked. "And then?"

"And I drove her home."

"I repeat, and then?" she pressed.

"When we got to her house, she said she wasn't sure when her brother would be home. Otherwise, she would invite me in."

"Now, that sounds like things are moving in the right direction," Luna said with glee.

"Except we were greeted by Abeo at the front door. He was quite toasted."

"Were you able to get in a good-night kiss at least?" Luna pushed harder.

"Yes."

"And?" Luna was becoming impatient.

"I don't kiss and tell." Cullen folded his arms in the "that is all I have to say" stance. "But there is something I can tell you. Jennine was at Chi-Chi's."

"I know!" Luna burst out. "She's coming over at six to give me all the gory details. Apparently she spent the night."

"Oh, that must have gone over like a lead balloon with Chi-Chi." Cullen cracked a grin.

"More like osmium." Luna was referring to one of the heaviest metals on Earth.

"Yeah. It's toxic, too." Cullen chuckled.

"I cannot wait to hear how that happened. Well, I can imagine the how part. When Jennine sets her sights on something, the only thing that can stop her is an antiballistic missile."

The two of them broke out in laughter.

Luna gave her brother a big hug. "I am so happy you had a good time."

Cullen gave her a kiss on the head. "Thanks to you."

"I gotta run. Come on, Wiley." Luna called her pooch over.

"Oh, no you don't. You haven't told me about your weekend, missy."

"I don't kiss and tell either. Ciao! See you tomorrow!"

She turned and trotted out the door with Wiley on her heels.

Cullen stood in the doorway. "Yeah, well, we're not done with this conversation." He waved and grinned.

Chi-Chi got to Luna's right at six. They greeted each other, hooting and hugging as if they hadn't seen one another in years.

"Let me feed Wiley and pour us some wine."

Luna plated Wiley's favorite food as he lovingly looked up and wagged his tail. Then she opened a bottle of Lorenza Rosé and poured each a glass. "Come sit. We have a lot to talk about. But first, what the heck was Jennine doing at your house? Besides the obvious?" Luna asked, as they clinked glasses.

"Evidently, my brother likes the taste of champagne and imbibed more than he should have. He claims Jennine kept filling his glass."

"Well, of course she did," Luna said.

"Yes, because he does not know how to say 'no.' He was too drunk to drive, so Jennine drove him to my house."

"Invited herself in, and . . . ?"

"And? He passed out!" Chi-Chi roared.

Luna almost spit out her drink. "Oh my

gosh. That must have put a real damper in Jennine's plans."

"I am sure it did. So what happened this morning?"

"I gave her a cup of coffee and told her we were going to church."

"Church?" Luna asked.

"Yes. I told Abeo he needed to go." Chi-Chi was snickering.

"And did he?"

"Oh yes. I was not going to let him get away with bad behavior."

"But you said they didn't do anything."

"Getting drunk and bringing someone into my house without asking me is bad behavior." Chi-Chi took a sip of her wine. "And it was my chance to torture him for a change."

"Church is torture?"

"When you have a hangover, it is." Chi-Chi grinned with a twinkle in her eye.

Luna chuckled. "Anything is torture when you have a hangover."

"Very true. That is why I limit my intake." She held out her glass for a refill. "Except for now."

Again, the women were laughing hysterically.

"You did a very impressive job singing last night." Luna raised her glass.

"I was very nervous, but I thought if I didn't do it then, I would probably never do it again. The musicians were very professional. So when I asked the keyboard player if he knew that song and would it be all right for me to sing, he was happy to oblige. I knew he thought he was taking a risk, but I sang the first few bars to him so we could figure out the right key."

"Well, it was utterly fantastic."

"Thank you. And thank you for being so pushy about Cullen and me going to dinner. It was a wonderful evening."

"And?" Luna gave her a sideways look.

"And I hope he and I can do it again."

"And without his little sister," Luna teased.

"No offense, but I see enough of you every day," Chi-Chi teased back.

"None taken."

"Now it is your turn, my friend. How was your weekend with the fine marshal?"

"More than fine." Luna could still feel the warmth of him. "It was like the best romantic movie ever made. Even the power went out!"

"That could be a good thing or a bad thing," Chi-Chi noted.

"Very true. Actually, the timing could not have been more perfect. We spent a couple of hours going over ideas for his place. Then he grilled steaks and we had dinner. After dinner, we sat on the sofa in front of a fire and just as he was about to kiss me my phone rang. It was Cullen with you serenading in the background."

"Oh no! I am so sorry I interrupted your evening."

Chi-Chi was genuinely distraught.

"No worries. I was a little shaken when I saw it was Cullen calling. I thought it was an emergency. Chris comforted me." Luna used air quotes for "comforted." "And then the power went out."

"Not between the two of you I am guessing?" Chi-Chi gave her a sly grin.

"Nope! There was enough heat and energy to light up the sky."

"That is truly funny. The power goes out, and you spark your own!"

"It was sweet and passionate." Luna was recalling the memory in her head. "And the best part? There were no awkward moments. Before, during, or after. It was as if we had been together before."

"Well, you have been together before."

"Yeah, but not like that!" Luna blurted.

"I believe you had been thinking about that moment for a very long time. You had it well choreographed in your head."

"How interesting you used the word 'choreographed' because that's exactly what I thought when I woke up."

"It should not surprise you that you function on a slightly different wavelength than most people." Chi-Chi smiled.

"I know. The funny thing is, I get excited whenever it happens. For me, it's a validation that there is a divine force, an energy that flows; and we are truly a part of it."

"You know I would agree with that."

"It's right in front of us, but most people, including me, miss the hints. The signs. The clues, so I get excited when someone else is experiencing it."

"Yes. It is very invigorating." Chi-Chi nodded. "And also reassuring. Speaking of reassuring, how did you leave it with the fine marshal? Are you in fight-or-flight mode? Que será, será mode? Which I doubt. Or, I am enjoying this ride and I will not pull the emergency brake because I'm in insecure mode?"

"I'm working on the insecure thing. Between you and Cullen, I am reminded to avoid the self-sabotage. I have very strong feelings for Chris. I know he has feelings for me as well. We're both a little jumpy when it comes to relationships, so it's good we waited until we got to know each other. We *like* each other!" Luna exclaimed.

"How did you leave it? Future plans? I know that is an anxiety trigger for all of us."

"Ya know, we didn't address the fact that we made love for the first time. There was no 'about last night' conversation. And we weren't all over each other this morning. We were affectionate, yes. A couple of hugs, kisses on the cheek, a pat on the heinie. I patted *his.*" Luna giggled. "It seemed so natural. Then we packed a lunch and took an hour hike." Luna went on. "Oh, and he made a copy of the note and a page of the diary and is going to hook me up with a handwriting analyst."

"You could not go an entire twenty-four hours without bringing up your sleuthing." Chi-Chi tsk-tsked.

"I am *me,* remember? Anyway, he's working on that piece, and Ellie and I are going to the library this week to look up fires between 1999 and 2001. There couldn't have been many. Or maybe? I guess we'll find out." Luna's excitement was growing. "I really think I'm close to figuring this out. At least a good part of it. It feels really close." Luna mused and thought about the woman Tori. "I am sure she is connected somehow. But I don't think she is aware of it. If I am making any sense."

"You lost me on that last sentence, but that is OK. Tell me, were you able to come up with some plans for Chris's house?"

"Yes we did. He had already started ripping down the wall between the kitchen and dining area but realized it was a load bearing wall and so he can't remove all the two-by-fours. I came up with an alternative. An island cabinet and countertop with a decorative pillar on each end. Not ideal, but less expensive than bringing in steel beams."

"How was the rest of the house? As bad as he described? Brown?"

"Yeah. Brown paneling. Again I came up with a makeover that didn't require ripping off the paneling."

Luna pulled out her sketchbook and showed Chi-Chi the rough drawings. "The yard is beautiful, and there's a large picture window in the living-room area, and a patio door in the dining area. I thought he was going to break out in a sweat when we started talking costs. But I explained unless he plans on selling the house in the next ten years, he doesn't have to do high-end appliances."

"Very wise."

"And I get to help him pick everything out." Luna clapped her hands together. "This is going to be so much fun!"

"I am very happy for you, Luna. You have a special glow about you. More so than you had two days ago and, believe me, your wattage is always higher than most people's." Chi-Chi chuckled.

Luna's cell phone rang. It was Gaines. She got all fluttery. "Hi," she answered.

"Hey. Just checking you got back all right."

"Yes. Sorry, I should have called, but I had to pick up Wiley, then Chi-Chi came by."

"No problem." He paused.

Luna grimaced, expecting that "about last night" conversation.

"Hey, I wanted you to know I'm really glad you came out here. I had a great time. With you." He wanted to make sure he was being clear. It was about her.

"Me too. It was comfortable. Easy."

"I concur," he replied. "I'm planning on getting paint to do something about these walls. You mentioned a fabric for the bottom? I wouldn't know where to begin."

Luna laughed softly. "I suggest you paint all of them first, then the fabric, then the chair rail. It will hide any ragged edges."

"You said gray? Are you sure that will make it brighter in here?"

"Actually, there are over one hundred and one shades of gray regardless of the book

368

title." She giggled. "Something light. Silver Satin or American Gray are very light and neutral. Depending on how well it covers the paneling, you may just want to go with the chair rail in a slightly darker color."

"I think I may need your help on that."

Luna raised her eyebrows with delight. "You let me know when."

"How about the week after next? I'm off Monday and Tuesday."

"Hang on. Let me check my book." Luna pretended to be looking at something, then responded, "That would work out perfectly. The center is closed, so I wouldn't have to find someone to work at the café."

"Excellent. Any chance you can come out on Sunday so we'll have all day Monday to figure this out?"

"What about Carter?"

"He has a game early that afternoon, so he'll be back at his mother's by four."

"I think that sounds like a plan." Luna was resisting the temptation to jump up and down. "Listen, I have to go. Chi-Chi is here."

"Tell her I was very impressed with her solo."

"Will do. Talk later. Ciao!" Luna disconnected the call.

Chi-Chi looked at her with the widest eyes

369

ever. "So? Another trip to Charlotte?"

"Yes!" Now Luna was jumping up and down. "He wants me to help him pick out paint and stuff."

"Things seem to be moving in the right direction!" Chi-Chi gave Luna a high five. "Now, where were we?"

"I forget." Luna laughed. "So much has happened in the past twenty-four hours."

"You have that right, my friend."

"I guess this will give you and Cullen an excuse to have dinner again."

"Perhaps. But I think I should invite him over for an authentic Nigerian dinner. We will start with *chin chin.* Little tiny nibbles of dough and sweetness. Then we shall have *suya,* spiced meat on skewers with *akara* fritters. Then *efo riro,* which is a stew made with spinach and vegetables and meat."

"Sounds delicious. How come you've never made that for me?"

"Because you didn't take me to Bouchorelle!" Chi-Chi laughed loudly. "Do you think he will agree to come?"

"Only if you *invite* him."

"That is something I can do." Chi-Chi smiled.

The women continued discussing the high points of the weekend. By the time Chi-Chi finished her story about Jennine, the two of them were practically rolling.

"I do not want her stalking me asking me too many questions about Abeo."

"I'm sure you will be able to nip it in the bud." Luna took one more sip. "Besides, you're much taller than she is. You can intimidate her with one of your cold stares."

Chi-Chi stood and folded her arms. She made a scowling face. "Like this?"

Luna was doubled over. "Exactly!"

CHAPTER SIXTEEN

Monday morning

Luna was unpacking her overnight bag when she decided to go through her wardrobe. She didn't wear half of what was in there. She didn't even know what was in there. It was time to refresh and renew. She wasn't sure if what she felt for Chris was love or a serious kind of like.

Either way, it pumped her endorphins. She was in a fine mood. She perused her schedule and remembered she owed the mysterious Tori an appointment. Luna swiped through her call history and pressed SEND. Two rings and a woman's soft voice answered. "Hello?"

"Hello, Tori?"

"Yes."

"This is Luna Bodhi. We met a couple of weeks ago."

"Yes. Of course. How are you?" Tori asked.

"I'm well, thank you. I was looking over

372

my calendar and am wondering if you are available next Saturday?"

"I should be. What did you have in mind?"

"Would it be possible for you to come around ten? It doesn't start to get busy until after eleven, so that should give us some time."

"Yes. Yes, that would be good." Tori was not going to tell her husband; nor was she going to ask. She did not want to miss this opportunity.

"Great. See you Saturday at ten. Namaste Café. Namaste."

"Nuuunuunamaste." Tori tried to pronounce it correctly. She was elated that Luna could see her so soon.

Luna was glad she had called Tori. She didn't want to wait any longer to dig deeper. She would ask her flat out if she had a fire in her past when she was young.

She kept folding and placing clothes in boxes. "Wiley, why did you let me buy all of these? What were you thinking?"

Wiley gave her a yawn punctuated with a moan.

"I really need to ditch some of these granny dresses. I can still be boho with less ruffles. And so much of it looks like so much of the rest of it. Yikes!"

Luna sized up the four Bankers Boxes. She was satisfied she wouldn't miss any of the items she had packed. "Want to go for a ride?" She spoke to Wiley as she began to move the boxes out to the car. Since it was one of his favorite things to do, he yapped a happy reply.

Luna stopped at a local thrift shop and dropped off her now-orphaned clothes. The clothes were in very good shape, so she felt they would go to a good home.

When she arrived at the center, she realized Alex would not be on doggie duty, so she couldn't leave Wiley outside by himself. "Come on. You can be my assistant today." Luna walked into her spotless café. "Wow. I should leave more often." Not that it was ever messy.

She saw the lights on in Cullen's workshop and headed in that direction.

"What's up, bro?" she asked.

"Working on the trunk. So did you get around to finagling Chris into helping you?"

She swatted him on the back with the newspaper she was carrying. "I'll have you know Chris is referring me to a handwriting analyst to compare the note and the page in the diary."

"How did you manage that?"

"I have the secret touch." Luna started

blushing, realizing what she said could have gone in a different direction.

"Oh, do you now?" Cullen gave her a one-eyed look.

And there it is. She thought. "I don't kiss and tell."

"You don't have to. You're not the only one who can read auras," he teased.

"Just zip it, please. Tell me more about this trunk. It's looking good, by the way."

"Not much to tell. Most of the smoke odor is gone. I'm wondering if we should have the blanket cleaned?" Cullen asked.

"I am sure the owner would appreciate that if we ever find out who it is." Luna thought for a minute. "Did you deposit the money order yet?"

"No. I'm not really comfortable about it. Can't say why, but it can keep until the rightful owner resurfaces. I have an e-mail address, so I will contact him/her/them when it's done."

"Yeah, but not until I've put all of the pieces of the puzzle together. We don't want to send it back without my reaching my objective." Luna was sitting on a bench and swinging her legs. "Ellie and I are going to the library tomorrow to check out the newspaper archives. See if we can find out anything about a fire."

"What makes you think the fire took place anywhere around here?"

"Because of the carnival stubs."

"But you said the guy told you they covered several states."

"Yes, and he narrowed it down based on the flyer."

"Are you sure you're not working under-cover?"

Cullen chuckled.

"Very funny. Let's not forget, I was a government employee at one time."

"You got me there." Cullen stepped back and looked at the final coat of sealant he had applied. "Check these out." He showed her the brand-new-looking hinges and the lock.

"Impressive. It's going to look great when you're finished. But do not e-mail the person until I get either a confirmation or rejection on the handwriting."

"You got it." He wiped his hands. "Now scram. I'm busy." Cullen had used that phrase with her ever since they were kids.

Luna shimmied off the bench and went back to her café. She opened her appointment book and jotted down her meeting with Tori for Saturday. Normally, she didn't read clients over the weekend, but she was making an exception. She knew Tori was connected to the trunk somehow and was more than anxious to find out how.

The next day, Ellie and Luna went to the county library. Much to their surprise, there were over sixty local newspapers in North Carolina. There were also dozens of weekly papers with special Sunday editions, and a number of dailies. But over the past twenty years, many of them had gone out of business, and the number of print editions had dwindled to around forty.

"Looks like we have our work cut out for us. Good thing we're only looking at three summers' worth," Ellie announced.

After three hours of coming up with nothing, they decided to take a lunch break. As they were leaving the library, Luna got a flash. More like a hunch. She stepped up to the information counter where the librarian was sitting. "Excuse me. My friend and I are doing some research. Are you familiar with the Stillwell Art Center?"

"I am indeed." She pulled off her reading glasses and let them hang from their chain. "It is so nice to have a place filled with so many talented artists."

Luna motioned for Ellie to come over. "This is Ellie Stillwell, the force behind the art center."

The librarian stood immediately. "It is a pleasure to meet you, Ms. Stillwell. You have done an absolutely marvelous job."

"Thank you." Ellie shook the woman's hand.

Luna leaned in. "As I mentioned, we are doing some research, but it occurred to me that you might be able to lend a hand."

"I would be delighted!" The woman could not have been more accommodating. "What do you need?"

"We've been looking through the newspaper archives to see if we can find any information about a fire that may have taken place between 1999 and 2001," Luna informed the helpful librarian.

"There are always a number of them, especially in the summer."

"I'm not talking about campfires or forest fires. A house fire perhaps? A business? A church? Something that would involve people."

"Let me think. Twenty or so years ago, you say?"

"Yes. Someone might have gotten hurt. I don't think there was a death, but it was some kind of accident." Luna was going with her gut as far as what she felt had happened.

The librarian shook her head. "I can't

recall anything specific."

"It was in the summer. Probably August. We think it might have happened when the carnival was in town, or thereabouts."

"Doesn't ring a bell. When was the carnival here?"

"Probably August of 1999, 2000, or 2001," Ellie interjected.

Luna got another flash. "Wait. The diary mentioned graduation. Maybe the tickets were from the summer before, and the fire was in June the following year."

"Good point." Ellie nodded.

"Oh well, if you're asking about a fire around the time of graduation, that I do remember." The woman ushered Ellie and Luna over to a table and chairs. "It was a very sad situation."

"Did anyone die?" Luna gripped the edge of the table. She hadn't felt it, but she could have been wrong.

"No, but a boy was burned."

Ellie and Luna sat up in surprise. Luna pulled out a pad and pen. "How old was he?"

"I think he might have been twelve or so."

"Do you remember what happened?" Ellie encouraged the woman's memory.

"From what I can remember, it happened at a large mobile-home community. Some people called it a trailer park, but it was a little nicer than most. The boy was supposed to be looked after by his sister. But when the fire department and police arrived, it was only the boy who was there. He suffered third-degree burns on the side of his face and neck."

"What happened to the sister?"

"No one knows for sure." The librarian leaned in farther. "I don't like to gossip, but from what I was told, the mother was a terrible drunk and the father was always on the road. Truck driver, I believe."

"And the sister was nowhere to be found?"

"That sounds very suspicious."

"That's what they thought at first. But the boy said it was a candle that set fire to the drapes. He ran from his bedroom to check on his sister and the flames got his shirt and his hair. Poor thing."

"Then what happened?" Ellie and Luna asked in unison.

"The state took the boy and put him in foster care." The librarian shook her head.

"So no one knows what became of the boy or the sister?"

"I'm afraid I can't help you there, and since then all the mobile homes got wiped out in a flood, and the land was cleared. There's a big-box store there now."

Luna was feverishly writing everything down. "Do you think it was covered by one of the newspapers?"

"I know it was. It was one of those incidents that left a lot of questions. There are probably a few articles about it, but like most stories, they eventually get boring, and the press moves on to something else."

Luna reached over and patted the woman's hand. "You have been extremely helpful. We are going to grab some lunch. Can we get you anything?"

"Oh no, I'm fine. I brought my lunch. Will you be coming back?"

"Yes. I want to find out everything I can about the fire."

"Any particular reason? You said you were doing research," the librarian asked.

"It has to do with an old mysterious trunk. We're trying to put the pieces together."

"Sounds intriguing. If I think of anything else, I'll let you know when you come back."

Luna and Ellie got up, thanked the woman, and scurried out the door.

"Can you believe that?" Luna was all atwitter.

"When you get a feeling about something, you are on the money, honey." Ellie put her arm around Luna.

"I don't know why it hadn't occurred to

me to ask her when we first got here. Librarians know everything!" They linked arms and practically skipped to the local tap house.

They both ordered cheeseburgers with fries. "I'm going to hate myself in a few hours, when the french fries start reminding me of what an idiot I was to eat them." Ellie dunked one into the ketchup.

"Yeah. Why is that everything that tastes good and feels good is bad for you?" Luna wiped her mouth.

"Speaking of what is good for you, you have had a very different aura about you since you got back." Ellie smiled as she slathered more ketchup on the crispy potatoes.

"Funny. That's what Cullen said. Imagine him using the word 'aura.'"

"I can. Because it's true. You and the marshal had a nice time together?"

"We did, indeed." She took another bite of her juicy burger.

"I don't mean to pry. But I know how fond you are of each other. I guess what I am trying to say is that you and Christopher seem well suited for each other."

"Let's not get ahead of ourselves." Luna pointed her pinky at Ellie as she chomped down on the meat.

"Goodness, girl. You aren't getting any younger. Isn't it time for you to . . ."

"Settle down?" Luna quickly interrupted.

"Not in the traditional sense of settling down. I know that's not your thing. But having a nice, warm relationship with someone isn't a terrible thing."

Luna wiped her hands on the checkered cloth napkin.

"You are right. There are no rules anymore. Sometimes that's a good thing and sometimes not so much."

"Have you made plans to see each other again?" Ellie asked.

"Yes! I am going back weekend after next to help him pick out paint and a few other things."

"Well, it sounds to me he surely wants your participation."

"And I am happy to do it." Luna reached over and grabbed one of Ellie's fries. "You're right. These are not good for you. I'll help you get rid of them."

Ellie smacked Luna's hand with a fry. "Don't get too handsy with me, little lady."

Luna laughed and motioned for the waitress to bring the check. "I don't mean to rush, but now that we have more pieces to the puzzle, maybe we can find a name or two in the newspapers."

"I should probably stop eating these things anyway," Ellie said.

After they paid the bill, Luna decided to change the subject. "Tell me about Nathan. You've known him a long time."

"I have. He's a wonderful man."

"So?" Luna peered into Ellie's eyes.

"My dear, he's gay. He has kept it on the down-low for years. It's only been a little over a decade that the LGBTQ community has become more visible. We don't have a gay district or a 'gayborhood,' but we're much more inclusive now."

"I really never gave it much thought," Luna contemplated.

"That's because *you* are an all-inclusive soulful being. You don't judge people by what they look like or their religion, whether in themselves or others for that matter. You accept people for their spirit."

"You're right. My energy checks out their energy. If the energies mix, I'm cool with it. If not, well, 'Don't let the door hit you on the behind.' "

Ellie laughed. "You wouldn't show anyone to the door."

"Oh, trust me. I have and I would. Granted, I give a lot of people a lot of latitude. But when they have stretched my patience and sucked me dry, it's adios, sayonara, arrivederci, toodle-oo, and good-bye."

"But you're not mean or cruel about it," Ellie said.

"Nope. I just tune them out psychically. Most people don't realize I've put up a force field to protect me from their kryptonite." Luna chuckled.

Ellie laughed. "You are such a delight, Luna Bodhi Bodman."

Luna did a little curtsy as she opened the big doors to the library.

The librarian bounced out of her seat when she saw them return. "I think I found some information for you!" The woman was elated. "I hope you don't mind. But you had me wondering about all of that, so I had to check a few things." She slid a copy of a newspaper article across the desk. "Here. It talks about the fire, the sister, the boy."

Luna's hands were almost shaking. She knew that this was going to be the tipping point. "I don't mind at all. My goodness, you've saved us hours of work."

"After you left, it started coming back to me, so I looked up the big local paper. They would have had the most coverage."

"Seriously, I cannot thank you enough. May we use the table?"

"Of course!" she said in a louder-than-acceptable whisper. Then she giggled. "Oops. Sshhhh."

Luna and Ellie sat next to each other as they read the article.

A fire broke out in the Shady Grove Mobile Park Community Saturday night. A young boy, approximately twelve years old, was found outside the home suffering from third-degree burns on his neck. His name has not been released at this time. According to his statement, a candle was left burning unattended. The youth was admitted to the burn unit of the hospital, where he is being treated for his injuries. His parents, Gina and James T. Conover, Sr., were out of town at the time. The whereabouts of his sister, Victoria, is not known. The fire has been deemed an accident and not arson.

"Conover?" Ellie looked at the article again.

She repeated, "Conover. James T. Conover."

"What about it?" Luna was on the edge of her seat.

"That's Jimmy Can-Do's name." Ellie stopped in her tracks.

Luna reread the article. She closed her eyes for a moment. "I think the trunk came from Jimmy."

"What makes you say that?"

"Well, the name for one thing. And, you have never seen his face, have you?"

"No, I haven't."

The librarian interrupted the conversation. "Here is a small follow-up article."

Several weeks ago we reported on a fire that took place in the Shady Grove Mobile Park Community. The county fire marshal has confirmed that the blaze was started by a candle left unattended. The boy has been released from the hospital and placed in foster care. The family has no comment at this time.

Luna peered up at Ellie. "Hear me out. Let's say it was Jimmy in the fire. He's sent to foster care. His sister has gone missing. He recovered the trunk, but it was in need of a makeover. Who does a better job than Cullen?" Luna was ticking off her summation. "Jimmy works with metal. Maybe it's his way of coping with the trauma." She took a breath. "The woman who came to see me was distraught. There was a sadness, a remorse about her. And she ran away with her boyfriend when she was in her teens, who is now her husband. And I am willing to bet, Tori is the missing sister."

"But the diary was signed with a *V*. Her name is Tori," Ellie reminded her.

Luna jumped up. "Yes, but Tori is a nickname for Victoria." She knew she couldn't keep her voice to a library whisper any longer. "Come on!" She grabbed Ellie's arm and turned to the librarian. "I cannot thank you enough. Please come by the art center. We will give you a personal tour and treat you to lunch."

"Really?" The woman's eyes lit up. "That would be splendid."

Luna fished one of her business cards out of her bag, and Ellie did the same. "Please get in touch."

Luna chimed in. "You have no idea how much this has helped. Thank you, and yes, please come visit."

Luna couldn't help but give the woman a big bear hug.

Luna and Ellie hurried out the door. Their excitement was overflowing.

They returned to the center to see if Cullen had finished the trunk.

Luna rushed in. She was out of breath. "Cul! Cul! You are not going to believe what we discovered!"

"Easy there. What's going on?"

"I'm pretty sure we solved this entire mystery." She pointed to the trunk.

"How?" Cullen looked skeptical.

"The librarian! She found an article about a fire that took place around twenty years ago. It was in a mobile home. A twelve-year-old kid was burned on the side of his face. The parents weren't around." She paused. "And the father's name was James T. Conover."

"So?"

"That's Jimmy Can-Do's name! Ellie said it's the name on the lease. James T. Conover, Jr."

"Holy smoke! For sure?" Cullen leaned against his workbench. "So now what?"

"I'm waiting for Chris to see when he can get the handwriting analyst to look at the note and diary. If it's a match, then that client is Jimmy's sister."

"That is some crazy theory."

"Cullen, I know it. I know it in my gut. The article said the sister's name was Victoria, and 'Tori' is a nickname for Victoria. It's as plain as day."

She went through the list of facts with him. The fire, the extent of the boy's injuries, the names, the sister, the metal craftsmanship. She explained working with metal was probably his way of coping with his burns. No one has ever seen his face, including Ellie. Now they surmised it might be due to some disfiguration.

"But why go to all the trouble of sending me this trunk?"

"That I cannot say, unless it was his way of reaching into the past and maybe hoping there were some clues to his sister's whereabouts."

"But you don't know if he even has a sister, much less that he's looking for her."

"But the name is James T. Conover, Junior and Senior. That cannot be a coincidence." Luna was emphatic about it. "I'm going to call Chris and bring him up to speed. Maybe he'll have some idea when we'll have something from the handwriting expert. If it's a match, then we'll know for sure. She's coming here on Saturday. I plan on prying more information out of her."

"But you're the psychic." Cullen was trying to put it together in his head. "Shouldn't *you* be telling *her* information?"

"Yes, and I will in so many words. I know I'm right about all of this. And I don't think Tori even knows her brother is here. I don't think she knows where he is at all." Luna's arms were akimbo.

"OK, let's say you are correct. What are

you going to do about it?"

"Ellie and I will figure it out."

Later that evening, Luna phoned Chris and told him everything that she had found out at the library.

"You are becoming quite the gumshoe." Gaines was only half joking.

"I know I'm being pushy about this, but do you think we can have an answer about the handwriting before Saturday? Tori is coming in the morning for a reading."

"Well, that should be interesting now that you have an idea."

"Yeah. I did the worst thing a psychic could do. Research. But it wasn't to cheat. It was to get to the bottom of the trunk, the diary, and the note. I'm not going to lie to her or pretend I pulled this information out of thin air. I will ask her about a fire, which, may I remind you, was in the sketch I did when I first met her. Then everything else seemed to fall into place. More or less."

"You were acting on a hunch," Gaines said.

"That is correct."

"So it wasn't really cheating." Gaines knew Luna had misgivings about exploring other people's background. "You were following your intuition about the fire and the connection."

Luna sighed. "You're right. I had all the best intentions."

"Now, don't get all wimpy on me. If you can bring a brother and sister together, then you've done a good thing."

"That's what worries me. What if they hate each other?"

"I guess you'll find out. Look, you are giving them an opportunity for reconciliation. They can choose to do whatever they want afterward."

"This is why I like you so much." Luna almost gasped at verbalizing her feelings for him.

"And I like you, too."

Luna could feel his smile coming through.

"I'll call my contact tomorrow and see if he can check out the handwriting before Saturday."

"You're the best. Thanks." Luna wasn't sure what to say next.

"You're quite welcome. I figure if I don't help you out, you're going to try to do it on your own, and I have enough work with criminal behavior."

Luna burst out laughing. "Me? Criminal?"

"Let's say unconventional. I'm sure you're all jazzed about this. Try to get a good night's sleep. I'll give you a call in the morning."

"Sounds good. And, Chris?" She paused. "I really do like you."

"Ditto, you lunatic."

CHAPTER SEVENTEEN

Saturday

The week following their heart-to-heart talk, Tori and her husband seemed to have turned a corner. He was home for dinner every night but Thursday. He even helped with the dishes. Tori was being cautiously optimistic that this was a new beginning for them. When she told her boss about their conversation, he was delighted to hear that she had taken his advice. "The offer still stands about the break room. You're still going to need to take care of the little one."

She told her husband where she was going but not exactly what she was doing. She needed some reassurance from Luna. She didn't know what she would do if Luna told her to "run like hell," but she was feeling hopeful.

Luna arrived at the center a little before nine. She was prepared to answer all of

Tori's questions. And then Luna had a couple of her own.

When Tori arrived, Luna offered her coffee and a pastry. Tori was happy to accept. Luna noticed a different vibe from the woman.

"Please sit." Luna motioned to the table next to the easel. She pulled out her marker and began to draw without looking at the paper. "Are things better with you and your husband?"

Tori seemed a bit surprised at the question. "Why yes. We had a very serious, long overdue conversation. I told him I wasn't happy, but that was after he asked me if I was having an affair!"

Luna knitted her eyebrows. "What made him think that?"

"I'd been acting differently. When I found out I was pregnant, I knew I had to take control of my life. I had let too many things happen to me without my own participation, if you know what I mean."

"There's a lot to be said about 'going with the flow,' but you can't let the current carry you away," Luna said.

"Exactly. And I was adrift. I didn't want to bring another child into the world, especially if I wasn't happy. That's something a child should not have to experience, a miserable parent." Tori started twisting her napkin again. "I work for a law firm and looked up divorce laws in North Carolina."

"And now?" Luna asked.

"Well, that's why I'm here." Tori looked up at Luna. "Do you think it's going to be all right? We're really going to work it out?"

"It seems like you already are." Luna peeked at the drawing. It was a little girl holding hands with a mother and father. The sun was shining. She ripped the page off the pad and handed it to Tori. "This is what I feel."

Tori's eyes welled up. "I feel the same way. It was a total lack of communication that was driving the wedge between us. I promised not to keep my feelings a secret, and he promised to be a better partner."

Luna sat down at the table across from Tori. She took both hands in hers. "OK, now I have to ask you something very personal."

Tori looked perplexed. "What is it?"

"Were you ever involved in a fire?"

Tori's eyes almost bugged out of her head. "How did you know?"

"It's a bit of a long story. Part intuition, part detective work."

"You were spying on me?" Tori's eyes got even bigger.

"No, not you specifically. Like I said, it's a long story."

Tori explained what had happened that fateful night.

"My parents were away, and my brother was home. Kyle and I . . ."

It was Luna's turn to have eyes like saucers. "Kyle?"

"Yes, that's my husband's name. Why? Is it important?"

"Very. I'll explain in a bit. Please continue."

Luna was very serious when her phone rang. It was Gaines. "Sorry. I have to take this." Luna got up and walked into Cullen's showroom. "Hey. How's it going?"

"You are something else, Luna-tic. The handwriting is a match. How you figured all of this out is beyond me."

"I knew it! I knew it!" Luna was beyond excited. "She's here right now. Let me finish up with her. I'll call you back. You are the best!"

Before Luna went back to the café, she called Ellie, using Cullen's walkie-talkie. "Ellie. It's a match. The handwriting is a match!"

"Incredible! I am going to call Jimmy and tell him there's an emergency and he needs to get here pronto. Do you think you can stall her?"

"I'll do my best." Luna went back into the café.

Luna sat down across from Tori. "Tell me more about that night. If you don't mind."

"It's been a terrible burden to carry. As I was saying, Kyle and I decided to take a walk. I stupidly left a candle burning. Kyle and I heard the fire engines, and when we got close to the house, we realized what had happened. We were both so scared, and he had been talking about us running away, so that seemed like the opportune moment."

"And your brother?"

Tori burst into tears. "I saw him running from the house. I could hear him screaming. I wanted to run to him, but Kyle thought we might get arrested because of the fire. So we took off. I wrote my parents a note and said not to look for us. And they didn't. No surprise there."

Luna handed Tori the box of tissues she kept handy for emotional readings. "And you have no idea what happened to your brother?"

Tori shook her head. "I have no connection with anyone from my past. It's kinda sad. I had a best friend who I cut out of my life. I was afraid she'd tell my parents. As the days became weeks, then months, then years, I thought it was too late to reach out."

She thought about Rita's story and how similar it sounded to Tori's. Luna wondered if that could be because they were part of the same story. It would be very bizarre, but synchronicity works that way.

"Give me a second, would you?"

"Sure." Tori sniffed.

Luna pulled out her walkie-talkie. "Hey there. Do you have a minute to stop by?"

The voice crackled back. "Sure. I also have photos to show you."

Within a few minutes, Rita walked into the café. A woman was sitting at a table. There was something familiar about her, but she couldn't put her finger on it. Luna nodded. Rita gave Luna an odd look.

"Victoria?" Luna asked in a hushed voice.

The woman jerked around. No one had called her Victoria in decades. She froze in place. Rita too had stopped dead. "Vic? Is that really you?"

"Rita? What are you doing here?" Tori got up and ran toward her friend.

"What am I doing here? What are *you* doing here?"

The women sat down and covered most of the past twenty years in about an hour. They cried, hugged, and cried some more. They were tears of joy.

Luna also got weepy at the unplanned reunion, and then her walkie-talkie crackled. It was Ellie. Jimmy was in the building. He was wearing a hoodie and sunglasses. "Meet me in the atrium," Ellie said.

"Ladies, can you both come with me?" Luna asked.

"Where?" Rita asked. Tori shrugged.

"Just into the atrium. Ellie wants to see us."

The three women walked out of the café and saw Ellie speaking to a man who could have been mistaken for a burglar. Nathan was standing by, so they weren't concerned. As the women got closer, the man stiffened.

Tori recognized her brother immediately in spite of his disguise. It was his stance. He always leaned more on one side and hooked his thumbs in his front pockets. "Jimmy?"

"Vic?" He gulped.

Victoria ran over and threw her arms around him. "J.T., I am so sorry. So, so, very sorry." She was bawling at this point.

He held her close and rocked her back and forth. "It's OK, Vic. I'm OK." Tears streamed down his hidden face. "You actually did me a favor. The family they placed me with were very nice people. They got me counseling, where I learned to deal with the trauma. That's when I began to make things with metal."

Tori couldn't stop sobbing. Luna jumped in. "Maybe we should take this inside." She motioned for all of them to follow her into Cullen's showroom. She led the way into the workshop. That morning, Cullen had finished putting the trunk back together with its shiny hinges and lock. "This is a big day for surprises." She pointed to the trunk. "I believe this belongs to you."

Jimmy was stunned. He stood there, silently taking in the events of the past few minutes. "How did you find out? And how did Vic end up here?"

"Let's go back to my café, and we'll start from the beginning. You know, the part where you had this delivered to my brother?"

"And the part where I found out about Luna because I was standing in the right spot in a grocery store I had never visited before?" Tori chimed in.

"This may take a while." Luna chuckled.

When they sat down, Tori told the story of her wandering into a huge food store and overhearing a few women talking about a psychic at Stillwell Art Center. It was a pinnacle moment. Tori knew she needed some kind of guidance and believed it was divine intervention that had brought her to that place at that time.

Rita pulled out the photos she had brought to show Luna. "Here's one of us with our mothers." Rita smiled. "It was a good day that day."

Tori picked up the photo and gulped. "This looks like a woman at a coffee shop who I apparently imagined." Everyone shot her a quizzical look, and Tori explained how this stranger told her to be at a certain place at a certain time. It had ultimately led to a dialogue between her and her husband. When Tori returned to the coffee shop, they said they knew of no one who fit the woman's description. Another inexplicable situation that had brought about a good outcome.

"Lots of synchronicity going on." Luna smiled. "I believe this belongs to you." She handed Tori the diary.

There was a moment of silence. Everyone was feeling the blessings that had been lost and now found.

Jimmy was the one to speak up first. "I knew Rita was here. That's one reason why I was always hidden. I didn't want to drag up the past. But now we are all together again, and there are no more secrets."

EPILOGUE

Several months later

Victoria was going into her third trimester. Things at home were better than she could have imagined. Kyle was a doting father-to-be, and Brendon was overjoyed that he was going to have a baby sister when he got back.

Luna, Ellie, and Rita thought it would be fitting for them to host a party at the atrium. After all, it was where it had all come together. They decided to make it a combo party, giving Victoria and Kyle a baby shower and the wedding reception they had never had.

Jimmy still kept a low profile to maintain the legend and mystique of the invisible honor-system metal sculptor. But he was always available for his sister and fellow artists. He was content in knowing he was no longer alone. He had a sister and a growing family.

The day of the party, Rita had gone overboard with the catering, to everyone's gastronomic delight. A small jazz combo played, and Chi-Chi's rendition of songs could make a strong man weep. Cullen was pumped up like a rooster knowing the exquisitely talented woman was his regular Saturday night date.

Suki brought several origami mobiles to decorate the atrium, including the one Tori had finished. She also gave everyone a pink origami crane as a party favor.

Jennine was tailing Chi-Chi, interrogating her about Abeo. After months of being cordial, Chi-Chi finally told Jennine to find out for herself. She could no longer deal with the aftermath of her brother's debauchery.

Victoria and Kyle truly looked like a happy couple, with Kyle managing any and all of Victoria's needs, wants, and desires.

Ellie was pleased as punch when George Layton arrived to cheer on the happy couple. Ellie had no idea Tori worked for the man. Another twist of fate. George and his late wife were fixtures at the many fundraisers she and Richard had attended years before. Now, with the two of them widowed, a new significance to their friendship could be found.

And then there was Luna, basking in the warmth and light of the love that surrounded all the people she loved, including the handsome Marshal Christopher Gaines, who stuck by her side like Velcro.

ABOUT THE AUTHOR

Fern Michaels is the *USA Today* and *New York Times* bestselling author of the Sisterhood, Men of the Sisterhood, and Godmothers series, as well as dozens of other novels and novellas. There are more than 110 million copies of her books in print. Fern Michaels has built and funded several large day-care centers in her hometown and is a passionate animal lover who has outfitted police dogs across the country with special bulletproof vests. She shares her home in South Carolina with her four dogs and a resident ghost named Mary Margaret. Visit her website at FernMichaels.com.

The employees of Thorndike Press hope you have enjoyed this Large Print book. All our Thorndike, Wheeler, and Kennebec Large Print titles are designed for easy reading, and all our books are made to last. Other Thorndike Press Large Print books are available at your library, through selected bookstores, or directly from us.

For information about titles, please call:
  (800) 223-1244

or visit our website at:
  gale.com/thorndike

To share your comments, please write:
  Publisher
  Thorndike Press
  10 Water St., Suite 310
  Waterville, ME 04901